Behind Closed Doors

Behind Closed Doors

Brian L Porter

Published 2014 by Creativia
Paperback design by Creativia (www.creativia.org)
Cover art by http://www.thecovercollection.com/
ISBN: 978-1497531987
Edited by Lorna Read

Dedication

Behind Closed Doors *is dedicated to the memory of Enid Ann Porter, (1914 – 2004), to Juliet, and to Jennie and the staff, volunteers, and four-legged residents of The Mayflower Animal Sanctuary, Doncaster, UK. Keep up the great work, people!*

Contents

Chapter 1
Introduction

The year 1888 remains memorable for many different reasons. In the USA, blizzards swept across the country, claiming the lives of hundreds of innocent souls. In Germany, Wilhelm II was crowned Emperor, and in London, in June of that year, Annie Besant organized the famed *matchgirls' strike,* which was to have future implications for the working classes within the great hub of the British Empire.

It was, however, within the annals of crime that the year passed most memorably into history, for 1888 was the year in which the city of London was rocked to its core by the most vicious and diabolical series of murders ever recorded in the history of such events in the United Kingdom. In the space of a few short weeks, the great metropolis was to be witness to a series of murders most foul, which, to this very day, have ensured lasting immortality and infamy for their perpetrator. The streets of the Whitechapel and Spitalfields areas, in particular, became streets of fear, as the unknown and, to this day, unidentified assailant, known only as *Jack the Ripper,* seemed to appear and disappear like a wraith in the night, leaving a trail of blood, death, and terror in his wake.

Little, however, is known of another series of murders which took place in London at that time. As *Jack the Ripper* struck with apparent impunity on the mean, filthy, rat-infested streets of London's East End, another, less spectacular, but no less dangerous killer was on the prowl, hardly a stone's-throw from the scenes of the Ripper's handiwork, the killer striking with unerring regularity, less than twenty-four hours after the murders of the Ripper himself.

With the Metropolitan police force's resources stretched almost to their limit in their search for *Jack the Ripper*, and with the banner headlines of the popular press screaming of his atrocities with almost daily regularity, it is little surprise that the story of the second, rather less newsworthy series of murders has been relegated to little more than a footnote in history. Yet, with political machinations taking place to suppress news of the second string of killings in an attempt to avoid a massive public backlash against not only the police, but the government too, and an investigation hampered by interference at many levels of authority, the story of the so-called *Underground Murders* is one that should, and will, be told in the following pages.

Today, the London Underground, known almost universally as *The Tube*, carries millions of passengers every year in relative comfort and safety, both above and below the streets of the capital. Back in the days of Queen Victoria, however, the Underground Railway was a new and innovative feat of engineering brilliance, which was yet to make its permanent mark on the infrastructure of the city. With steam locomotives and cold and often uncomfortable carriages plagued by noxious fumes from the locomotives and the tunnels, it was nonetheless popular, especially with the working classes, for whom it provided a cheap and for the most part ultra-reliable means of travelling far greater distances to and from work – or at least, the search for work – than had hitherto been possible. This new transport system was also to become the unfortunate setting for the murders which feature within the pages of this book.

Only the release of certain documents from Scotland Yard's archives, under the United Kingdom's recent Freedom of Information Act, has made the telling of this little-known murder mystery possible, so, without further ado, I ask you accompany me on a journey back in time, back to the autumn of the year 1888, and a cold, rather misty London morning. . .

PART ONE

Chapter 2
An Early Morning Caller

"Albert, the dog."

"Eh, what?" came the muffled response from a sleepy Albert Norris, his head tucked away under his pillow, as the first wash of morning light encroached through the curtained window into the bedroom.

"I said, the dog needs to go out. He's scratching at the door."

Norris emerged from under the pillow. His hair was tousled from a night's tossing and turning and he looked at his wife as she nudged him forcibly in the ribs with her elbow.

"Okay, Betty, I'm going," he replied, as he slowly extricated himself from the warmth of his bed, his feet slipping, almost as if by magic, into the carpet slippers which sat in their usual place beside the bed. Norris trudged sleepily across the room, stopping only to pick up and pull on his plaid dressing gown, a Christmas gift from his wife the previous year, then opened the door, allowing the entry of a scruffy black terrier of indeterminate parentage. The mutt immediately bypassed Norris and jumped on the bed, smothering his mistress's face with affectionate licks as his tail wagged non-stop with excitement.

"Bert!" she shouted at her husband, who, as was usual upon Billy the dog's daily entrance to their room, stood watching the performance with a huge grin on his face.

"Alright, I know. Billy, come on, you mad hound," he called, and the terrier leaped from the bed and quickly followed Norris as he went down the stairs and opened the back door of their neat terraced home, to allow the dog to roam freely in the small back garden.

Albert Norris spent the next five minutes making a pot of steaming hot tea, then, leaving Billy to enjoy himself in the garden, he returned to the bedroom with cups of tea for his wife and himself.

"One day, Bert, that dog will learn not to jump on the bed in the mornings. I'm sure you encourage him."

"Oh, come on, d'you really expect him to change? We've had him five years, and he's hardly likely to stop showing you his affection after all that time, is he?"

"I suppose you're right." Betty Norris smiled at her husband. "The tea's good, Bert, as always."

"My speciality, eh, my love," he replied, his voice soft and soothing as he reached out and touched his wife's hair, stroking her long auburn locks and caressing her gently behind her ear.

"Now, Bert Norris, that's enough of that. You've work to go to, my lad. You can forget all that amorous stuff and put it aside for later."

"Well, then, you'd best be getting out of that bed and seeing to my breakfast, don't you think? Or do you want me to go to work on an empty stomach?"

"Bert Norris, you're a slave driver," she said, laughing.

Betty thumped her husband playfully and finished her tea, returning the cup and saucer to the tea-tray. Five minutes later, she was in the kitchen, boiling two eggs and buttering two thick slices of bread for her husband's breakfast. Before the eggs were ready, their morning routine was interrupted by a loud knocking at the front door.

"I'll go," said Norris. He walked briskly from the kitchen and along the narrow hallway. He paused at the door to turn the key in the lock and then opened it to reveal a young and seemingly agitated uniformed police constable, who stood almost to attention as the bulky figure of Albert Norris filled the open doorway.

"Constable Fry," said Norris, recognising the young man as one of the constables from the station, though not one he'd worked closely with in the past. "What one earth brings you to my door at this early hour?"

"Inspector Norris," said Fry, "I'm so sorry to disturb you, but Chief Inspector Madden sent me. Well, that is, the chief inspector gave the orders and Sergeant Wilson actually sent me, but..."

"You're babbling, Fry. Pull yourself together, man and tell me what's happened. By the look on your face, something serious is afoot."

"Yes, sir, sorry, sir. Anyway, Sergeant Wilson said I was to fetch you right away. All hell's broke loose, sir. You know as how the Whitechapel Murderer struck again last night? Well, the night before last night, really, and..."

"Whoa, hold your horses, man! I'm not involved in that case. I thought Inspector Abberline was leading the local investigation into that one?"

"Yes, I know, sir, but it's not about that."

"Well, why mention him then? What's this about, Fry?"

"The beast killed again in the early hours of yesterday morning, as you know, and the mutilations were even worse than the others, sir, I mean Tabram and Nichols, and there's hardly a constable to be spared. Everyone is being drafted in to intensify the search, as Sergeant Wilson put it. That's why they need you for the other case."

"What *other case*?" asked Norris, his face suddenly setting into a hard and professional stare as he waited for Fry to get to the real point of this early morning summons.

"There's been a killing on the new Underground Railway, sir. A woman, stabbed and left in a carriage, I've been told to tell you. The chief inspector wants you to take charge of the case. Someone has already been sent to fetch Sergeant Hillman to the station, too."

Dylan Hillman was Norris's sergeant, the only man in the entire world he would admit to having absolute faith and trust in. Hillman and Norris had worked closely together for five years, and the bond between the two men had grown ever stronger with each passing year. At least, Norris thought, he wasn't the only man being summoned into the station at the crack of dawn. He could only imagine the scowl on Hillman's face when a constable knocked him up at such an ungodly hour.

"I take it I've no time for breakfast then, Fry?" asked Norris, knowing the answer already. If Madden had sent for him, it meant he was needed right away, not after enjoying a leisurely breakfast with his wife.

"The sergeant said I was to tell you that the chief inspector said, '*Now means now*,' if you'll forgive me, sir."

"Don't worry, constable. I'm not in the habit of shooting the messenger. Just give me a minute to let my wife know I may be out for a long while."

Norris closed the door. Constable Fry stood waiting, fidgeting and fretting as one minute turned into two, then three, and then four. Surely, he'd be in trouble with the sergeant if the inspector didn't get himself down to the station in double-quick time? After all, the chief inspector himself had summoned him.

A full ten minutes had passed by the time Norris eventually opened the front door once again. Betty had wrapped two slices of buttered bread in a slice of grease-proof paper, which he carried under his left arm. She had also made sure that Norris had eaten the two eggs she'd boiled before he rejoined Fry. They'd gone cold while was standing at the door talking to the constable, but at least they were a source of nourishment for her husband, who, she knew from past experiences, could be away for many long hours when in the early stages of a murder investigation. Norris had kissed his wife on the cheek, patted the dog, who'd returned from his patrol of the back garden to scrounge any leftovers from the breakfast table, and was now ready to face whatever the day held in store for him.

"Right, Constable Fry, lead on," said a cheery Albert Norris, as he rejoined the young constable. He'd had no time to shave, and his coat appeared more than little crumpled, but, as he walked at a brisk pace beside the inspector, Fry felt that Detective Inspector Norris, who he knew solely by reputation, was definitely not a man he'd like to cross. Norris had a 'past', so he'd learned –

though quite what had happened that had left the inspector in a sort of promotion limbo, no one at the station either knew or was prepared to say. All Fry knew, as he cast his eyes in the inspector's direction as they walked, was that the man had a certain air of authority about him; one that would brook no argument from a humble P.C. such as himself. Norris could be difficult to get along with, that much he'd learned, and he made a conscious decision not to get on the inspector's wrong side, if he could help it.

The two men soon left behind the neat suburban terraces where the inspector had made his home and found themselves walking along an already busy thoroughfare, as early morning omnibuses rattled along the cobbled streets, horses snorting and hooves clattering as they carried the early morning workers to their destinations. They were passed by three such omnibuses, each filled to the brim on both the upper and lower decks with passengers. Clearly, the advent of the new underground railway hadn't entirely stolen too much business from the omnibus company, as had been expected. There were still many residents of London who feared the new railway, preferring to travel above ground rather than risk the tunnels and darkness of the new transport system. Even though much of the rail network ran above ground, they still considered it too risky and avoided it as though certain death would visit itself upon anyone foolish enough to hazard a journey along its gleaming metal rails.

Street sellers were already at work setting up their stalls, a hot chestnut seller firing up his brazier, a match seller preparing his pitch and all manner of others making an early start as they went about the business of earning a living. For many, that living would be a hard one, as thousands of the capital's residents fell into the lowest category of society, that of the poor.

Fifteen minutes after leaving the inspector's house on Allardyce Street, on the morning of 9th September, 1888, just over twenty-four hours after the man who would later be dubbed Jack the Ripper had killed and mutilated the unfortunate Annie Chapman, Norris arrived at New Street police station, where his involvement with *the underground murders*, as the killings would eventually be dubbed, soon began in earnest.

Chapter 3
The Body at Aldgate

Approximately four hours before Constable Fry knocked on Albert Norris's front door, at just after 2 a.m., twenty two-year-old Arthur Ward, employee of the Metropolitan Railway, began his systematic check of the carriages of the last train of the night to have arrived and terminated at Aldgate station. Ward's job entailed opening each carriage door and making sure that all passengers had safely alighted and vacated the train, and to check for any property left behind on the train, which he would then deliver to the lost property office. At such a late hour, it wasn't unusual for the odd late-night reveller to fall asleep in their seat and either miss their stop, or carry on to the end of the line where Arthur Ward, or someone like him, would gently awaken them and coax them from the train.

Each carriage could hold a maximum of ten people, on somewhat uncomfortable bench seats covered in a bare modicum of cloth material that added little in the way of comfort for those travelling on board this latest innovative mode of travel within the capital. As he reached the third carriage of the late night train, Ward opened the door and quickly spotted the reclining figure of a young woman in the corner of one of the bench seats, her head resting against the window of the carriage. She wore a green dress, with a pale brown shawl covering her shoulders. Her boots were well-soled, almost new in appearance and she had the appearance of a respectable young working woman, perhaps a nurse or a midwife, he thought, on her way home from a late shift at one of the local hospitals. He knew that not all nurses lived on the premises in some of the city's larger hospitals. His own cousin, Maude, was a nurse at Charing Cross, and 'lived out' at her parents' home.

"End of the line, my dear." Ward spoke loudly, wanting to wake the woman and see her on her way. "This is Aldgate, lady," he tried again. "We don't go no further tonight. This is the end of the line."

When his repeated entreaties received no reply from the apparently sleeping woman, Arthur Ward stepped briskly into the compartment and placed a hand on her shoulder, shaking her gently.

"Please, Miss, it's late and you ought to be getting off home, now," he appealed. Receiving no response, he shook the woman a little harder. This time, he was shocked as, instead of waking and perhaps reproaching him for his familiarity in touching her while she slept, the woman instead slipped slowly away from the window, off the seat itself, then rolled in ungainly fashion onto the floor of the carriage.

Up to that date in his young life, Arthur Ward had never seen or been in close proximity to a dead body. Yet, as he stared down at the figure lying at his feet on the carriage floor, he was in no doubt whatsoever that the young woman was indeed deceased. The blank, staring eyes and pallid appearance of her face were unmistakable clues, and if they needed reinforcing in his mind, that reinforcement came from the small but significant red stain, almost centrally placed on her chest, which was revealed as her shawl slipped back with the movement of her body onto the floor. Arthur knew blood when he saw it; he'd seen enough accidents amongst some of the labourers on the railway to recognise it for what it was. Strangely, his first thought was that there should be more blood, if what he was looking at was a fatal wound, but then, he was no medical expert.

He realised he was shaking. Shock perhaps, he thought, and his legs felt like lead, though he knew he couldn't stand there staring at the woman's body all night. He had to get help, to report his grisly find and so, with a superhuman effort, Arthur Ward forced his legs to move, as he beat a retreat from the carriage and made his way along the platform to the station master's office. The station master, Edgar Rowe, had long since left for the night and his office was currently occupied by the night-time supervisor, Maurice Belton. Belton was also preparing to finish work for the night, as soon as Arthur Ward reported to him that the train was clear and the station could be locked up until the early morning shift arrived, in little less than two hours' time.

Belton smiled as young Arthur entered the office, but the smile soon turned to a look of worried puzzlement as he saw the shocked look and pallor clearly apparent on the younger man's face.

"Arthur? What's wrong? You look as if you've seen a ghost."

"Worse than that, Mr. Belton, I've found a body!" Arthur shouted.

"A body? What sort of body?" asked Belton, realising as he spoke that it was probably the stupidest question he'd ever asked in his life.

"The dead sort, Mr. Belton. A woman, a young one, in one of the carriages. It's horrible, really. She's got a red bloodstain on her chest. I think she's been shot."

"All right, Arthur, calm down a bit, there's a good lad. I think you'd better show me this body of yours before we go any further."

"T'ain't no body of mine, Mr. Belton, that's for sure."

"Yes, well, anyway, you'd better show me," said Belton. He extricated his slightly ponderous bulk from the space behind the desk and made his way with Arthur Ward to the carriage where the recumbent body of the young woman lay.

After confirming what Arthur Ward already knew, in other words, that the woman was beyond any help from the living, Belton sent the hapless young man to find a constable, or, if one couldn't be found, he instructed the young man to run to the nearest police station, some ten minutes' walk away, and bring back a policeman.

Glad to be out of the claustrophobic atmosphere of the underground station concourse, Arthur Ward gulped in huge lungfuls of air as he arrived on the street outside Aldgate station. He was glad to escape from the all-pervading smell that always lingered within the confines of his place of work; a mixture of stale smoke, steam, coal dust and other noxious elements that hung like a pall on every yard of the railway. As luck would have it, within two minutes of leaving the station he turned a corner to find himself face to face with a uniformed police constable, and the young man quickly blurted out his story.

"There's been a murder, on the train, in the station," he babbled at the surprised police officer, who, seeing the man's agitated state, took hold of his arm.

"Now, then," the officer said, soothingly. "What murder is this you're referring to? Which station do you mean? Give me the facts, man, and we can sort this out sooner."

"Aldgate station. Yes, of course, I'm sorry. I found the body in a carriage. It's a young woman and there's a big red wound in her chest."

"Is there anyone with her now?" asked the constable.

"Yes, Mr. Belton the night station supervisor's with her."

"Right then, here's what I want you to do, young fellow. What's your name, by the way?"

"Ward, sir. Arthur Ward."

"Right, Arthur. I want you to run to New Street police station, it's not far from here. D'you know it?"

Arthur nodded.

"Good. Tell the sergeant on duty that Constable Wilkinson sent you to report the murder of a young woman. Give him all the details you can, and he'll send someone to Aldgate as soon as he can. I'll be there, waiting for them."

"Yes, right. I'll be as fast as I can," Arthur replied.

Police Constable Bob Wilkinson quickly made his way to Aldgate, where he found Maurice Belton standing on the platform, outside the carriage that Wilkinson assumed held the body of the deceased. Indeed, Belton had seen enough of the corpse and had spent little time with the body after sending Ward on his mission. Rightly, he'd also suspected that the less he encroached upon the scene, the less chance there was of him compromising any evidence the killer might have left behind.

"Mr. Belton, is it, sir?"

"Maurice Belton, yes, that's right, Constable."

"The body, sir?"

"In there." Belton pointed at the appropriate carriage door.

Wilkinson stepped past the night supervisor, into the murder scene and within minutes, he was joined by both a uniformed sergeant and a young plain clothes detective, accompanied by Arthur Ward, who waited on the platform with Belton. The detective, a Sergeant Dove, appeared to take charge of the scene, and it was he, a short time later, who soon sent Wilkinson back to the station with instructions that would see the crime reported to higher authority in rapid time.

Even Dove was unaware just how high his message would be passed in a short space of time, or that within hours, he would be joined at the scene by Detective Inspector Albert Norris, who himself was being summoned from his home and given some rather unusual instructions regarding the investigation that was being handed to him.

For now, Detective Sergeant Dove and Sergeant Lee made sure the scene was as secure as they could make it, and Constable Wilkinson was put to work taking preliminary statements from both Arthur Ward and Maurice Belton, though Dove was certain that whoever arrived to take charge of the case would need to speak to both men, too. For that reason, the sergeant forbade the two men from leaving the station until an inspector arrived.

"But my wife will worry," Belton protested. "I'm already late home from work and if I have to hang around here for hours, she'll be certain I've been murdered or met with an accident."

"Too right," added Arthur Ward. "And my mum and dad will wonder what's become of me, too."

Dove pondered for a moment.

Sergeant Lee provided the solution they required.

"I'll run back to New Street and arrange for a constable to get messages to their homes, if they'll provide me with their addresses," he volunteered. "I can do that and be back here in no time."

Belton and Ward provided the information Lee required and he set off to arrange for their families to be told simply that there'd been *an incident at work* and that they were both assisting the police with their inquiries and would return home soon.

Tobias Dove was soon hard at work, searching the carriage and inspecting the woman's body to the best of his ability. He wanted to locate as many clues as possible, to present to whichever inspector might arrive to take charge of the case. He quickly found himself baffled by the apparent lack of any substantive evidence, either on the body of the deceased, or in the carriage itself.

Joined soon afterwards by Sergeant Lee, who'd brought two more constables with him to help in the search for clues, Dove continued in his investigation until the arrival, an hour later, of the police surgeon, Doctor Roebuck. The surgeon had been summoned from his bed by a uniformed officer, sent by Lee as soon as he'd returned to New Street with confirmation that a body had indeed been discovered, and that foul play was suspected.

Doctor Roebuck busied himself with an examination of the body, during which time Constable Fry had been despatched by the chief inspector, himself woken from his slumbers by a runner, to bring Inspector Albert Norris into his office for a briefing on the case. As the ever-growing official contingent assembled on the platform at Aldgate, Albert Norris found himself seated opposite his superior officer, receiving a rather strange briefing. It was certainly one such as he'd never heard the like of before, in all his years on the force.

Chapter 4
Instructions

Chief Inspector Joshua Madden sat cradling his unlit pipe in the palm of his right hand, as Albert Norris sat down on the opposite side of his desk, as instructed. Aged almost sixty, a little under six feet tall, with a waistline just giving way to obesity, and hoping to retire before the year was out, Madden stroked his greying beard and waited for the inspector to settle himself before speaking.

"Well, Bert, we've a real to-do on our hands, that's for sure. Sorry for calling you out so early, by the way."

"Not a problem, sir," Norris replied, though he knew Madden's apology would never stand up in a court of law. It had probably given the chief inspector great delight to summon Norris from his bed at the crack of dawn. "Young Fry told me there'd been a murder?"

"Yes, a bad business by all accounts. A young woman's body was discovered by a Metropolitan Railway employee a few hours ago."

"On the railway track, sir, or on a train?"

"In a carriage, standing at the platform on Aldgate station."

"Ah, so we can't be sure if the victim was actually killed where she was found?"

"Well, it's fairly certain she was killed in the carriage."

"No, sir. I mean, if she was on a train, she could have been killed at any point along her journey. As you said, the body was discovered at Aldgate when the train was stationary. There's nothing to suggest that she was killed there, I suppose, as opposed to anywhere else along the train's route?"

"I don't have a lot of details, yet, Inspector. Sergeant Dove is on the scene and is carrying out a preliminary investigation of the carriage and the body, in the presence of the police surgeon."

"I see, sir. Can I just ask why I've been drafted in for this one? I mean, I'm hardly flavour of the month around here, or anywhere else in the city, am I? Surely Scotland Yard will want to get their hooks into this one."

Madden looked hard at Norris, his cheeks puffing out with barely concealed anger, which he did well to stifle before replying to the inspector's question.

"Listen to me, and listen well, Inspector. As long as you're on my team, you follow my orders, is that clear?"

Norris nodded but said nothing. Madden continued.

"Scotland Yard have got their work cut out in the search for this so-called Whitechapel Murderer. You know as well as I do that they've drafted in uniformed constables from every station in the city to help in the investigation. Stations like ours are being denuded of officers we can ill afford to lose if we're to police the rest of London effectively. We've lost five men to the Whitechapel investigation and I have to make the best of the resources left at my disposal. You, Norris, made a mistake ten years ago, one that cost you your place at Scotland Yard. Since then, you've done a pretty good job in my opinion, but you have a bloody bad habit of carrying that awful big chip around on your shoulder. Forget the past, Bert, and concentrate on now. You're the best man I have for this job, and I want you to lead the investigation."

"I see, sir. When you put it like that, I can't really refuse, can I?"

"No, you bloody well can't. Now, are you going to listen to what I have to say, or not?"

"Yes, sir. Please, do carry on."

Madden ignored the slight condescension in Norris's voice, but, as if to reinforce his superiority over his subordinate officer, he removed a box of Swan Vesta matches from a drawer in his desk and spent a whole minute lighting his pipe, puffing on the stem until the tobacco in the bowl was burning to his satisfaction. Satisfied at last, he spoke once again.

"How much do you know about the Metropolitan Railway, Bert?"

"Well, as far as I recall, it was opened in the early Sixties... "

"1863, to be precise," the chief interjected.

"Right, sir, 1863 it is, then. It runs above and below ground and the steam locomotives that haul the carriages are specially adapted for running through the long tunnels underground. I've never travelled on it myself, but I've heard it's fast and efficient as well as being cheap. The downside, from what I've heard and read, is that it's smoky and draughty, and the smell of the smoke and other substances produced by the locomotives can be positively gut-wrenching for the passengers. The smoke fills the carriages, seeping in through every crack and tiny hole in the coachwork, and some people claim that riding on the underground railway can be bloody hazardous to a person's health. That's about all I know, sir."

"Some of what you say is quite true, Bert, but there's more to it than that. The government is committed to seeing a great expansion of the underground railway system. It already carries millions of passengers every year, and has revolutionised the movement of the labour force around the city. Workers can now travel into and out of the city, to and from jobs they might never have obtained before the coming of the railway. Yes, there are still those who doubt the long-term future of the railway, and those who tell of so-called *choke damp* as being a terrible affliction travellers place themselves at risk of catching if they use the system regularly, but the Metropolitan is here to stay. Not only that, but the company has plans to expand the system so that it reaches even further afield, into the suburbs and beyond. Before long, it will be possible for workers to travel into the city from country villages and towns, and vice-versa, of course. Think of the economic virtue of such expansion, and what it may do to assist in the growth of the industry of the nation."

"Sounds like you're an expert in the workings of the Metropolitan Railway, sir."

"I'm telling you what I know, and what I've read in The Times in recent months, Inspector, nothing more."

After hesitating for a few seconds, Madden then went on.

"Well, there is something more, in fact, though what I'm about to tell you is completely confidential. You may, at some point in the investigation, reveal this to your sergeant, but only if you feel it to be a necessity for him to share this knowledge, understood?"

Not sure what the chief inspector was about to reveal, Norris could only nod in agreement, and shifted in his chair, slightly uneasily. He had a feeling he wasn't going to like what he was about to hear. Madden opened a drawer in his desk, and extracted a slim brown file. Placing it on his desk, he opened it and removed a single sheet of paper, covered, as Norris could see from his side of the desk, in neat typewritten script.

"Sadly," Madden began, "there have been a number of threats made against the Metropolitan since it opened over twenty years ago. Most of the older ones can, I believe, be easily discounted as irrelevant to today's investigation. Others, however, can't be dismissed quite so readily."

"Threats, sir? What kind of threats?" Norris was intrigued.

"There are people, Norris, who believe that the underground railway is not a good or proper thing as far as London is concerned. Here are a couple of examples."

He began to read from the paper in front of him.

"'Men have met their maker as a result of the greed and avarice of those who would turn the people of this fair city into denizens of the underworld. Be warned that their deaths will be avenged.' It's true that a number of workers were killed in accidents, mostly cave-ins, during the excavations of the original tunnel and some of the newer ones. This could be a valid threat from someone with revenge in mind against the company, perhaps a friend or relative of one of the dead men. 'God will not allow this fiendish contraption, this infernal machine of the devil to prosper. We will bring about its ruination and force the Metropolitan Railway to cease its operations forthwith, in the name of The Almighty,' says another one. There are more, but they mostly follow the same theme."

"But surely, sir, these are cranks, fools and idiotic protesters with more time and ink on their hands than real intent?"

"You're probably correct, Inspector. But, and we must be careful here, if even one of these is a genuine threat and someone has taken to murder to try and scare the good people of the city from the railway in order to force it to cease operations, or at least in a move designed to hit the company's profits, then we must be alert to the danger."

"Yes, sir, I think I see. But if this is a random, motiveless murder designed simply to hit the reputation of the Metropolitan railway, we are going to find it even harder to track down the killer."

"I'm afraid there's more. The final paragraph of this document, which was circulated to all senior officers in the Metropolitan Police, states quite firmly: *'Any act of wilful sabotage, or potential wilful sabotage, violence against the person or persons of those employed by or being carried as passengers by the Metropolitan Railway, will be viewed in the gravest light by Her Majesty's government, such is the importance placed by said government on the future economic success of the underground railway and its implications for the future prosperity of the country itself. It is therefore imperative that any investigation into any such acts be carried out with extreme tact and diplomacy, with the minimum publicity being granted to the act, and with the outcome kept as close and private as can be allowed within the confines of the law.'*

"In other words, Norris, you are to keep your investigation as low-key as possible, reporting only to me, and discussing the case only with those directly involved in the investigation. That includes your wife, and even your dog. Do I make myself clear?"

"Yes, sir, you do. I didn't realise this was such a high-profile case."

"It isn't, really. And that's how we have to keep it."

"But surely, sir, the press will be onto the murder in no time?"

"The government has certain powers to limit press coverage of cases which are deemed a matter of national security. This will be classified as such and all editors will be instructed, under the Special Powers Act, to co-operate in a partial news blackout. There will be minimal information printed, enough to make sure that there will be no embarrassing leaks of information from anyone privy to the fact that the murder did in fact take place, but the details will be closely guarded and any press articles censored by the Home Office."

"Bloody hell, sir. What you're effectively saying is that I'm to be working with one hand tied behind my back, so to speak."

"I'm afraid so, Norris. That's the way things stand, and you'd better be extremely careful where you tread with this one. Now, I think we've wasted enough time here in the office. Your sergeant has already been despatched to Aldgate to take over from the responding officers, so I suggest you get over there post-haste and assert your authority on the situation. Remember as well that the Whitechapel Murderer is getting all the publicity and attracting massive press coverage. Let's keep it that way, eh?"

"In other words, let the boys in Whitechapel run rings around themselves, while we keep a low profile and work in the shadows?"

"Something like that, yes. Now, you were about to leave?"

"Yes, sir, but, just one question?"

"Which is?"

"What about any witnesses? Won't they be free to relate what's happened to their families, the press perhaps?"

"They will be taken care of too, Norris. Never fear. They will be sworn to silence under pain of prosecution. A member of Special Branch is already on the way to Aldgate to ensure they sign the necessary papers that will ensure their silence."

"They, whoever 'they' are, seem to have this all sewn up, sir, if you don't mind me saying so. Do you really want me to find this killer, or just go through the motions and let the whole thing be buried under the carpet?"

"We are the Metropolitan Police, Inspector Norris. You will do all you can to unearth and apprehend the killer, and then leave matters in my hands. Clear?"

"Yes, sir. I'd better be going then."

Norris rose to leave and Madden stared at him for a second before standing himself, offering a handshake across the desk and saying, simply, "Good luck, Bert."

"Thank you, sir. I've a feeling I'm going to need it."

Norris took his leave of the chief inspector, and made his way on foot to Aldgate, where he knew his sergeant, and indeed his close friend, Dylan Hillman, would be waiting. *What*, he wondered, *am I to tell Hillman?*

For the first time in many years, Albert Norris envied the role of the humble police constable who simply followed orders, did his job, and went home at the end of his shift. Whatever he and Hillman were about to become embroiled in, would, he felt sure, leave a bitter taste in his mouth. Already, the feeling that he'd be subject to political manipulation as his investigation proceeded was strong in Norris's mind. As he entered Aldgate station and headed for the crowd of police officers already gathered on the platform, he had the sensation that this case, like one a long time ago, might not really be in the best interest of his career, such as it already was.

Chapter 5
No Bloody Footprints

As he walked along the platform towards the gathering of officers already in attendance, Norris found himself struck by an alien sensation, as though in walking from the daylight into the rather subterranean atmosphere of the station, he'd entered a new world, one with which he'd rapidly need to become familiar. His nose twitched as the smell he'd heard so much about rose to meet his nostrils. Without doubt, the combined odours of steam, soot, coal smoke and sulphur produced an all-pervading and unpleasant miasma that, Norris thought, could hardly be worth anyone taking the time and trouble to travel on the new-fangled transportation system. He'd never been tempted to try the underground railway, never having had need of it, and now, he felt even less inclined to sample its services.

As he drew closer, his sergeant, Dylan Hillman, raised a hand in greeting. Norris waved back as he passed the deep-burgundy-red locomotive that stood quietly at the front of the death train. Norris was struck by the rather strange, ungainly appearance of the loco, its funnel taller than he'd imagined and the odd pipes at the side of the boiler, that he'd later discover were part of the unusual and unique steam condensing system particular to the underground railway.

"Morning, sir," called Hillman, as Norris came within speaking distance.

"Morning to you, too, Dylan. Seems we've a bit of a rum do on our hands today."

"Yes, a nasty one, this, she's in there," said Hillman, pointing at the open carriage door where the body lay. "The doctor's still in there with her. I thought it best to wait for you before allowing anyone else to touch her, or move the body."

"Good thinking, Dylan. Who's the doctor on duty?"

"Doctor Roebuck."

"Ah, a good man. Good morning to you, too, gentlemen." He directed his words to the other officers who stood waiting for him to complete his conversation with Hillman.

"Good morning, sir," both Dove and Lee echoed in unison, the two constables to their rear simply touching their helmets in salute.

"Sergeants Dove and Lee were the first officers on the scene, sir," said Hillman.

"I see. Anything you can tell me, Dove? Or you, Sergeant Lee?"

Dove replied on behalf of the two of them.

"Not really, sir. She's dead, that's for sure, and Doctor Roebuck said a few minutes ago that she'd been stabbed, though there ain't a lot of blood in there to testify to that conclusion. The railway staff on duty say they either can't remember, or simply didn't see if any other passengers exited from the carriage she was found in when it pulled in to the station."

As Dove spoke, the head of Doctor Roebuck appeared in the doorway. Norris had known Roebuck for some years. He was tall, slim and every inch a medical man in speech and demeanour, and Norris knew him to be a meticulous and reliable examiner of such scenes on behalf of the police.

"Ah, Sergeant, that's because you're not a medical man. You're expecting to see blood splashed all over the compartment, are you not, in order to bear witness to a fatal stabbing?"

"Well, Doctor, I'm not trying to tell you your job, of course, I'm just a humble policeman, but I did think there'd be more blood, yes."

"Sergeant Dove, in most cases of death by stabbing, you'd be quite correct. But in this case, it would appear our murderer either knew exactly what he was doing, or simply got lucky."

"Meaning what, Doctor Roebuck?" Norris asked.

"Meaning, Inspector, that the heart stops pumping blood around the body at the exact instant of death. In this case, the poor woman was stabbed directly in the heart, causing immediate massive shock, the heart ceasing to do its job, and almost instantaneous death. Consequently, the blood loss was minimal, and the small amount of blood that did leak from the wound was, for the most part, immediately soaked up by the fabric of her dress and shawl."

"No bloody footprints to follow, then, eh, Doctor?"

"Not one, I'm afraid. Would you like to see her?"

"I think I'd better. Come on, Dylan."

With that, Norris and Hillman stepped into the death scene, joining the doctor as he crouched over the body of the victim.

"She's young," said Norris.

"Looks like a working girl of sorts. Not too poor, not too affluent, I'd say," said Roebuck.

"Anything on her to give us a clue to her identity, Doctor?" asked Hillman.

"Nothing yet. But wait, what's this?"

Roebuck pushed his hand into a semi-concealed pocket in the woman's dress and removed a piece of paper, the only item contained within it. He passed it straight up to Norris who was standing slightly to his side.

"'*Bible Study for the Young Ladies of London, at St Giles's Church, Clerkenwell, every Thursday night,*'" Norris read.

"Last night," said Hillman.

"Someone at the church might know her, Dylan."

"We'll need a photograph, sir," the sergeant replied.

"Organise it please," said Norris. "There's no purse or handbag lying around, is there, Doctor?"

"Sorry, Inspector. She had nothing with her at all, unless the killer took it with him. Listen, if there's nothing else you want here, can I have the body removed to the mortuary? I can get on with a full autopsy then, as the law requires."

"Of course, Doctor, you can proceed with the removal. Please let me know what you discover as soon as you've completed the post mortem examination."

"Yes, I'll do that," Roebuck replied. He stepped from the carriage, back onto the platform and scurried off to summon the mortuary assistants to remove the body.

"Inspector?" a voice called out from the platform, and Norris leaned through the doorway in response to the call which emanated from Sergeant Dove.

"Yes, Sergeant. What can I do for you?"

"The railway people want to know about the trains, sir."

"What trains?"

"The line re-opens in less than an hour, sir. There'll be thousands of people wanting to come down here to catch trains to work and so on. Do we let them in, or close the station, or what?"

Norris thought long and hard before replying, his mind fixed on the warning he'd received from Chief Inspector Madden. *Keep it low-key for now*, he thought.

"Tell them they can open for business as usual. But I want this train moved to a siding or whatever, and the carriage sealed so that only we can access it until we're done with the investigation of the murder scene. Has the man from Special Branch arrived yet?"

"Already here, sir. An Inspector Small. He's been talking to the railway employees, as he didn't want to disturb you while you were making your examination of the carriage."

"Very thoughtful of him, I'm sure." Norris smiled at the sergeant. "I'd better go and have a word."

He's in the station master's office, sir."

"Thank you, Dove."

Ten minutes later, Norris re-emerged from the stationmaster's office. Inspector Small, a rotund and slightly bellicose fellow who Norris took an instant dislike to, had obtained signatures from the railway employees which would ensure they didn't blurt out the story of the murder, unless of course they sought a place behind bars in one of Her Majesty's prisons. Norris was uncomfortable with such coercion, but knew there was nothing he could do to prevent it. Far bigger fish than he had their hands in the pond, and he was, despite being in charge of the investigation, nothing more than a political pawn in this game, of that he was sure.

Rejoining Hillman, who was organising the removal of the train from its current position with the day supervisor, who should have relieved the unfortunate Belton some hours ago, Norris took a last look inside the carriage.

"There's nothing more for us here, Dylan," he said, gruffly. "Come on, leave Dove in charge of the scene. We've got work to do elsewhere."

"Where are we going, sir?"

"Why, Sergeant Hillman, we're going to church!"

Chapter 6
Identification

Sadly, the site of St. Giles's church no longer exists in the modern world in which we live. The hundred years and more that have elapsed since the underground killings have seen the eradication of many streets and once common landmarks from the old city of London. Such, as seems too often the case, is the price of progress and urban growth. Anyone visiting the site today would find nothing more architecturally exciting than a large, sprawling, underground car park, topped with nothing more salubrious than a small parade of shops, serving fast food, selling motor parts, or second-hand clothing.

At the time of our story, however, St Giles's remained a beacon of Christian virtue within its local environment, its spire rising to tower over the streets around its position on the corner of Bremner Street (now sadly vanished) and Victoria Road. Each Sunday, its pews would be filled with pious Victorians, both from the middle class community it mainly served, and those from the lower echelons of society, servants and menial workers who lived on the periphery of local society. Even those who worked long, gruelling hours on the most tedious and back-breaking work imaginable, would somehow find the time to garb themselves in whatever constituted their 'Sunday Best' clothes, and would spend their Sunday mornings, or evenings perhaps, on their knees, praying to God and listening to the sermons preached from the pulpit, that would invariably warn of the dangers to their immortal souls, from all manner of sins.

Sexual promiscuity always ranked high on such lists of forbidden pleasures, as the Victorian ethic of propriety and abstinence showered down from myriad pulpits around the country every Sunday. Such words appeared to have little effect on the poorer members of society, however, evidenced by the burgeoning population of the great capital of the British Empire. Even so, the prospect of eternal damnation would far outweigh the chance of a few extra hours in bed on a Sunday, even if such a luxury were available to some. The church would resound to the sound of up to two hundred voices raised in praise of the Lord, as hymns were sung with great gusto and feeling. After the service, the congregation would go home filled with the self-righteous piety of the Victorian generation, the belief that they were indeed the children of God, and that they would find eternal peace and happiness as long as they followed the instructions of that most revered member of society, the minister.

After leaving Aldgate, Dylan Hillman hailed a passing cab and he and the inspector joined the ever-growing early morning throng of traffic as London, and Londoners, awoke from their slumbers, and the business of grinding out another day's existence began in earnest. The few clouds that had greeted the dawn were clearing from the sky, and the streets of the city became suffused with a warmth unusual for the time of year. Norris hoped that the mortuary attendants had worked swiftly to get the corpse of the murder victim to the morgue before the heat began to affect it. The cabbie dropped them off on the corner, about a hundred yards from the entrance to the church, allowing the two men the chance to stretch their legs a little before entering the building.

Albert Norris and Dylan Hillman arrived at St. Giles's, not far from Farringdon Street underground station, just as the minister in question, the Reverend Martin Bowker, dressed in his usual attire of black frock-coat, his white dog-collar prominent against his sombre black shirt, stepped through the heavy oak doors and appeared on the outer steps of the church. He was taking the morning air, or so it appeared to the approaching detectives.

"Good morning, gentlemen," he said cheerfully as the two men drew nearer.

"Good morning to you, too, sir," Norris replied. "May we have a word with you?"

"God's house is always open and, as his servant, I'm always ready to hear from members of his flock," the minister replied, smiling benignly at the two detectives.

"I'm Detective Inspector Norris, this is Detective Sergeant Hillman, from New Street, and I'm afraid it's a matter of police business, rather than God's work, that we wish to discuss with you, Reverend. . . ?"

"Bowker, Detective Inspector, Martin Bowker. I thought I didn't recognise you two gentlemen as being members of my regular congregation. Please, shall we step inside the church and discuss whatever you wish to see me about, out of the public gaze?"

"Yes, thank you, sir. A good idea." Norris replied.

* * *

Ten minutes later, while seated on of the church's rear pews, Norris and Hillman had jointly given the vicar of St. Giles's as much information about the events of the previous night as they deemed it necessary for him to know. It was time to find out if he knew the dead woman.

"She had this in a pocket in her dress," Norris said, showing Bowker the Bible Study advertisement that Doctor Roebuck had discovered on the dead woman.

"Ah, I see. This is the reason you came to see me. I was beginning to wonder, Inspector. You think she may have been a member of my congregation, perhaps even one of my Bible Study Class?"

"Why else would she be carrying one of your leaflets?" Hillman asked.

"My dear Sergeant, anyone in the parish could have got hold of one of those. See. . . " He pointed to a set of wooden pigeonholes affixed to the wall of the church porch. "There are dozens of those leaflets placed in there, where it is quite easy for anyone to simply enter the church, pick one up and take it with them, without me or anyone else even knowing they've been here. As I said before, God's house is. . . ."

"Always open," Norris completed the vicar's sentence. "Yes, that's all very well, Reverend, but, does the description I've given you remind you of anyone in your congregation?"

"Well, we did hold a class last night, and there was a woman in a green dress present. Do you have one of those modern photographic images, perhaps? I'd hate to send you on a wild goose chase to the wrong place, especially if I'm wrong and you find whoever it may be alive and well. What a shock they might receive, to think you believe them to have been the victim of a violent murder!'"

This was one of the occasions Norris hated. Dealing with men of the cloth could be frustrating at the best of times. Their self-righteousness could be annoying to a practical and level-headed investigative mind, so Norris thoughts ran. Now, the vicar's sensibilities were beginning to grate on the detective.

"Reverend Bowker, I assure you we will be diplomatic and sensitive about any information you provide us with. As for a photographic reproduction of the deceased, that will be dealt with at the mortuary. For now, you must base your identification solely on the description we've given you. I know it's not much, but surely there can't have been many ladies present dressed in similar attire last night?"

"Yes, well, there was such a lady here last night. It was, I believe, her third or fourth visit to the study class."

"Do you have a name for us, sir?" asked Hillman.

"And perhaps an address?" added Norris.

"I believe her name was Clara Forshaw, Inspector, and I understand she held a secretarial position with the Bellhaven family, who, I believe she mentioned once, live in the Holborn area. Clara was very pretty, and intelligent and even helped me out with some administrative tasks in respect of the study class, such was her kindheartedness."

"Do you mean Laurence Bellhaven?" asked Norris, his ears pricking up at the mention of the name.

"In all likelihood, one and same," the minister replied.

"You know the man, sir?" asked Hillman, a note of surprise in his voice.

"Let's just say I know of him, Sergeant."

"I'm sorry. Does the name cause you some disquiet, Inspector?" asked Bowker.

Norris's demeanour appeared to have changed almost instantaneously at the mention of the Bellhaven name and his reply to the minister ensured a speedy end to the interview.

"I thank you for your time, Reverend Bowker, and for the information, which I'm sure will be helpful. We must now check and see if the lady in the carriage was indeed the secretary of Mr. Bellhaven, so, if you will excuse us, Sergeant Hillman and I must go about our business, and leave you to yours. Come, sergeant, we have much to do."

With that, Norris led Dylan Hillman from the church, leaving a rather befuddled and confused minister in their wake. On the street outside St. Giles's, as they made their way to the nearest cab rank, Hillman grabbed his inspector by the arm, causing him to stop in his tracks.

"Bert, come on, talk to me. We've worked together for a long time, and been friends long enough for me to know when something's rattled you. What's the significance of this Laurence Bellhaven character? Is there something I ought to know about him?"

"I'm sorry, Dylan," Norris replied. "Yes, there is something you need to know, not just about Bellhaven, but about this bloody case we've been saddled with. Let's get a cab first, then it's time I gave you a few details about what we're dealing with."

Hillman knew Norris well enough not to question him further on the open street. Instead, they waited the two minutes it took for them to find a cab, whereupon Norris ordered the driver to take them back to New Street police station.

As they rattled along the cobbled streets, with the sounds of the horse's hooves, the cab's wheels and the sundry sounds of a now fully awake London encroaching on the interior of the cab,

Norris decided that they had enough privacy for him to begin. It was time for Dylan Hillman to share some unpleasant facts.

Chapter 7
Laurence Bellhaven

"Bloody hell, Bert! What have you got us into this time?" asked Hillman, five minutes later.

"Don't blame me, Dylan, old chum. I have to follow orders, just the same as you."

"But, you're basically saying that we have to conduct an investigation, quietly and without ruffling any feathers, and without letting the public know any of the details of the case?"

"Well, not many details, anyway. The Chief, and those in authority above him, will see to the press blackout, using the Special Powers act. They can do that, though I've never heard of the act being used in a case like this before. We have to do the best we can, and hope we can catch this bastard quickly and quietly. As the Chief said, the murders in Whitechapel are taking up the front pages of the press every day, and the public clamour for an arrest in that case will deflect any public interest away from our case. One woman dying on a train isn't going to push the Whitechapel Murderer off the front pages, is it? I've heard they've even got a so-called *vigilance committee* in Whitechapel now, sending out street patrols at night, in addition to our official police patrols. I don't think Abberline and his boys will be too happy about that."

"Hang on, Bert. You said, 'one woman dying on a train'. Don't you mean, *murdered on a train*?"

"I've a feeling the press report will be doctored a little to reflect what I just said, Dylan. Nothing to do with me, but that's the way I see it happening. They can't deny that something happened last night. Too many people will have noted the police presence at Aldgate, so they'll doubtless cook something up for the press to release. You mark my words."

Hillman whistled through his teeth. He understood right away that they were involved in a case that could have far more serious ramifications than he could possibly have ever imagined.

"And Laurence Bellhaven? Who is he, Bert, and what does he have to do with the case? You couldn't get out of that church fast enough, once the vicar told you who he thinks the victim worked for."

"Listen, Dylan. I told you about the document Madden showed me, right? Well, the paragraph at the bottom, the one that gave the instructions for the handling of any incidents of this particular nature on the underground railway, was signed by the Metropolitan Police Commissioner himself, with instructions that any such incidents would require the powers-that-be at Scotland Yard to liaise with the railway company's director of operations, *Mr. Laurence Bellhaven*, or his successors."

"Bloody hell," said Hillman. "So we really might be in a very tricky situation if that is his personal secretary lying on a slab in the morgue."

"I'm telling you, Dylan. This bloody case is getting more perplexing and potentially more political by the hour."

The cab slowed, the driver calling down to announce that they were arriving at the police station.

Leaving Hillman to pay off the cabbie, Norris stepped briskly up the steps that led into the station and made straight for the office of Chief Inspector Madden. Hillman caught up with him just as after he'd knocked on the door and received a loud "Come in," from within the room beyond.

* * *

The two men emerged from the office of Chief Inspector Joshua Madden fifteen minutes later. The chief inspector had expressed surprise at learning of the potential connection between the victim of the previous night's murder and a senior member of the Metropolitan Railway's management.

"This certainly casts a grim face on things, Inspector," he'd said. "This definitely makes me think there's a connection between the killing and a possible threat against the railway. I appreciate you bringing me the news before going to the Bellhaven home. That shows you appreciate the gravity of the situation."

"Actually, sir, I came back to the station to obtain his address. All I know is that it's in the Holborn area."

"Hmmph," the chief grumbled. "Yes, well, you were still correct to come back and report to me. This is a sensitive case, as I told you."

Norris and Hillman left the chief's office and used the police's own copy of the local electoral roll to locate the address of Mr. Laurence Bellhaven. Ten minutes later, seated in yet another cab, they were on their way once again, their destination being the Holborn home of Laurence Bellhaven.

"Do you think he'll be at home at this time of day?" asked Norris, as the cab rattled along the now busy London streets.

"Probably not, Dylan," Norris replied, "but I'm sure Mrs. Bellhaven will be in the house, and the servants, too. There's bound to be someone there who can recognise the description of the dead girl. We can always catch Bellhaven himself at the company offices if we need to, after we've spoken to the family."

As their cab drove into the elite and salubrious area that contained the homes of many of the local members of affluent society, the streets themselves took on a cleaner, less cluttered appearance. There was far less in the way of horse dung present on the road surfaces, and the cobbles themselves were rather more even, giving their cab a smother ride than in the previous few minutes. Looking through the windows of the hansom cab, the two men could see pristinely painted lamp posts, their glasses clean and polished and what appeared to be new, or nearly new, gas mantles in each of them. Clearly, this would be a well-lit neighbourhood by night, in contrast with some of the meaner, less affluent areas of the city, Whitechapel springing clearly into the mind of Norris. The man who was currently terrorising the poor unfortunates of that particular borough would find it extremely difficult to achieve similar results here on Lewisham Place.

Some twenty minutes after leaving the police station, the cab pulled up right outside the front steps of the Bellhaven home. Norris and Hillman stepped from the cab and looked up at the house, which rose from the ground like a pristine white testament to the wealth of its owner. The impeccably painted brickwork glinted in the morning sunshine, the brilliantly lacquered black-painted front door with its ornate brass knocker and door handle contrasting starkly with the gleaming white of the building itself. On either side of the four steps that led to the front door, two columns rose four feet upwards from the pavement, each adorned with a reposing lion, painted in shining gilt, casting a golden glow over the steps as they reflected the sun's rays. Norris knew these Georgian-styled homes. Despite being situated on the busy thoroughfare of Lewisham Place, he was well aware that to the rear it would possess a large, well tended garden, with perhaps a kitchen garden, where Bellhaven's private gardener would grow many of the fresh fruits and vegetables that doubtless formed a large part of the family's diet.

"Nice place," said Hillman.

"Give me my little terrace any day," Norris replied. "I'd hate to have to pay for all the painting and polishing that keeps this place looking the way it does."

"Ah, but then, if you had his wealth, you probably wouldn't miss the money he spends on keeping it like this."

"Very true, Dylan, very true."

Norris's knocking was answered in double-quick time by a smartly uniformed butler. After introducing themselves and stating the reason for their visit, the man, who gave his name as Roland Soames, showed them into the parlour. Less than a minute after they'd entered the room, they were joined by Laurence Bellhaven himself, who was clearly not, as Norris supposed, busily engaged in company business at his office. Tall, slightly overweight, though immaculately dressed as though for a board meeting, his full beard and sideburns giving him the look of the captain of an ocean-going clipper ship, Laurence Bellhaven appeared every inch the wealthy and successful business man that he indeed was.

After introductions were exchanged, Norris wasted no time in getting down to business.

"Good morning, sir. I had imagined that you'd be at work today."

"I should be, Detective Inspector, but my private secretary, who lives on the premises, failed to return to the house last night. Aside from the inconvenience to my work schedule, her disappearance has caused my wife to worry about the girl's safety, a worry I share to some extent."

"Have you reported her failure to return to the police, sir," asked Hillman.

"No, Sergeant, I have not. I believe it is not unusual for the police to ask people to wait at least twenty-four hours before assuming a person to be missing?"

"Quite correct, sir," said Norris. "However, we have reason to believe that your secretary may have met with a violent death some time last night, whilst travelling home on the underground railway."

Bellhaven appeared to pale with shock at Norris's words.

"Death? You mean the poor girl has been...?"

"Murdered, sir. Yes, we do. Was her name Clara Forshaw?"

"Yes, Inspector, it was. But how...? Where...?"

"She was killed by a single stab wound to the heart, and her body was found in a carriage at Aldgate Underground Station in the early hours of this morning."

"Oh God, poor girl. At the station, you say?"

"Yes indeed, sir, though we don't know for certain if she was killed in the carriage or perhaps murdered elsewhere, with her body simply left there to be found. Tell me, was she wearing a green dress when she left home last night?"

"I don't know. Perhaps one of the servants or my wife saw her leave. I was at my office until after seven p.m. and she'd already gone out by the time I returned home."

"Perhaps my sergeant could go and speak to the servants while we talk?"

"Yes, of course. Please, Sergeant, feel free. You'll find Soames in the Butler's Pantry, along the hall on the left as you leave the room. He'll help you find and speak to the staff."

"Thank you, sir," said Hillman as he left the room.

"Do you know where Clara went last night, Mr. Bellhaven?" asked Norris, as soon as they were alone.

"For the last few weeks, she'd been attending a Bible study class, I believe. Clara had recently found strength in religion. She was in sore need of consolation after the death of her mother some few months ago, and the church appeared to be providing her with whatever solace she sought. I presume that was her destination last night, Inspector."

"I see. How long had she been your secretary, sir?"

"My *private* secretary, Inspector. Clara dealt with my personal and private correspondence and also aided me in scheduling my workload, which can be quite arduous at times. She was not an ordinary secretary, concerned with taking dictation and everyday matters of trivia. In many ways she could have been more aptly described as my personal assistant. She'd been in my employ for just over two years."

"And to your knowledge, she had no enemies, no one who might wish her harm?"

"Certainly not. Clara was a very proper and upright young lady, otherwise she would not have been employed in my household."

"Of course, sir. Were there any gentlemen friends in her life that you know of?"

"Again, most certainly not, Inspector, for the same reasons I have already given you."

"She had no problems here in the house, with other members of the staff, for example, that you may have been aware of?"

"None at all. She was, of course, not a servant as such, so she kept a distance from most of the household staff, though she would speak with them regularly and they all appeared to like her, as far as I could ascertain. You must understand that

I do not take great pains to engage in long conversations with the servants, Inspector. There are limits, even in our modern, enlightened age, you know."

"Yes, Mr. Bellhaven, as you say," said Norris, feeling a growing dislike for the man, who now moved from his position in front of the fireplace to take up residence in a large and comfortable armchair nearby. Norris hated those who looked down at their fellow men, simply because of the fact that some were less fortunate than others. Bellhaven slipped a little further in the inspector's estimation when he did not invite Norris to sit.

At that moment, there came a knock on the door and Dylan Hillman walked back into the room. Bellhaven was about to say something, but Norris forestalled him.

"Anything, Sergeant?"

"It's her, sir, without doubt. The servants all described her perfectly and if that weren't enough, there was this."

Hillman passed a small photograph frame to Norris. Contained within its imitation silver filigree border was a picture of a smiling young woman, together with an older couple.

"Her parents, sir, according to Soames. Seems her mother died recently."

"Yes, Mr. Bellhaven has informed me of her family tragedy. So, the identity of our victim is confirmed, Mr. Bellhaven. I must ask you if you believe this crime could have been perpetrated as part of some twisted scheme to hurt the Metropolitan Railway, by perhaps frightening people off your trains and thus hitting your profits?"

Bellhaven appeared to pause in thought for a few seconds before answering.

"I see where you're heading with this, Inspector, and yes, perhaps that is the intention of whoever has committed this terrible crime. Poor Clara. I grieve for her, I really do, but even you must realise that it would take far more than one isolated incident of violence on the underground railway in order for any such event to have any lasting effect on the profits or the running of the Metropolitan."

"That's precisely what I'm afraid of, sir," said Norris, gravely.

"You don't mean. . . ?"

"Oh yes, I do, sir. I mean that this may only be the beginning of a campaign of terror targeted against your company."

"But that's monstrous, Inspector! No one could be that mad, that wanton, to do such dreadful things simply to force us out of business."

"You've received many crank letters over the years, from those who see the railway as the devil's work, or as a destroyer of streets and houses for its new tunnels, thus making the poor even poorer and so on. This could be someone who has decided to take their angst a stage further than mere letter writing."

"But, even if that were true, Inspector, the killer cannot know of the government's total support for the expansion of the underground system, or the pains it has gone to in order to ensure that events such as this will receive nothing in the way of sensationalist publicity, as I must assume you know. Further killings would avail him nothing."

Norris had wondered if and when Bellhaven would bring up the special measures he himself had learned of only that day.

"True, sir, but, as you say, he may not be aware of it and, as a consequence, those very measures may serve only to fuel his anger, if he feels his actions are being neither reported to the public, nor having the desired effect upon the company."

"You speak eloquently of the dilemma, Inspector. Either way, there is a risk of further killings, but surely, you and the good sergeant here will be doing all you can to apprehend this vile monster before he commits any further atrocities?"

"We shall indeed, sir," Norris replied, "but, for now, we have little to go on, and without being able to appeal for public or press support, we may well find our efforts hampered by such constraints as we must work under."

"Then, Inspector, I wish you well in your endeavours, and now, if there is nothing else, I must go and inform my wife of this sad news, and I do have work that must be done. Sad as I am at Clara's demise, her loss will be truly felt not only in terms of her place in this household, but in terms of the fact that my personal workload has just doubled with no one here to assist me in its execution."

Norris knew when he was being summarily dismissed. Bellhaven had answered all the questions he was going to, at least for the time being.

"Yes, of course, sir. Sergeant Hillman and I will be on our way. As you rightly point out, we have much to do, and I'm sure you are as anxious as we are to see Clara's killer brought to justice."

"Yes, Inspector, quite so. Now, if you will excuse me?"

Bellhaven rose and strode across to a small bell-push set into the wall beside the fireplace. He pressed the white button to summon the butler, Soames, who appeared in seconds and was instructed to see the detectives out.

Norris and Hillman both felt far more comfortable in the cleaner, fresher air of the street than they had in the almost stultified atmosphere that pervaded the home of the wealthy, but probably very boring, Laurence Bellhaven. On that point, they were both agreed. As to the next step in their investigation, however, neither man could, at that point, see where their next move lay.

"It's as if she was killed by a wraith, Dylan. There's no footprints, very little blood, the carriage doors were closed when she was found, so whoever did it must have casually exited the carriage without fear of being discovered. Her employer saw her as a paragon of female virtue, by all accounts. She was a churchgoer, and had no known enemies, male or female, as far as Bellhaven can tell us. If it wasn't for the connection to Bellhaven and the Metropolitan Railway, I'd be tempted to see her as the random victim of a lunatic."

"I suppose there's a chance of that, Bert. Her connection to Bellhaven could be a horrible coincidence."

"Oh yes, and since when did you and I start believing in coincidences, my dear old chum? Next stop, The Spotted Hound, Dylan. We've got some serious thinking to do."

Dylan Hillman groaned, inwardly. When Albert Norris suggested his favourite pub in the middle of the day, Hillman knew that such thinking was about to be followed by a serious headache. If there was one thing that Norris could do with far greater aplomb than the sergeant, it was to hold his ale with little if any ill-effects. *Still, orders are orders*, he thought, as Norris hailed the first passing cab that came their way.

It was only the first day and so far, the investigation was not going too well, and that, thought Hillman, was a bloody great understatement.

Chapter 8
Post Mortem

The all-pervading smell of the mortuary assaulted the nostrils of the two men as they entered the autopsy room, where Doctor Roebuck was just completing his post mortem examination on the remains of Clara Forshaw. For once, Dylan Hillman felt a sense of gratitude towards his inspector for having dragged him along to The Spotted Hound in the middle of the working day. At least the effects of the three pints of ale he'd consumed went some way towards alleviating the overwhelming queasiness that usually accompanied a visit to the autopsy room. Even so, he still felt a wave of nausea as the odors of disinfectant, blood, and human entrails rose to greet his nostrils as he and Norris entered and drew closer to the table where Roebuck stood over the body, apparently impervious to any malodours that may be present.

Hearing their approach, the doctor looked up and hailed the two detectives.

"Gentlemen, good afternoon. I'm just finishing up here."

"Hello again, Doctor Roebuck," Norris replied. "I'm hoping you've found something that may be of help to the investigation?"

The two men now stood close to the table, waiting for the doctor to reveal the results of his examination. Roebuck, experienced not only in his work as a police surgeon, but also in his dealings with Albert Norris, wasted no time in coming to the point.

"Very well, Inspector, Sergeant. I'll give you the results of the post mortem examination as they stand at present, though I see little reason why anything may change in my final report. First of all, the victim. . ."

"We've identified her as Clara Forshaw, Doctor, aged twenty-three," Norris interrupted.

"I see," said the doctor, before continuing. "The victim, Miss Clara Forshaw, aged twenty-three years, was, until the time of her death, a healthy and well-fed young woman. Her organs show none of the signs of malnutrition or disease that one might expect to find in the poorer members of our society. Her teeth do show signs of minor decay, but that is not unusual.

"Ascertaining the cause of death was not difficult. As I hazarded a guess on my first examination of the body, Miss Forshaw was despatched by a single stab wound to the chest, which instantly perforated her heart. Death would have been almost instantaneous. Of course, the heart ceases to pump blood as soon as it is stopped, which explains the lack of any significant amounts of blood at the scene. What there was, I also rightly assumed, was soaked up by her clothing, as you can see."

He pointed to the young woman's clothes, which had been removed and neatly laid out on an adjoining table. As he'd indicated, her chemise, the upper part of her dress and her shawl bore bloodstained marks, consistent with the doctor's findings.

"Any guesses as to the type of weapon used?" asked Hillman. His nausea passed as he concentrated on the sad and pathetic naked corpse laid out before him, the chest and abdomen laid open by the surgeon's knife. Dylan Hillman never would get used to the sight of those brought to an untimely end by the use of violence. He'd become a policeman precisely because he hated violence and wanted to do something to counter the criminal element of society who all too readily resorted to such means.

"The weapon, Sergeant Hillman, in my estimation, was a long-bladed knife, perhaps about five or six inches in length. The entry wound appears clean and there are no signs that the weapon had any serrations on its edges. It's my guess that the killer may have used a very sharp and thin kitchen knife, the type used in thousands of homes across the city, which I know doesn't help you a great deal."

"It was too much to expect you to be able to tell us exactly what the weapon was, Doctor," Norris interjected. "Please go on."

"Yes, well, as I was about to say, there was one single stab wound, which penetrated the chest cavity and went directly into the heart. The poor girl would hardly have known what was happening. There were no signs or evidence of sexual assault, as I'm sure you would have asked me in a moment or two. She certainly wouldn't have suffered a great deal, if that's any consolation to her family..."

"I doubt her father will take much consolation from anything we tell him. His wife, Clara's mother, died only a short time ago," said Norris.

"He doesn't know yet?"

"We've only just found out who she is, Doctor. I wanted to speak to you before tackling that particularly unpleasant task."

"Mmm, yes, of course, Inspector. Anyway, you might not want to tell him the other thing I found, that might, on the other hand, be of great interest to you and the sergeant, in terms of your investigation."

"Go on," said Norris, intrigued at the physician's statement.

"Take a look at this, gentlemen."

Roebuck led the two detectives across the room to another, smaller table, where a metal dish stood, its contents obscured by a thin muslin cloth. As he removed the cloth, Norris's eyes bulged in surprise. Hillman's previous nausea returned and he was forced to place a hand over his mouth to prevent an involuntary urge to vomit.

Lying in the dish, in a small pool of blood, was a forlorn-looking, five to six inch long foetus.

"She was pregnant!" Norris exclaimed.

"Bloody hell," added Hillman.

"From the size of the foetus, I'd say somewhere in the region of three months," the doctor informed them.

"This puts a whole new complexion on the case, wouldn't you say, Dylan?" said Norris, turning to his sergeant, who could hardly take his eyes off the miniature human being, now as deceased as its mother, lying pathetically in that lonely-looking, cold, impersonal mortuary dish.

"Oy, did you hear me?" Norris nudged him.

"What? Eh? Oh yes, sorry, Bert. Yes, I heard you. I think it definitely puts a new slant on things."

"I thought you'd find it interesting," said Roebuck.

"It certainly is, Doctor," Norris replied.

"She wasn't married," Hillman added, "so it's possible this wasn't some random killing after all, or one aimed at the railway in particular."

"My thoughts, exactly, Sergeant," said Norris. "We need to find the girl's lover, whoever he was. If he was a married man, or one who was in no position to support her and a child, we could be looking at the real motive for the girl's murder."

Doctor Roebuck stood back as he listened to the two men, and the excitement that had crept into their voices.

"Anything else I can do for you, gentlemen?"

"I don't think so, Doctor Roebuck, unless you can give me the name of the man who made her pregnant." Norris smiled, for the first time that day. The doctor had at least given them something that could provide an alternative motive for murder, a line of inquiry that didn't necessarily add up to a crime directed primarily against the underground railway.

"What now, Inspector?" asked Roebuck, seeing the look on Norris's face that spoke of a determination to get things moving, and fast.

"First, the sergeant and I have to pay a call on the girl's father. He deserves to know what's happened before we go any further."

"And then, sir?" asked Hillman, almost anticipating what his inspector was about to say.

"Then, Dylan, old chum, we go back to Lewisham Place. I think it's time we had a rather more detailed chat with each and very member of the Bellhaven household. Someone, one of the staff perhaps, has to know something. The girl was three months pregnant, for God's sake, and I want to know who was responsible, and fast!"

Chapter 9
A Father's Grief

Locating the home of Clara Forshaw's father hadn't proved a difficult task. The Bellhaven's butler, Roland Soames, had previously informed Dylan Hillman that the man ran his own small bookstore, situated in the middle of a small parade of shops in a side street somewhere off Clerkenwell High Street.

Arriving on the high street, the detectives took less than five minutes to locate the store, easily identified by the sign that read *M. Forshaw, Rare and Antiquarian Books*. The two men knew the type of premises well. The store would be rented, and the family, such as it was now reduced to, would live in accommodations immediately above the business. Not quite the affluent façade or trappings of the home of Laurence Bellhaven, but, Norris concluded, as he opened the door, setting a bell ringing to announce their arrival, one that suggested an honest and hardworking aspect with regard to its proprietor.

Norris's first impressions on entering the store were the smells of polished wood, emanating from the bookshelves and shop counter, and the unmistakable odour of the leather bindings of the many books that lined the shelves. There was also a faint, musty scent of dust, which Norris assumed would be coming from some of the older, less saleable books on the shelves that spread over all four walls of this literary emporium.

Within seconds of the over-door bell announcing their arrival, an interior door at the rear of the shop swung open and the proprietor stepped forward to greet them. The man was aged around fifty to fifty-five, his head bald in the centre, but with wispy white tufts of hair clinging almost precariously to the sides. He was clean-shaven and gave off an air of studious professionalism as he approached Norris and Hillman. Despite the apparent cheeriness of his greeting, Norris could see, in the man's eyes, a great sadness within, and now, here he was, about to add to the burden of the man's grief so soon after the loss of his wife.

"Good morning, gentlemen. How can I help you today?" he asked of his visitors.

The next ten minutes proved to be traumatic for the detectives and even more so for the recipient of their terrible news.

"You must be mistaken, Inspector. My daughter is so young. She cannot be dead!" Merton Forshaw protested, as denial at first refused to give way to reality.

"I'm sorry, sir, her identity has been confirmed. The dead woman is Clara, your daughter."

"Oh, God, please help me!" the man suddenly sobbed, holding his head in his hands as he did so. "I lost her mother but a short time ago. She was so beautiful, as was Clara, who took after her in so many ways."

"I'm so sorry, Mr. Forshaw, I really am, but I need to ask you something rather delicate. It is very important."

"Delicate? *Delicate*, you say? My daughter is dead, you tell me, Inspector, and you speak of *delicate*? There can be nothing delicate about what has transpired, and whatever you need to ask of me in order that you may find the beast that has brought this evil deed upon her, and this grief to me, you must ask."

Norris felt great respect for the man who stood quietly sobbing in front of him. In the midst of his personal trauma, Merton Forshaw had an inner strength that Norris mentally applauded. This man, he knew, would do anything to help the police find the killer of his daughter. Sentimentality would be pushed to one side until he had done what he could to help the inspector in his investigation.

Sadly, that determination showed signs of rocking when Norris mentioned Clara's pregnancy. Even Forshaw's stoic determination to assist the police visibly wilted a little, as his face registered the shock and shame that such an event normally provoked in polite Victorian society. He soon regained a modicum of composure, however, and was unable to offer any help on the subject. His daughter, to the best of his knowledge, had no close gentleman friends and the fact of such a pregnancy was more than a surprise to him. Clara, he assured them, had always been a 'good girl' and he knew her recent affiliation with the church and religion would have certainly given her cause for guilt at such an eventuality, assuming, as he put it, that his unworldly offspring was even aware of her 'condition', as he delicately put it.

By the end of the interview, it was clear to Norris that, despite his desire to be of assistance, there wasn't much Merton Forshaw could tell them that might be of help. Clara would regularly visit him on Sunday afternoons, her day off, having spent the mornings at church. They would take a walk together, usually in the nearby park, where Clara loved to watch the ducks and swans that resided on a small island in the middle of the ornamental lake. She would always take her leave of her father a little after six p.m., after which she would return to her room at the Bellhaven home, where she would prepare herself for the coming working week.

According to Forshaw, his daughter had little or no time for men friends, as her days and evenings were spoken for almost exclusively with work, church, or reading. Like her father, she had a passion for books and would happily spend hours reading in the privacy of her room, to the exclusion of even the company of the other members of the household. Norris's final words to Forshaw were instructions on how to go about the business of obtaining his daughter's body from the mortuary in order to arrange for a Christian burial. The finality of those almost clinical instructions were enough to leave Forshaw, head bowed, and shoulders hunched, in a posture of abject despair.

Leaving the sad and heartbroken man alone with his thoughts and his collection of musty, dust-gathering books, the two men once more stepped into the outside world, where the warmth of the sun contrasted with the rather grim and dingy interior of Forshaw's book store. As they stood on the pavement, surrounded by the hubbub of the gathering crowds that made up the typical high street scene on any given day of the week, Dylan Hillman made an observation that Norris had rather hoped he'd pick up on, much as he had.

"You know, Bert. What he couldn't tell us about Clara almost gave us as much information as if he'd given us chapter and verse of her daily movements."

"Go on, Dylan."

"Well, if Clara was such a good girl, and her time was spent working, praying, or reading, it kind of leads us away from the thought of her having a lover somewhere outside of work, don't you think?"

"I was hoping you'd deduce that, too, old chum. That's where my thoughts were led, as well. If she had no time for a liaison outside of work and church, then the father of her child has to be located in either of those two locations. Agreed?"

"Can't be any other explanation as far as I can see," Hillman concurred.

"You know, Dylan, I have to say that it's looking more and more as if this isn't a crime against the Metropolitan Railway, and could be something of a far more personal nature."

"Doesn't help the dead girl much though, does it?"

"True, sergeant, very true."

"So, where next, then? Church or the Bellhaven residence?"

"On the basis that the vicar of St.Giles's should be above reproach. . ."

"Ha!" Hillman interjected.

"Oh, shut up, Dylan. As I was saying, unless one of the congregation is our man, I think we stand a better chance 'closer to home', if you know what I mean. I think we should begin at the Bellhaven home and talk in-depth to every male servant in that household."

"And Laurence Bellhaven?"

"Oh yes, we'll have words with the great man himself, never fear, old chum."

"We're not going to have time to do both today, Bert. Time's marching along, you know."

"Don't worry, Dylan. We'll do the Bellhaven house today, and the Reverend Bowker can wait until tomorrow. After all, it's as he said, isn't it? God's house is always open. I doubt he'll be too far away when we want to speak to him."

"Do you mean God, or the vicar," asked Hillman facetiously.

"Well, both, I suppose, Dylan," Norris replied. "I'll take all the help I can get on this case, and if the Almighty cares to lend a helping hand, then who am I to turn him down? Anyway, that's for tomorrow. Let's make tracks and get to the Bellhaven house. I'd like to get this done with and actually get home to my wife sometime before dark tonight, if that's at all possible. It's been a bloody long day so far."

"You can say that again," the sergeant replied. "Hey, look, here comes a cab. Shall I hail it?"

"You need to ask?"

In seconds, the detectives found themselves seated in the rear of yet another hansom cab as it carried them back towards the Bellhaven residence. Norris allowed himself to hope that they just might be on the verge of finding something concrete in their search for Clara Forshaw's murderer. At the same time as that inkling of optimism crept into his mind, he cautioned himself, mentally, against jumping to conclusions. After all, hadn't he got things badly wrong once before in his career? And hadn't that mistake wrought tragic consequences?

Norris tried to shake off thoughts of the past as the cab rattled along, but even so, his mind was in a kind of fug as they drew up outside the pristine, white-walled home of Laurence Bellhaven for the second time that day.

Chapter 10
An Interview with
Florence Bellhaven

"Preposterous! I refuse to believe such slanderous lies!" Laurence Bellhaven thundered, at the news of his deceased personal secretary's pregnancy.

Once again, they stood in Bellhaven's parlour, having been ushered in by Soames, the butler, who quickly left the detectives alone with his employer.

"I assure you, there is no mistake, Mr. Bellhaven. The sergeant and I have seen the evidence for ourselves."

"But, Clara was a good girl, Inspector. How could such a thing have happened?"

"She won't have been the first young woman who fell for a few smooth words, or who was influenced by an older, perhaps married man into believing he was in love with her. Maybe she thought he'd leave his wife for her, he refused to do so, and he killed her when she threatened to reveal their affair to his wife."

"Or maybe she just fell for the wrong man, someone her own age, who got her pregnant and then refused to take responsibility for her and the child," added Hillman.

"Yes, but either way, what has this to do with me, Inspector?"

"Quite simply, sir, we need to speak to all the men she came into contact with on a regular basis, and that includes your staff. How many males do you have in your employ?"

"Apart from Soames, there are only two. Nicholson is my valet, and we have a gardener, Abraham Peacock. He only works here three days each week. He has another position as gardener with one of my close neighbours, Mr. Travis Wilde."

"How old are the two men, and are they married?"

"Nicholson is twenty-four or five, I believe, and betrothed to be married to a girl in service at the Wilde house, as it happens. Peacock is at least a hundred years old. I jest, of course, but he is a venerable old soldier who served his country for many years and now lives a quiet life tending the gardens he loves so dearly. He certainly can't be your man, inspector."

"Even so, I need to speak to each of them. And Soames, your butler."

"Ah yes, Soames, of course. He is married to my cook. They have both been in my employ for over ten years, and both are excellent at their jobs. Mrs. Soames is a simply wonderful cook. My wife would not be without her, running the kitchen and producing such wonderful meals for us every day of the week."

Norris cast a glance at Hillman, who caught the meaning of his look right away.

"Are Mr. and Mrs. Soames happily married, Mr. Bellhaven?" Hillman asked.

"What? Well, how should I know? I suppose they are. They've been together a long time, as far as I'm aware, Sergeant."

"That's no guarantee of fidelity in my experience," said Norris, darkly.

"That's a ridiculous suggestion," Bellhaven went on. "Soames would never do such a thing, I'm sure of it. Adultery is not something I could ever see him being capable of."

"Even so, we must speak with him and the others, as soon as possible, Mr. Bellhaven."

Laurence Bellhaven at last acquiesced to Norris's request and quickly summoned Soames, giving him instructions to make both Nicholson and Peacock available immediately to the detectives. "And you can use the kitchen for the interviews. Please, keep it brief, Inspector. I'm sure Mrs. Soames will want to begin preparations for dinner very soon."

* * *

"Well, that wasn't very productive, was it, old chum?" said Norris, as the last of the male Bellhaven servants, Peacock, the gardener, left the kitchen, leaving the two detectives seated at the large kitchen table. They'd learned very little that would be of help from the interviews with the three men.

"I'd have to agree with that, Bert," Hillman replied. "Bellhaven was right about old Peacock, for sure. I doubt the old boy has had a sexual thought in his head for years. He's too devoted to his dahlias, foxgloves and the cabbages in the kitchen garden to even have time to think about young women less than half his age."

"And Soames?" asked Norris, inviting his sergeant's opinion once more.

"Ah, yes, Roland the butler. Well, I have to say that of all three, he's the one who showed the most emotion with regard to the girl's death. Though I have to say, I think that had more to do with him looking at her in a fatherly light, rather than a lustful one."

"I agree with you, Dylan. He appears to oversee the whole household in just such a fatherly fashion, quite rare in a butler nowadays, I think. I've a feeling our Mr. Soames may harbour the odd socialist tendency in that quick and obviously intelligent brain of his. He certainly seems keen on improving the lot of his fellow workers, and genuinely seems concerned for their welfare. Unless I'm mistaken, I'd also say he's very much in love with his wife. His eyes sort of shone each time he mentioned Mrs. Soames."

"I suppose he could have had a short dalliance with the girl, if she got very close to him and mistook his fatherly supervision for something more?"

"I don't think so, Dylan. Upright and honest as the day as long, I'd say."

"And you don't think young Basil Nicholson could be our man either, sir?"

"Oh, come on, Dylan. That young fellow might be engaged to a young lady along the street, but have you ever seen such a blatantly effeminate example of manhood in your life? That betrothal is purely for cosmetic purposes if you ask me, a cover to disguise his true sexual predilections, though I doubt the young lady in question has even thought of it that way. I don't think it will be too long before our boys will be finding young Basil in the arms of some other young fellow in a house of ill repute and he'll end up behind bars for his inclinations, you mark my words."

"So, what's next?"

"Now we go back and talk to Bellhaven again, and his wife."

Laurence Bellhaven had left the house, bound for the company offices, by the time the two detectives left the kitchen. The ever-efficient Soames did, however, arrange for them to speak to Mrs. Bellhaven, who, he informed them, would see them in her private sitting room, which stood just along the hall from the parlour where Bellhaven had received them.

As the detectives entered the room, Florence Bellhaven rose from the soft, chintz-covered armchair in which she'd been sitting. Norris estimated that the woman was at least ten years younger than her husband, perhaps more, but, even so, she had a gaunt and haggard look about her. Norris hoped it was a reaction to the death of Clara Forshaw that had rendered her in such a condition. He'd hate to believe that Mrs. Bellhaven was such an unhappy soul that her current demeanour was a permanent state. The woman, in truth, looked positively wretched! She was dressed in black, as befitted a state of mourning, and her blonde hair was tied in a rather severe bun, reminiscent of Her Majesty Queen Victoria herself. Her blue eyes appeared dull, almost lifeless, as though the very life, her vitality, had been drained away by either the current, or some other, personal tragedy.

"I'm so sorry, Inspector. I should have spoken to you earlier but I'm afraid I quite fainted away on hearing the terrible news about poor Clara."

"That's quite understandable, Mrs. Bellhaven. This is Sergeant Hillman, by the way."

"Good morning, Sergeant. Welcome to my home."

"Thank you, Ma'am," said Hillman.

Norris took up the conversation once again.

"Mrs. Bellhaven, may I ask if you were particularly close to Miss Forshaw?"

"Not close as such, Inspector. She was my husband's personal secretary, after all, and it wouldn't do to become over-friendly with an employee, as I'm sure you understand."

"But, you were on good terms with her?"

"Oh, yes. Clara was a very upright and respectable young lady. On occasions, if she wasn't too busy with work on my husband's behalf, I would invite her to take tea with me, and we would discuss matters of the day, books and, lately, religion, to which she was particularly committed."

"So I understand. But did your conversations ever stray to the subject of men, particularly men friends that Clara may have had?"

"Oh no, Inspector! That would not have been proper conversation for two respectable ladies."

"And would it be a surprise to you to learn that Clara was three months pregnant at the time of her murder?"

At that, Florence Bellhaven looked as though she were about to faint again. Her legs appeared to lose their strength and the woman sagged back towards the armchair she'd so recently risen from. Dylan Hillman moved quickly to her side and politely took the woman's elbow in his hand, solicitously guiding her to the chair, where she sat and began to sob quietly into a white linen handkerchief she'd pulled from the sleeve of her dress.

"I'm sorry if that came as a shock to you. I thought your husband just might have mentioned it before leaving the house."

"My husband tells me very little, Inspector," Florence confessed and, in those few words, Albert Norris read much about the life of the woman who sat in front of him. Florence Bellhaven might live in a large house, with all the trappings of wealth and status around her, but he recognised a lonely and perhaps neglected wife when he saw one.

He imagined Florence and Clara, mistress and secretary, enjoying almost clandestine conversations and social intercourse while Bellhaven himself was absent from the house, enjoying whatever manly pleasures he chose to indulge in. Now, he believed he understood the reasons for her wretched and doleful appearance. Laurence Bellhaven had lost his personal secretary, but Florence, whether she cared to confess it or not, had in all probability lost perhaps the only friend she was likely to be able to make within the household. A personal secretary was, after all, not one of the household servants and therefore sat a rung or two above the likes of Soames and young Nicholson.

"I see, Mrs. Bellhaven," Norris replied. "If there's nothing more you can tell us which might throw some light on this tragedy, then I think we'll leave you now."

"Thank you, Inspector. You're most considerate, but there is one question I'd like to ask you, if I may?"

"Of course."

"Do you think that poor Clara may have fallen foul of that vile monster who is stalking the streets of Whitechapel?"

"I don't think that's a possibility at all," he replied. "There is nothing to suggest such a connection. The methods of the two killers are too different for us to even consider a link between Clara's murder and that of the unfortunates murdered so horribly in Whitechapel."

Florence Bellhaven quickly thanked Norris for his consideration and apologised for being of little help, at which point he and Hillman took their leave of the woman, leaving her to her thoughts in her own private sitting room, where Norris though she might also be constructing her own private hell.

"There's something I don't like about that house, Dylan," he said to Hillman, as their cab rattled its way back to New Street. "There's an air of repression about the place."

"I felt that, too, but isn't that the way with lot of these upper crust nobs? All propriety and stiff upper lip and no bloody feelings, no emotions?"

"You're probably right, Dylan, old chum. Trouble is, no matter what we might think about the Bellhaven household, we've learned very little today that's helpful in trying to track down Clara's killer."

"Yes, and what about old man Bellhaven just sauntering off to the office like that, as if we weren't even there?"

"The great man probably thought he'd said all he had to say to the likes of us, and had better things to do in keeping the bloody underground railway running. Never mind about the death of one young woman. God forbid that it should interfere with the Metropolitan Railway, Sergeant, yes indeed, God forbid."

"So, what do we do now?"

"Now, we return to the station, report to Madden, and then, Dylan, I'm going home to my wife. She'll be wondering where I am, after me disappearing this morning at the crack of dawn. I'll be lucky if the dog remembers who I am. I suggest you go home, too, and get some rest. Maybe tomorrow we'll get a break, when we visit the good reverend at St. Giles's."

On returning to New Street Police Station, Norris was saved from making his report to his superior officer by the fact that Chief Inspector Madden had been called to Scotland Yard an hour earlier, and wasn't expected back at New Street until the following day. Norris assumed the chief inspector's summons had something to do with the Forshaw case, but, in the absence of any message being left for him by Madden, he instructed Hillman to go home. Norris himself left the station a short time after his sergeant and trudged wearily home, where he was welcomed by an over-exuberant Billy the terrier, who certainly hadn't forgotten his master, and a worried-looking wife. Betty Norris knew her husband well enough to be certain that he wouldn't have spent so long at work unless he was involved in something big. Well aware of Chief Inspector Madden's instructions that morning, Norris could only tell Betty that he was investigating a murder, and that for reasons of internal security, he was forbidden from discussing any matters relating to the case with anyone, friend or family.

"Well, that's a fine kettle of fish, I don't think," said Betty, after trying every method she knew to force her husband into revealing details of the case he was working on. "I'm your wife, Albert Norris, and if you can't trust me, then who can you trust?"

"Sorry, Betty. Like I said, I have my orders."

"Hmmph," said Betty. "I'll bet you've been drafted in to that damned Whitechapel Murderer case."

Before he could answer, she added, "It's alright, you don't have to say yes or no. I know when I'm beat. Did you see the evening paper before you came home, by the way?"

"No, why?" asked Norris, relieved that Betty hadn't given him too hard a time.

Betty passed the evening edition of *The Star* to her husband.

"More about the Whitechapel murders, is it?" asked Norris.

"Oh no, the front page is full of that story, of course, but look here."

Betty pointed to a short article on page five, having already opened the paper at the relevant place. Norris read: *The body of an unidentified woman in her early twenties was discovered today by staff at the underground railway station at Aldgate. It is thought that the woman may have suffered a heart attack shortly before the last train of the night pulled in to the station. Every effort is being made by the police to identify the woman so that her next of kin can be informed of her untimely death.*

So, he thought, *that's all they think Clara Forshaw's death worthy of. A few lines that don't even go so far as to ask the usual; anyone with any information should contact the police.*

He looked up at Betty.

"What about it, Betty? There's not much of any interest in this, is there?"

"Oh, it's just that when I first saw it, I thought maybe it had something to do with why you were called from your bed so early this morning. Aldgate is on your manor, isn't it, Bert?"

Norris knew then that Betty had worked it out. She wasn't stupid. They'd been married long enough for her to be able to read him like a book, and she was also very aware of police procedures and the way things worked at New Street.

"I won't tell if you don't," she winked at him. "Just tell me, and I'll shut up. Are you working on this case, Bert?"

He nodded silently, thinking that if he didn't actually say anything, Madden could never accuse him of talking out of turn.

"And there's more to it than the article says, isn't there? Those few lines are a load of rubbish. Anyone with half a brain and knowledge of how things work in the police force could work that out, Bert."

"Yes, Betty, and that's all I'm allowed to say, okay?"

"Okay, Bert. As long as you know you can talk to me if you need to. I can understand some cases are a bit sensitive and this must be very sensitive indeed if Madden's forbidden you to speak to your own wife about it."

"Betty!" he implored.

"I promise. I'll not say another word," she replied. "Now, how does meat and potatoes with some nice fresh carrots sound for your tea?"

The rest of the evening passed quietly in the Norris household. Betty was as good as her word, and never mentioned another word about the case. Norris went to bed a little after eleven and he and Betty snuggled together in a loving embrace that helped wipe the trials and tribulations of the day from Norris's mind. *Tomorrow,* he thought, *we may just make some progress.* Before he could think anything else, sleep claimed him and he was soon snoring gently beside Betty, with Billy the dog snoring far louder, but in tune with his master, on his blanket at the bottom of the stairs.

Chapter 11
An Interview with
Reverend Bowker

Norris and Hillman made an early start the following day, reporting the results of the previous day's interviews to Chief Inspector Madden, before heading over to St. Giles's church. Sadly for them, the Reverend Martin Bowker was in the process of conducting a morning service when they arrived and the two men took places in one of the rear pews and listened, along with a small congregation, to the latter part of the service.

At the conclusion of the service, the detectives waited as the vicar stood at the door, shaking hands with most of the departing congregation. As the last of the worshippers disappeared down the steps of St. Giles's, Martin Bowker walked straight across to where the detectives stood waiting.

"Good day to you, Inspector, and you too, Sergeant. Delighted as I was to see you in the congregation this morning, I have a feeling your presence here has more to do with police business than that of the Lord."

"I'm afraid so, Reverend Bowker," said Norris. "We need to ask you a few more questions about Clara Forshaw."

"Ah, so it was her, then? You're sure of it?"

"Her identity has been confirmed, yes. The doctor who conducted the post mortem examination also discovered that Clara was three months pregnant at the time of her death."

"What? But that's simply outrageous! It's impossible. Well, not impossible in a physical sense of course, but, spiritually, Clara was a devout and respectable young woman, Inspector."

"I don't doubt it, sir. But, the facts are inescapable. Clara was with child, and it's vitally important that we find out who the father of that child was."

"And you think I can help you?"

"You knew her well, Mr. Bowker, perhaps as well as anyone in the last few months of her life. You may know more than you realise. For example, did Clara make any special or close friends during her time at your church, or in your Bible class, perhaps?"

"If she did, I was singularly unaware of the fact, Inspector. I don't pry into the lives of those who come through the doors of God's house, and I only offer my help and counselling to those who request it."

Norris wondered why the vicar had mentioned counselling. Had the reverend made an unfortunate slip-up? He seized on the moment.

"Did Clara come to you for counselling, Mr. Bowker?"

"What? Well, yes, of course, though when I speak of counselling, I refer to God's counselling, Inspector. Like many of the students at my Bible class, Clara sought further knowledge and counselling on the subject of the good book, and of God's word in greater detail."

"I see. So, you were not aware of any personal matters that may have been giving Clara cause for concern?"

"If you're asking me if I knew she was with child, then the answer is no. My relationship with Clara was purely a spiritual one, and her personal life was never an issue of discussion between us."

"And she had no special female friends that you know of, someone in whom she may have confided such personal issues?"

"I've already told you, Inspector. I do not interfere with my flock's personal lives. If Clara had any friends here, male or female, I am in ignorance of the fact."

It was rapidly becoming clear to Norris that he would receive no helpful information from the Reverend Bowker, and he and

Hillman thanked him for his time, and left the church some fifteen minutes after arriving, allowing the vicar to go about his business.

Standing on the street outside the church, Norris turned to Hillman, voicing his thoughts to his sergeant.

"I don't know about you, Dylan, old chum, and I know he's a man of God and all that, but there's something about Martin Bowker that I don't like."

"I admit he's a bit of a cold fish, Bert, and seems a bit too reserved for my liking, but you don't really think he could be mixed up in all this, do you?"

"I really don't know. All that we do know for sure is that he knew the dead girl and apparently spent some time counselling her on matters of religion, according to his account of the facts. It's just that he seems a bit evasive in his answers to our questions, as though he's hiding something."

"You mean, something like an illicit love affair with a member of his congregation, for example?"

"He wouldn't be the first man of the cloth to have fallen from the path of righteousness, Dylan, and I doubt he'll be the last, either, if it turns out that's what he did."

"I know, but we don't really have any authentic reasons to suspect him, do we?"

"Not yet, Dylan, not yet."

"In that case, I've a feeling we haven't seen the last of the Reverend Bowker, eh, Bert?"

"Correct. I want you to look into his past. Get one of the constables from the station to help you. I want to know everything there is to know about the Reverend Martin Bowker; where he comes from, and his history both in and out of his priestly garb. I want to know if he's married, happily or otherwise, and if there's ever been a whiff of scandal, major or minor, attached to his name."

"How about we take him down to the station and question him a bit more deeply?"

"No, not yet. Like you said, we don't have anything more than my gut feeling to go on at present. I want us to have something to confront him with before we question him any further."

* * *

So began Norris and Hillman's investigation into the life of Martin Bowker, who remained, for the time being, Norris's chief (and only) suspect, based on nothing more than an evasive attitude and Norris's thought that there was simply something 'not quite right' about the vicar of St. Giles's church. Hillman had decided to use Constable Simon Wilkinson to assist him with his probe into the vicar's background. Wilkinson had been first on the scene at Aldgate Underground Station on the night of the discovery of Clara Forshaw's body, and Hillman, bearing in mind what Norris had told him about the politics of the case, considered it prudent to use an officer who'd already been involved in the case, rather than bringing in a fresh face. Norris applauded his sergeant's decision and also knew Wilkinson to be an effective and diligent officer.

Unhappily, even the combined talents of Hillman and Wilkinson failed to dig up anything that might be construed as evidence of wrongdoing, or even a hint of scandal, when it came to their probe into the life of Martin Bowker. The reverend gentleman, as Wilkinson insisted on calling him out of respect for his position, had never married, and although that was unusual for a Church of England minister in his mid-thirties, it couldn't be taken as any sort of indictment against him as a man. They both knew that it was possible that Bowker simply hadn't met the right woman yet.

He'd been born and raised in Exeter, and had gone to university in London, after which he'd attended the seminary from whence he'd moved on to become a minister of the church. He appeared to have led a particularly blameless life and had moved to the parish of St. Giles's after spending six years as the vicar of a country church near Basingstoke, in Hampshire, following on from a successful spell as Vicar of All Saints Church in Weymouth, Dorset. Not a whiff of scandal of any description had attached itself to the young vicar, at least, none that the two police officers could discover. Bowker lived alone in the vicarage, a small, terraced home provided by the Church of England for the incumbent of the position of minister at St.Giles's and situated less than five minutes walk from the church. Two ladies of the parish, both in their late fifties, had assumed the joint role of caretaker of the vicarage and between them, they ensured that Bowker's home was kept spick and span, as befits the home of a minister of the church.

As for the church itself, the congregation of St. Giles's was on the large side, a visible testament to the popularity of the man who wore the dog collar. Many churches in the surrounding area failed to boast such a throng as regularly gathered at services conducted by Martin Bowker. Similarly, his Bible Classes for ladies of the parish had proved a spectacular success, attracting women from miles around who appeared attracted to the charismatic vicar and his direct and straightforward approach to the teachings of God.

This, then, was the man whom Norris held suspicions about, but who, it appeared, possessed a squeaky-clean record and could also call upon a church full of character witnesses if need be, to testify on his behalf. Norris knew that if Bowker were at all implicated in the murder of Clara Forshaw, he would need evidence, good solid evidence before proceeding further with his investigation.

"I wish we could get someone on the inside, Dylan," he said to Hillman, as the two men sat in Norris's small office at New Street, two full weeks after the death of Clara Forshaw.

"You mean, under cover?"

"Yes, at those Bible Study classes of his."

"But, sir, you know as well as I do that those classes are for women only."

"I know, Dylan, that's what makes it so bloody frustrating."

It was a fact that at the time of the underground murders, the Metropolitan Police Force did not employ women as police officers. It would not be until 1914 that Margaret Damer Dawson, an anti-white slavery campaigner and Nina Boyle, a militant suffragette journalist, founded the Women Police Service. Set up by the women to help deter pimps and thus discourage women from entering prostitution as a way of life, and, through Boyle, as a way of allowing women into a men's world during the war situation that existed at that time, this was not an official force and it received little help and recognition from the official police force. Dawson wanted to found a uniformed organisation of women, whilst Boyle wished to take advantage of the war to put women temporarily in men's places, with the expectation that their usefulness would lead to their permanent continuation after the war. Not until 1923 would the women of the force be granted official, though somewhat limited, powers of arrest.

"So, what do we do?" asked Hillman, after each of the two men had spent a couple of minutes lost in thought as they tried to devise a means to infiltrate Bowker's study classes.

"I don't know, Dylan. There's just no way we can get anyone into one of those meetings. I'd like to see how he handles things when he's surrounded by an audience of ladies, as opposed to his demeanour when he faces a regular congregation."

"In other words, we're on a loser with that idea."

"'Fraid so, old chum."

"So, what do we do?"

"We watch him, Dylan, that's what we do. I want you, me, Wilkinson and a couple of others to place him under twenty-four hour surveillance for a week, at least. Let's observe his comings and goings and see if Mr. Bowker has any little secrets we can uncover by simply keeping a close eye on him."

Unfortunately for Norris, Joshua Madden refused to allow him three constables for his surveillance operation, given that he had so little to go on in terms of his suspicions against Martin Bowker. As Madden reminded Norris: "You must not lose sight of the bigger picture, here, Bert. You have a theory, and it might prove a good one, but you have to consider that this could still be a case of an attack on the Metropolitan Railway, and not a personal crime against this poor young woman. Her pregnancy might have been coincidental to the circumstances of her murder. You can have constables Wilkinson and Fry, and that's it, I'm afraid. You and Hillman can make up the rest of the time, if you want to give up your own time in pursuit of this man – who, I would remind you, is a man of the cloth, an ordained minister, and hardly the type of man one would expect to be involved in the murder of an innocent young woman."

"Not quite so innocent, as she was up the duff," muttered Dylan Hillman, from his position just behind his inspector.

"I'm sorry, what did you say, sergeant?" said Madden.

"Er, sorry sir, I was just saying it's sad when the innocent ones get done, that's all."

"Yes, quite, Sergeant. Now, I suggest you both get along and do the best you can. This case is going nowhere fast, Inspector Norris. The commissioner wants to see results. He's already getting enough aggravation on a daily basis due to this damned Whitechapel Murderer. He'd like to see this one closed without any undue hue and cry."

"Right, sir, and just who do *you* suggest I arrest, then? Someone who we can fit to the crime, just to keep the commissioner happy?"

"How dare you speak to me like that, Norris? Just get out there and find this bloody killer, and just remember not to go about it with blinkers on. Follow your theory, but don't be blinded by it. Just remember there are serious political implications attached to this case, if it can be proved that the railway is being directly targeted. Now, get out, and get on with your jobs, both of you!"

"Yes, sir," Norris replied quietly, satisfied, from Madden's reaction, that he'd made his point successfully. Madden knew that Norris wouldn't be pushed into some easy solution to the case just to satisfy someone in higher authority. If they wanted the killer, they'd have to wait until he'd tracked him down, the good, old-fashioned way, by honest police work and detection.

"And, Sergeant," said Madden, as the two detectives were walking out through the door to his office.

"Sir?"

"I may be getting on a bit, but I'm not totally deaf. She may have been up the duff, as you so eruditely put it, but she was a young woman, an innocent victim of a violent and vicious crime. Don't forget that."

"Yes, sir, I mean, no, sir. Of course, sir," said a rather flustered Dylan Hillman, as Norris finally closed the chief inspector's door behind them.

"You silly bugger, Dylan. He's not daft, you know." Norris grinned at his sergeant.

"I know, but he is a bit of a pompous sod, don't you think, Bert?"

"Now, now, old chum. That's no way to speak about a superior officer, is it? Mind you, you're right, he is a pompous sod."

The two men laughed all the way along the corridor as they walked to the canteen for a cup of tea, after which, they'd get along and recruit their helpers in the coming surveillance operation on the Reverend Martin Bowker. After a series of groans from Constables Wilkinson and Fry at being 'saddled', as Fry put it, with an endless round of almost idle activity in watching the activities of the Reverend Bowker, Hillman quickly mapped out a schedule of shifts that would see the four men share the surveillance workload. At least Wilkinson and Fry would be able to do their share, and then go home at the end of their shifts. For Norris and Hillman, however, any time spent in following or simply observing Martin Bowker, would be in addition to their normal working hours. Neither man was under any illusions as to the lack of sleep that lay ahead for both of them. As a gesture to the team, Norris agreed that the operation would swing into action at dawn the following day, giving his men one last night of relative peace and restful sleep before commencing their task.

Norris returned home and spent a quiet half hour walking Billy, before settling down to a meal with Betty, and finally retiring to bed relatively early, at 9 p.m. Betty specifically avoided asking any questions of her husband that might compromise his orders from the chief inspector, and, satisfied that he was making some progress, and that his investigation now had something and someone to focus upon, Albert Norris slept well. Likewise, a few streets across town, Dylan Hillman, though without a wife or dog for company, also enjoyed an early night, conscious of the gruelling hours of work that lay ahead in the coming days.

As the two men slept that night, with the promise of a possible resolution to their case slowly taking shape (in Norris's mind, at least), neither Norris nor Hillman could have foreseen the events that were soon to follow.

Chapter 12
The March of Time

At the time of the underground murders, the Jack the Ripper killings and other Victorian manifestations of murderous evils, it was a sad fact that unless the perpetrator was caught in the act, or the police succeeded in obtaining a confession from the killer, the apprehension of many murderers remained difficult for the official police force. Although many scientists and criminologists had begun to experiment with and use a rudimentary form of fingerprinting as a means of identification, it was not until 1900 that fingerprinting was introduced in England as a positive means of identifying those responsible for criminal acts. Similarly, it would be many years before forensic science, as we now know it, would be introduced and used as an aid in the solving of crime.

So, for Albert Norris and Dylan Hillman, their investigation revolved around whatever suspicions they could justifiably build a case on. If, during the course of their inquiries, they could unearth any evidence linking the victim to a particular suspect, then they would leave no stone unturned in an effort to discover if that person had the motive, the time and the opportunity to have carried out the murder. If so, they would bring the suspect in for questioning, and hope to elicit a confession of guilt. Failing such a confession, they would hope to at least uncover some form of evidence that would reasonably assist in obtaining a conviction in a court of law. In short, the police needed to get lucky.

Unfortunately, luck, as with evidence, appeared to be in short supply for the two dogged detectives. Try as they might, they could make little progress with the case. Days turned into a week, then two, and the surveillance on Martin Bowker had so far failed to produce anything that might add to Norris's original feeling that the reverend gentleman from St.Giles's might not be all he first seemed to be. The vicar conducted his services in church, went home, attended a couple of Bible Class meetings, went home, and in short, work aside, Martin Bowker appeared to do nothing more than spend his time at home, perhaps writing his next sermon. He'd deviated only a couple of times from this daily, boring, routine. Constable Wilkinson reported that Bowker had used the underground railway system to travel to a Diocesan meeting on Portland Road, and had thus travelled as far as the Portland Road underground station, and back again at the conclusion of the meeting. Likewise, Constable Fry had observed the vicar using the underground system to travel to St. James's Park station, where he'd alighted and then walked as far as Green Park, where he attended an open air prayer and worship meeting. Again, he returned home immediately afterwards.

The newspapers continued to berate the Metropolitan Police Force and clamoured for an arrest in the case of the Whitechapel Murders. More and more officers were drafted into the search for the killer of the East End prostitutes, whose names now gained a degree of fame in death that they could never have attained in life. Suddenly, everyone knew who Annie Chapman, Mary Ann Nichols and Martha Tabram were, as vigilantes took to the streets of Whitechapel in an effort to assist the police in the hunt for the killer.

Thanks to the political sensitivity of the underground murders, however, and the government's ploy to avoid a panic by using its special powers to limit the press's reporting on the case, little more appeared in the popular press in relation to the death of Clara Forshaw. A couple of updates were released to the press, which simply stated that the woman found dead at Aldgate station had been identified (without giving her name), and her family informed. Police inquiries, it stated, continued.

The ploy succeeded handsomely, with the entire press hulla-baloo related to the Whitechapel murders being more than enough to satisfy an avid reading public, eager for news of the latest developments of the police investigation in the East End.

Time continued to pass with unerring certainty, day to night, night to day, and the frustration was beginning to take its toll on Norris and Hillman, who were both aware that Chief Inspector Madden would be breathing down their necks very soon, unless they could provide him with some positive results to their investigation. He, after all, continued to believe in the theory of a conspiracy against the railway company, rather than in Norris's belief that the murder of Cara Forshaw had been a rather more personal and well-directed crime.

So it was that on the afternoon of the 29th September, Norris and his sergeant were summoned to Madden's office. Three weeks had elapsed since Clara's murder, and Madden was growing impatient.

"Well, gentlemen," he began, seated comfortably in his chair as the two men stood respectfully in front of his desk, "we don't seem to be getting very far, do we?"

"No, sir, we don't," Norris replied.

"And why do you think that is, Inspector?"

"Well, sir, we've tried all we can to trace any connection between Clara Forshaw and either Reverend Bowker or members of his congregation, but without much success, I'm afraid."

"I think you mean without *any* success," said Madden, sternly.

"Well, that's correct, sir, but we have been hampered a little by not being able to call on the usual avenues of assistance in the case. The press have been kept quiet, all the usual appeals for help from the public have been denied to us and we simply can't conjure up evidence if we don't know where to look for it."

"Have you considered that this might be because you're barking up the wrong tree with this investigation, Bert? I've given you plenty of leeway and resources to follow up on your theory implicating Reverend Bowker, as opposed to this being a politically motivated crime, but I'm afraid my patience has worn out. Can you tell me here and now whether you've discovered one shred of evidence that might reinforce your theory?"

Norris and Hillman exchanged glances, before the inspector added, simply, "No, sir, I can't."

"Then the time has come for you to end this ridiculous surveillance operation. I'm pulling Constables Fry and Wilkinson off the case, and you and Hillman had better start looking for evidence in other quarters. Do I make myself clear?"

"Yes, sir, but. . ."

"No buts, Inspector. My decision is made."

Then, in a slightly more conciliatory fashion, Madden added, "Look, Bert, you've played your theory out and it's come to nothing. Try going back to the beginning. Look for a connection with the underground railway. I'm certain that's where you'll find this killer."

"But if that were the case, sir, don't you think that the killer, seeing the lack of press coverage of the crime, would have done something to try and draw public attention to his crime, to publicise it and gain a degree of notoriety and thus emphasise his point, whatever it is?"

"Ah, but that's just the point, isn't it? You've so far ignored the possibility entirely, so you can hardly have an inkling about what this killer's motives are, can you, Bert?"

To his shame, Norris had to admit his superior officer had a point. Could he, through his own well-documented stubbornness, have jeopardised the investigation by ignoring a viable avenue of inquiry? Plus, there was always the possibility that he'd been set up to fail. Was it possible that someone, somewhere, didn't want this killer caught, thus explaining why Madden had allowed him to follow his theory for so long before pulling the plug on his surveillance of the vicar of St. Giles's? As these thought ran through his head, he murmured a quiet, "Yes, sir, I mean, no, sir." in reply to Madden's last statement.

"Good. Now, Inspector, Sergeant, please go away and find some more productive line of inquiry. I'd like to see progress on the case, as indeed would the Superintendent and, I may add, others in far higher positions."

The meeting at an end, Norris and Hillman left the office of Chief Inspector Madden, feeling suitable chastened.

"Well, that's us well and truly told, eh, Bert?" said Hillman, as soon as the two of them were together in the corridor outside Madden's office, the door closed and the chief inspector now out of earshot.

"'Fraid so, Dylan. I'm still damned if I believe in this conspiracy against the railway theory, but, as we've drawn a blank in every other direction, we're going to have to give it a go."

"So, where do we start?"

"I don't know. I suppose the only thing we can do is go back to the scene where the body was discovered. Let's speak to the staff at Aldgate again. I know they all said they saw and heard nothing, and no one could even tell us if anyone else alighted from the carriage, but damn it, someone must know something, even if they don't realise it."

"Do you want to head over there, now?"

"No, Dylan. Let's be prepared. I want the two of us to go through all the notes made by those who attended the scene on the night of Clara's murder. Let's see if we can spot anything that might give us an idea of where to start. Then, first thing tomorrow, we'll go down to Aldgate and speak to as many of the staff as we can."

"You know, Bert, even some of the staff who weren't actually on duty that night might have seen her in the past. Maybe she was seen with someone, maybe even the man who made her pregnant."

"That's a bloody brilliant idea, Dylan, old chum. Well done. Yes, we'll speak to every bloody Metropolitan Railway employee at Aldgate and see if anyone recognises a picture of the girl. Do you still have that photograph her father gave to us?"

"I do indeed."

"Right then, let's go read those notes, and tomorrow we start afresh, as the old man wants us to."

"You sound incredibly positive, Bert. I thought you didn't hold with the chief's theory?"

"No, but if we're going to crack this damned case, we need to look at all the angles. We've been blanked off from Bowker, though he's not in the clear yet as far as I'm concerned. I'm hoping someone at Aldgate may have seen Clara with the vicar and can give us a link to the two of them as a couple."

"You crafty bugger," said Hillman.

Norris winked at his sergeant.

"Aren't I just, old chum!"

With that, the two of them made their way to the office, where they began to read through the notes made by every officer who'd attended Aldgate station on the night of Clara Forshaw's murder. Tomorrow, they'd begin Norris's new line of inquiry with renewed optimism.

Unfortunately for Norris, the events of the coming night were about to throw a very large spanner in the works. Long after he and Hillman had left New Street Police Station and returned to their respective homes, and as darkness cast its shroud over the streets of the capital, murder returned to the streets of Whitechapel, not once, but twice in a single night. The Whitechapel Murderer had returned!

Chapter 13
A Double Event

As Albert Norris slept soundly beside Betty that Saturday night, with Billy the terrier snoring in his usual place at the foot of the stairs, events in Whitechapel unfolded at an alarming pace. At around 1 a.m., Louis Diemschütz drove his horse and cart into Dutfield's Yard, off Berner Street, Whitechapel and discovered the freshly murdered body of Elizabeth Stride. Theorists have since put forward the idea that the killer may have been lurking in the shadows of the yard as Diemschütz entered the premises and that his arrival may have prevented the murderer from carrying out the mutilations already perpetrated on earlier victims. Certainly, Elizabeth Stride had not been subjected to the same degree of mutilation as Annie Chapman or Mary Nicholls, but the same could not be said of the victim of the second, most gruesome murder that took place that night.

At 1.45 a.m., police constable Edward Watkins was to discover the horribly mutilated body of Catharine Eddowes in the south-west corner of Mitre Square, close to Aldgate. Eddowes had been subjected to the most appalling mutilations seen to date in the series of murders that were causing such fear and terror in London's East End. Despite the horrific nature of the mutilations to her face, abdomen and genitals, perhaps the most significant injury applied to her body was the severing of one of Catharine's ears, such significance becoming apparent some days later when a letter purporting to be from the killer was made public.

The location of the second murder of the night was also to lead to one source of confusion in the case, in that Mitre Square fell within the jurisdiction of the City of London Police Force, as opposed to the Metropolitan Police, and so resulted in two separate forces becoming involved in the investigation, with all the procedural complications that such an event merited.

Thus, when Norris arrived at New Street police station the following morning, he was to discover an air of fervent activity and an almost cacophonous din, as the hubbub of voices that greeted him reflected the fever pitch at which everyone appeared to be reacting to the latest horrendous murders in what was fast becoming the most serious case of multiple murder to have struck the streets of London. The press had already got hold of the story and the 'double event', as it became known, was being whipped into a frenzy by the headline-grabbing journalists, who had taken to goading the police and holding them responsible for their failure to apprehend the murderer who, they contended, was able to walk and stalk the streets of Whitechapel with complete impunity, due to the ineptitude of the police force.

"Bloody hell, Bert. The world's gone mad!" exclaimed Dylan Hillman, the moment Norris entered the door to their office.

"Looks like it, Dylan. Seems our friend in Whitechapel has been at work again."

"Yes, but not just one, two bloody victims in one night. The whole force is being mobilised in an effort to catch the bastard, or so they're saying."

"Well, old chum, mad as it appears to be, you and I have our own murder to investigate. They can pressgang as many men onto the Whitechapel murders as they like, but I don't think Madden is going to move us on to that one, at least not unless, or until, we can clear this one up."

Norris was quickly proved correct in his assumption, though not perhaps in the way he'd have liked. As the hubbub continued, Norris gestured to Hillman, who followed his inspector into his own office, where Norris intended to outline his own plan of action for the continuation of their investigation. No sooner had the two men sat down, however, when the office door abruptly swung open and Chief Inspector Madden strode purposefully into the room.

"Sorry to interrupt, Inspector," he spoke, almost breathlessly. "We have another murder on our hands."

"Yes, so I've heard, sir, and a double murder too, by all accounts."

"No, Bert. I'm sorry to say I'm not referring to the Whitechapel case."

Norris and Hillman both managed to look bemused at the chief's words.

"Then what. . . ?"

"The railway, Bert. Another murder on the underground railway. I told you this wasn't a personal crime. Now we have another body to add to poor Clara Forshaw's. He's struck again. If the public begin to get wind of all this, they're going to know we have two killers stalking the streets of London, and you can imagine the public outcry if that became the general feeling amongst the populace."

"Yes, quite," said Norris, a little uncaring of his superior officer's obvious discomfort. "But, where and when did this killing take place, sir? Do you have any details?"

"I don't know exactly when the murder took place, but, I've just been informed by a runner sent by Inspector Hall at Moorgate Street, that a body has been found in one of the tunnels that run into Moorgate Street Underground Station."

"Bloody hell, sir. Moorgate Street is only a couple of stops down the line from Aldgate. Man or woman? Do we know?"

"A woman, young, and not too poorly dressed, is all I know for the moment. Inspector Hall is a good man. Although we've kept this case pretty close to our chests, he was aware that we are investigating the previous death on the underground railway and thought I should be told about this latest state of affairs. I want the two of you to get down to Moorgate as soon as you can. I've sent the runner back with instructions to Hall to keep this as quiet as he can for the time being. Obviously, he'll have to be told something before too long, enough to make sure he and his men are aware of the 'special' aspects of the case, but for now, I've also sent written instructions that he is to cede responsibility in the case to you."

Norris simply nodded in response to Madden's last statement. He knew it wouldn't be long before leaks began to appear in the secrecy surrounding the case, if many more people became involved. He was sure that Hall would soon be receiving a visit from the man from Special Branch, in order to ensure his silence, but for now, that was the least of his concerns.

"You say this woman's body was found in a tunnel, sir. How do we know this isn't merely a case of suicide, perhaps? The poor woman may have been deranged or ill, and thrown herself under a passing train."

"Oh, come on, Sergeant Hillman," said Madden, in response to the sergeant's suggestion. "I think the locomotive driver or his fireman would have noticed if their engine had hit a human being on the line, don't you?"

"Under normal circumstances, I'd agree with you, sir, but Sergeant Hillman may have a point. In the darkness of those tunnels and with the way those trains rattle along, there's so much noise that maybe they wouldn't notice a collision with a body, not unless it was directly under the wheels and caused the loco to leave the rails. That, they most certainly *would* have noticed," said Norris, in defense of his sergeant.

"Yes, well, anyway, we can sit and conjecture the point all day, Bert, but that won't get us anywhere, will it? I suggest you and Hillman get across to Moorgate as fast as you can. A constable will be waiting to escort you to where Inspector Hall should be waiting with the body."

"Yes, sir. You're correct, of course," said Norris. "Come on, Dylan, let's get down there. The staff at Aldgate will have to wait for another time."

"Eh, Aldgate? What about the staff at Aldgate?" asked Madden, unaware of Norris's plan for the next stage of the investigation.

"Oh, just another line of inquiry, sir. It can wait," Norris replied. "Come on Dylan, let's go."

With that, the two men strode from the office, leaving the chief inspector standing in the doorway. They were soon in a cab on their way to Moorgate Underground Station, where, as they were soon to discover, their case had definitely taken a turn for the worse.

PART TWO

Chapter 14
Moorgate Street

Inspector Thomas Hall had positioned a constable at the entrance to Moorgate Street Underground Station for the sole purpose of meeting Norris and guiding him to the location of the newly discovered body. The fresh-faced officer, who Norris thought looked barely out of his teens, greeted him with a crisp salute as he and Hillman approached him.

"Constable Jennings, sir. Inspector Hall said as I was to meet you and take you to him at once."

"Very well, Constable, lead on," Norris replied, and he and Hillman quickly fell into step behind Jennings.

"What about the trains? Are they still running?" asked Hillman, as they descended the steps towards the station platforms.

"Yes, they are, but we're quite safe in the tunnel. They're routing the trains along the other track, causing a few delays, but Inspector Hall insisted we could only work if the railway people made it safe for us to do so."

"A wise man," said Norris.

"You know him, sir?" asked Hillman.

"Archie Hall was a constable, and I was his sergeant, a long time ago, Dylan. He's always been a capable sort of bloke. A bit younger than me, of course, but good at his job, always has been."

A minute later, as they arrived at the edge of the platform, bright with the light of what appeared to be hundreds of gas lamps affixed to the tubular-shaped walls, Jennings spoke once again.

"He's down there, sir, with Sergeant Willis and two constables – oh, and the doctor, of course – about a hundred yards or so inside the tunnel. You'll see the light from their lanterns when you get a little way along the track."

"Thank you, Jennings. You'd better go on with whatever you have to do next."

"Yes, sir. I'm to speak to some of the station employees, see if anyone knows anything, like."

"Good man. Off you go then."

Jennings left the two detectives to descend onto the track, and they slowly made their way into the cavernous subterranean hole that carried the tracks of the underground railway far beneath the streets of London. Even more so than on their visit to Aldgate, they were struck by the smell, as, this time, they were denied the luxury of conducting their initial investigation on the platform. Here, where the paying public never ventured, the stench of stale smoke, sulphur and steam mingled with coal dust that hovered in the air like a dense black cloud, forming a foul-smelling and pungent concoction that overpowered the olfactory senses of all those unfortunate enough to be forced to inhale it. Norris and Hillman could truly understand why so many thought the underground railway to be a demonic, satanic place, where noisy, foul-smelling engines of vast power plied back and forth, leaving trails of noxious fumes in their wake.

As they ventured into the almost stygian darkness, only occasionally broken by the faint glow of the tiny lamps that provided almost no light at all in the tunnel, they were careful not to trip over the steel rails that lay beneath their feet, somewhere in the gloom. Constable Jennings had omitted to inform Norris that the tunnel entered and exited the station via a small bend and so the lights from the lamps carried by Hall and his men didn't become apparent until Norris and Hillman rounded the bend and found themselves almost on top of the little group gathered at the side of the track.

As they drew closer, Norris recognised his one-time colleague, now Inspector Thomas Hall, and Sergeant Willis was easily recognisable by his uniform. The two constables in attendance were searching the immediate area, presumably, Norris thought, looking for anything to identify the woman, or perhaps for a murder weapon. On his knees beside the body was Doctor Marcus Roebuck, who had evidently been the police surgeon on call when the body had been discovered.

"Morning, all," said Norris, as he and Hillman stepped closer to the scene.

"Ah, Inspector Norris," said the doctor, returning instantly to his examination of the body.

"Well, this is a nice surprise, Bert," said Thomas Hall as he recognised his old friend. "When we sent word to New Street, I'd no idea it would be you who was in charge of the earlier case. Chief Inspector Madden appears to be playing this one close to his chest. He hardly told me a thing, apart from the fact I'm to cede responsibility to you and keep all details of the case to myself, and that applies to my men, too. Can you tell me what's going on here?"

"Sorry, Tom, I'm afraid I'm not at liberty to tell you any more than Madden. Let's just say there are some potential political considerations at stake in the case, and leave it at that for now, eh?"

"If you say so." Hall shrugged. "I can't say I'll be disappointed to hand over a murder case right now. We've more than enough keeping us busy as it is. I suppose you've heard about the double murder in Whitechapel last night, too?"

"I think everyone on the force has heard of that one by now. I'm glad to leave it to Abberline and his boys. Anyway, come on. Tell me what you've got here so far."

"See for yourself." Hall pointed at the body. "Young, I'd say, perhaps no more than twenty-four, or five. She's a bit of a mess, I'm afraid."

As Norris bent down to get a better look at the corpse, aided by one of the constables, who'd appeared as if by magic with a lantern to assist him, he asked, "Any chance it's a suicide? Maybe she threw herself under the train or something?"

"Not a chance in the world," came the fast reply from Roebuck, who continued to work by the light of two lanterns placed either side of the body. "Not unless she managed to stab herself to death, and somehow managed to throw the knife away, so far from her body that the constables haven't managed to find it yet."

"Ah," was all Norris said in reply.

"Exactly," said Roebuck.

"Am I missing something here?" asked Thomas Hall.

"Just that we've kind of been down this road before, Tom," Norris replied.

"You don't mean to tell me that in addition to the maniac stalking the streets of Whitechapel, we may have another one on our hands?"

"Precisely, which is why Madden and the brass up top want this kept as low profile as possible."

"I can see why," said Hall, nodding in understanding.

"I've no doubt Special Branch will be here soon, Tom. They'll want assurances from you and your men regarding your prudence with regards to anything you see or hear down here."

"Bloody hell, Bert. Sounds serious."

"You could say that, but for now, we need to find out what we can about this latest victim. Is there anything on her that could give us an indication of who she is, Doctor Roebuck?"

Roebuck slowly rose from his kneeling position until he stood face to face with Norris.

"Sorry to disappoint you, Inspector, but there's nothing. She was stabbed to the heart, that much is for sure, so I can say you're probably looking for the same man who killed Clara Forshaw, but this one was also struck by a passing train, by the looks of it. There's a lot of damage, as you can see, to the right side of her body. She probably wasn't directly on the track or the driver of the train would have felt something, but she must have been so close to it that the train struck her body with a glancing body and threw it up in the air, and she landed here, about twenty yards from the point of impact."

"How can you be sure of that?"

"Because, just before you got here, Constable Merryweather over there found the woman's purse and an amount of blood, just noticeable, by the side of the track, twenty yards along the line. I'll show you in a minute."

For the first time, Norris and Hillman took a close look at the body. Even in the darkness of the tunnel, the lamps provided enough light for them to ascertain that the woman's body had indeed suffered great trauma from a blow, caused, as the doctor had probably guessed correctly, by being struck by a train as it approached or departed from Moorgate Street station. The right-hand side of the body was badly mutilated, churned perhaps by the wheels of the train as it sliced through the portion of her body closest to the rail. It hadn't been necessary for the body to be placed on the line in order for damage of this nature to occur. Norris had seen previous victims of railway accidents, and knew only too well just how much damage could be caused to the human body by even a mild glancing blow from a fast-moving leviathan such as a railway engine and its coaches.

"My God, the poor woman looks like raw meat," said Hillman, grimacing as he took in the sight. The majority of the right side had been cleaved open, the abdomen and guts open to the world. Internal organs protruded from the massive gash in the woman's side, and, if they hadn't been sure that the injuries were caused by a passing train, one might almost have associated them with the Whitechapel Murderer. That, as Hillman knew, was preposterous of course.

"Afraid so, Sergeant," Roebuck replied. "We're lucky the chest was relatively unscathed, or I might not have been able to discern the stab wound, and the cause of death might have been indeterminable."

"I suppose we must be grateful for small mercies, eh?" Hillman added.

"Not that this poor young woman received much mercy, by the looks of things."

"Quite so, doctor," Norris interjected. "I'll need the results of your post mortem examination..."

"As soon as I can possibly get them to you. I know, Inspector Norris. I shan't let you down."

With that, Norris left Roebuck to conclude his on-scene examination, as a scurrying sound from round the corner heralded the arrival of the mortuary attendants, ready to remove the body to the morgue for the post-mortem to be carried out. Norris gestured to Hall to follow him and the two men walked a little way together, away from the immediate area where the body lay. Hillman remained close to the body, ready to oversee the scene until Norris returned. After spending five minutes filling Hall in with as much background information on the case as he dared, Norris responded to Doctor Roebuck's call, indicating that he could now carry out his own examination of the body.

Together, Norris, Hall and Hillman squatted close enough to the body for them to make out most of the details of the scene. As he stood back to allow them easier access, Roebuck said, "I'm sorry there doesn't appear to be anything else to tell you at present, Inspector. My first instincts appear to be correct and I'll confirm everything after the post mortem examination at the mortuary."

"She's a real mess, Bert, that's for sure," said Hillman, as he managed his first very close look at the dead woman.

"With no apparent identification on her, it could take a while to find out who she is, or rather, was," added Hall.

"One thing's for sure, she's young, like Clara Forshaw, and her clothes indicate she's a cut above the working girls of Whitechapel," said Norris. "It looks as if the same killer has struck again, Dylan, old chum. Now, we have to perhaps accept Madden's premise that this is something to do with a grudge against the railway."

Thomas Hall, having received a brief introduction to the peculiarities of the case from Norris, said nothing, and just continued to stare at the body. The blonde-haired woman was dressed in a waist-length black cloth jacket of reasonable quality, over a dark grey dress, with two outside pockets, both empty, according to the doctor. The dress had ridden up her legs somewhat to reveal a pair of black stockings, torn, apparently, by whatever trauma she'd sustained in the blow from the train, revealing the pale white flesh of her legs, as high as her thighs. Hall and Hillman, both single men, blushed a little at the sight of such an expanse of feminine flesh, though, as experienced police officers, both had seen such sights before. Still, they couldn't help but feel a little like pornographic voyeurs as they surveyed the ravaged corpse of the victim, and the neat, white drawers that were revealed at the tops of her thighs. This was the age of the Victorians, and such sights were, of course, improper by their very nature.

Norris felt no such instincts, however, as he bent closer to the woman and tried to take in every aspect of her facial features. Somehow, he had the strangest idea that he'd seen this woman before. He wanted to see her in daylight, as soon as he could, perhaps at the morgue, to try to confirm his odd conception of recognition. For now, though, he said nothing of such thoughts.

Suddenly, there came the sound of a shrill, continuous bell ringing, a sound that reverberated through the tunnel.

"That means a train's coming!" shouted Hall. "Everyone over here, against the wall."

Quickly, the entire group gathered at the side of the track, near the wall of the tunnel. In mere seconds, the sound of the approaching train could be heard, followed by the sight of a distant headlight as the locomotive rounded the bend and thundered towards them. In the cloistered confines of the tunnel, the sound of the approaching train grew with gathering intensity until the cacophonous din seemed fit to burst the eardrums of those present, these interlopers in the underworld. The train appeared large and threatening as it loomed ever closer, and then, with a mad, rushing wind accompanying it, the locomotive hurtled past the policemen and the doctor, followed by its rattling entourage of carriages, the whole caboodle resembling a terrifying beast of Hades, all speeding by in a few seconds, leaving a sudden silence as it disappeared from view and on into Moorgate Street Station. The driver and fireman had been visible on the exposed footplate at the loco flew past, captains of the beast, as exposed as the fearful spectators in the tunnel to the noxious cocktail of smoke and gasses that belched from the funnel. All around, the dust and residual smoke from its passing cast swirling clouds around the tunnel, causing the men to choke and gasp until, a minute later, the airborne mayhem began to subside and the tunnel returned to its original state, though the sulphurous stench had increased tenfold.

"Bloody hell!" exclaimed Hillman, and his statement was echoed in similar vein by the others.

"Can you imagine having to work on one of those things?" asked Norris, of no one in particular.

"Not good for one's health, I'm sure," said the doctor. "Our clothes will stink for a week, and our hair. Look at us! Our faces are filthy."

Even in the gloom of the tunnel, they could all see that the doctor was correct. It was time to move things along.

"Look, let's get on with it, before another one comes along," said Norris, and there was universal agreement.

Norris and Hall quickly regrouped to continue their conversation.

"If this is some sort of gruesome conspiracy, Bert, it means we have a second sick, perverted bastard running around London. I'd have thought we'd enough to contend with, with the bloody Whitechapel Murderer," said Hall.

"Well, Tom, just be grateful you can hand this one over to us, eh? I'll ask you to make sure your men are tight-lipped about this until you've been visited by the man from Special Branch. I don't like this bloody secrecy any more than you do, but, as they say, orders are orders."

"Don't you worry, Bert. I have no desire to jeopardise my pension. I'll speak to the others and make sure they're aware that we're involved in a sensitive case, which will require all of their discretion, until they've been spoken to by higher authority."

With the constraints of the case having been made apparent to his colleague, Norris looked once more at the corpse lying forlornly in the gloom at his feet. The mortuary attendants arrived and, as he could do little more at the scene, Norris allowed them to remove the body from its location by the side of the track. He, Hillman and Hall spent half an hour scouring the darkness around the immediate area in the search for clues, but found nothing. Three more trains passed in that time, causing them to run to the side of the tunnel for safety again, and further inflicting noise, dust and smoke-filled, choking tunnel air upon them.

As they made their way back towards the light some time later, relieved to be moving back into the world of daylight and fresh air, Norris continued to be dogged by a single thought.

Where on earth have I seen her before? Though the answer continued to evade him.

Chapter 15
Sudden Revelation

"Is there something wrong, Bert? I can tell when you've something on your mind," said Dylan Hillman, as the two detectives stood at the back of the room while Doctor Roebuck completed his post mortem examination of the latest victim of the underground railway killer. "You've hardly said two words since we left Moorgate Street, apart from the odd grunt now and then."

Norris sighed, and decided to entrust his odd feeling about the victim to his trusted sergeant.

"Sorry, Dylan, old chum. I've been lost in thought. When I looked at that poor woman beside the tracks, despite the darkness down there, I had the feeling I'd seen her someplace, and recently, too."

"Bloody hell, Bert, where?"

"That's just it. I can't sodding well remember. Even seeing her here, in the light, I can't quite place her. You know, it's like one of those things where you might have caught a glimpse of someone, their face has registered in your mind, and then, when you really want to recall the time and place you saw them, your mind just goes a blank."

"She's not a neighbour, or the daughter of someone you know or anything, then?"

"No, nothing like that. I think I saw her briefly a few days ago, but, where, Dylan, bloody well where?"

"I'm sure it'll come back to you. These things usually do. You've been working bloody hard lately and it's no surprise if you can't remember every face you see on the streets of London, Bert."

Roebuck chose that moment to leave the corpse on the table and walk across to where Norris and Hillman stood.

"Well, gentlemen, there's not a lot I can add to what I found at the scene. She was in her mid twenties, perhaps a little older, and certainly not from the lowest echelons of society. Her stomach contents reveal that she ate a meal of kidneys, potatoes and turnips some time before her death, and her overall condition indicates she was generally well-fed, and in good health. There are no diseases present which one might expect to find in the poorer classes, so my assumption is that the young lady was, like your previous victim, rather better off than the underclasses found on the streets of Whitechapel, for example. Her hands and fingers also display no signs of calluses or the effects of heavy manual work, so, maybe, like Clara Forshaw, she was in private employment of some kind. She was of course, killed by a single stab wound to the heart, just as in the previous case. I've no doubt you're seeking the same killer in both cases."

"Thank you, Doctor," said Norris. "It does seem as if our man is seeking a certain type of woman on whom to prey. I just wish we had some idea of her identity."

"I'm sorry I can't be of help with that one, Inspector. There's nothing on her to provide any clues as to who she is, or *was*, I should say."

At that, Norris walked slowly across the room, and spent a good two minutes scrutinising the face of the dead woman, trying to recall where he'd seen her before. He hardly noticed the approach of Hillman, who touched his elbow and released him from the turgid lethargy into which he'd allowed his mind to fall while he searched his memory, without success.

"Don't try and force it, Bert. You'll remember where you saw her eventually, I know you will."

"Sorry, Dylan. I was miles away, racking my brains and trying to retrace my steps over the last few days, or weeks in fact. It's bloody maddening to know I've seen her and yet, I don't think I ever knew her name."

Before they could continue their discussion, the door to the autopsy room opened to admit Inspector Thomas Hall. His facial expression immediately told Norris that the man had news.

"Tom, what is it? You look out of breath."

"I damn well am. I got here as quickly as I could. Sergeant Willis recently returned from a visit to the Metropolitan Railway's marshalling yard. I had an idea that, if we could find blood on the wheels of any of their locomotives or carriages, we could find out what time that train ran through the tunnel last night, and that would give us an idea when she was killed. We just have to look back from then to the time of the previous train, from which she was presumably dumped, and we should have a good idea when she murdered."

"And?" said an expectant Norris.

"Willis found it! Engine number 34, complete with nice, fresh bloodstains on the left side driving wheels of the engine. They were just about to clean the damn thing when Willis got there, so we were lucky. I checked with the controller on duty and number 34 ran into Moorgate Street at ten minutes after eleven last night. The previous train that passed through the tunnel and from which the body could have been thrown, bearing in mind the side of the track she was found, passed only twelve minutes earlier."

"Bloody well done, Tom, and to your Sergeant Willis, of course. So, she was killed around eleven p.m. and that gives us something to start with. If we can find out who she was, and where she boarded the train, that might help us to narrow down a suspect or two. For now, we have to try and track down anyone who was on that train. Er, Tom?"

"I know. You want me to put a couple of my men on it, while you and your team get your teeth into the bones of the investigation, right?"

"You know me too well, Tom, but, yes. Could you do that for me?"

"Don't worry, Bert. I've had a visit from Special Branch and me and my men have been told to keep our lips tightly sealed. I don't know why, and to be honest, I don't care. We'll get on with the job, and my gaffer says I'm to help you in whatever way I can."

"Ah, yes, Chief Inspector Murray. How is he, Tom?"

"He's as cranky and awkward as always, and still hates your guts for some reason. I could tell he hated it when he told me he'd had a visit from Special Branch, too and that they'd told him all information on the case had to go to you, and that his men would report to you in the first instance. In fact, his face was so red I thought he might explode. What on earth did you ever do to him, Bert?"

Norris smiled a wry and knowing smile that conveyed nothing to the man on the receiving end.

"Forget it, Tom. That's between me and him. For now, I'm grateful to you and your sergeant for what you've already done. Now, that train. . . ?"

"Right, Bert, enough said. We'll see what we can find out, where she got on, who else was on it, and anything else we can rake up."

With Hall gone, Norris soon returned to the perplexing problem of where he'd seen the girl before. He took Dylan Hillman with him as he decided a walk in the fresh air might revive his flagging memory. As the two men walked in a companionable silence, the sound of church bells striking the hour broke into the thoughts of the inspector, who suddenly became highly animated, much to Hillman's surprise.

"Bloody hell, Dylan. What a fool I've been. I should have remembered right away!"

"You mean. . . it's come back to you? You know who she was, Bert?"

"No, not who she was, but I do know where I've seen her before. Come on, Dylan, old chum."

Norris literally grabbed Hillman by the arm and began to drag him towards a nearby cab stand. Jumping into the nearest cab, he pulled Hillman in after him.

"Bloody hell, Bert, slow down. What's the panic?"

"No panic, Dylan, but guess what? I know it, now. I saw that girl the day you and I went to interview Reverend Bowker at the church and we had to wait for the service to finish. She smiled at me as she was leaving. She was one of his congregation, for God's sake!"

The cabbie took that moment to lean down and ask where Norris and Hillman wished to go.

"St. Giles's church, please, cabbie, and, as quick as you can, there's a good man."

Norris turned to Hillman, who sat beside him with a stunned expression on his face.

"I told you, old chum. Didn't I bloody well tell you? Our friend the reverend gentleman has got some serious explaining to do, and I aim to give him every opportunity to do so."

"Bert, I know it looks bad for him, but please, let's remember what Madden said. Don't go at it like a bull in a china shop. For God's sake, take it easy when we get there."

"Don't worry. I'll be as professional as it's possible to be with Bowker, Dylan. But this is a coincidence, and you know what I think of coincidences, eh?"

"I know. That there's no such thing."

"Dead right! We're going to talk to him and then he's going to come back to the station with us, and we're going to stand there while he looks at that woman's body, and I want to see how he reacts."

"And then?"

"And then, old chum, with a little bit of luck, he'll crack, and we'll charge the sanctimonious bastard with two murders."

Chapter 16
A Meeting With The
Commissioner

"This whole situation is getting completely out of hand, gentlemen."

Commissioner of the Metropolitan Police, Sir Charles Warren, sat behind his solid mahogany desk, his face an angry mask, as Chief Superintendent Walter Morrow and Chief Inspector Joshua Madden stood, appearing for the entire world like a pair of naughty schoolboys being berated by their headmaster. Warren hadn't invited either man to sit, despite the presence of two comfortable leather armchairs in the plush, carpeted office; a sure sign of his growing angst.

"I already have what seems to be half the police force of London searching for this damned Whitechapel Murderer, and now you have the effrontery to tell me that we've had a second murder on the underground railway and yet you have not a single clue as to who the perpetrator could be, despite having had over two weeks to investigate the case. Not only do the public appear to view me as incompetent in my handling of the Whitechapel case, but that epithet is being applied to the entire force, gentlemen, and another case of multiple murder, should it become public knowledge, will, I'm sure, lead not only to my forced resignation, but perhaps to that of others, too, if you take my hint. It simply isn't good enough."

Warren's implied threat certainly wasn't lost on the two men. Morrow, Madden's superior, replied as deferentially, and at the same time as positively, as he could.

"Sir Charles, I know it appears as though no progress has been made, but the Chief Inspector here has assured me that he has his best man on the case, who has been painstakingly following every possible lead, not only in the hunt for the killer but also in order to eliminate others from the inquiry."

"Ah, yes, Madden," said Sir Charles. "I understand Detective Inspector Norris is a man with a past. Are you so sure he's the best man to be handling what could turn out to be a highly sensitive and politically damaging case?"

Madden cleared his throat before replying. Defending Norris didn't exactly come naturally to him, but at the same time, his respect for the man's capabilities demanded no less.

"Sir, I have complete faith in Inspector Norris. Yes, he was the victim of a certain incident in the past, but that has no bearing on the present case. His skill as a detective is in no doubt and, though he can be argumentative and a little gruff in his manner towards authority, he has a record for getting the job done that is perhaps second to none. True, he sometimes goes into a sulk when confronted about some of his wilder theories, but that's simply because the man sincerely cares about the job he does. As fellow policeman, we can surely ask for no less."

"Well said, Madden," said Warren. "Believe me, I have no intention of undermining either you or Detective Inspector Norris. I merely wished to ascertain your own confidence in the man to whom this case has been entrusted. I'm well aware of the incident that led to his removal from Scotland Yard and, like you, I do not for one moment think that his past has any bearing on the present case. Better to let sleeping dogs lie, eh, gentlemen?"

"Er, yes, quite, sir," Morrow replied for both men.

"Then pray tell me, where is Inspector Norris at this moment? Is he following a new line of inquiry? On the second murder?"

Madden was silent and Morrow nudged him.

"Well, you heard Sir Charles. Where is Norris at present, Joshua?"

"Sir," said Madden, "the last I heard, Inspector Norris and Sergeant Hillman had gone for a walk in the fresh air, as it was put to me, in order to think."

Morrow almost visibly shrank into his own shoulders, and Sir Charles's face assumed that sternest of expressions once again as he said, "A walk in the fresh air, you say? Is this how we conduct murder investigations nowadays, Chief Inspector?"

"I'm sure Inspector Norris just felt the need to clear his head, sir. I understand he'd just left the post mortem examination on the latest victim and maybe just needed time to collect his thoughts as to which way to proceed with the investigation."

"I certainly hope so," said Warren. "We don't pay our detective division to go swanning around the streets of London, taking the air, when there's a murder to be solved."

"Norris had a theory that the murder of Clara Forshaw may not have been directly connected to the railway, Sir Charles," said Morrow.

Madden groaned inwardly, wishing Morrow had kept that bit of news to himself.

"Oh yes?" said Warren.

"Tell Sir Charles, Joshua, why don't you?"

"Well, sir, it was just a theory which I did my best to dispel, that the murder of the first victim may not have been linked to a campaign against the Metropolitan. When he discovered the victim had been pregnant at the time of her death, he thought the killer may have been the father of the child, perhaps a married man attempting to cover up an indiscretion with a young woman. I told him to forget such ideas, particularly as his chief suspect was none other than the vicar of St. Giles's church."

Warren's face immediately glowed red. The Commissioner was a devout evangelical Christian, and thoughts of a man of the cloth being responsible for heinous murder were simply anathema to him.

"Well, Chief Inspector, I'm certainly happy to know you've guided our Inspector Norris back on to the straight and narrow. A vicar? Certainly not! I've never heard of such a thing. I presume he is now conducting the investigation in a proper manner? We must find out who has a grudge against the Metropolitan, and now that we've had this second murder, it will be even harder to keep the hounds of the press at bay. Sooner or later, the story may break, and if it does, together with the murders in Whitechapel, there may be no holding back on both the public's disquiet and disaffection. There could be riots, gentlemen, d'you hear me? Riots, I say, if they feel the police are incapable of ensuring public safety."

Both Morrow and Madden appeared at a loss for words for a few seconds. It was the Chief Superintendent who eventually responded to the Commissioner's words.

"Sir Charles, I think I can say that every officer under my command will do all in their power to prevent any such loss of public confidence taking place. I know that Chief Inspector Madden can offer his personal assurances that, even as we speak, Detective Inspector Norris will be pursuing every avenue of investigation to find the link that will lead us to the killer, and I'm sure he will be able to prove, without a doubt, that the killer is, as you have long suspected, some kind of Fenian or Socialist agitator with a grudge against the modernisation of the transport system and the benefits it can bring to the people of London."

Warren looked directly at Joshua Madden as he spoke his next words.

"Is that true, Chief Inspector? Can you give me such an assurance?"

Madden took a deep breath.

"Sir Charles, I can state unequivocally, that, after my last interview with him, Detective Inspector Norris is well aware of the correct direction to take with regards to the investigation. I'm sure we'll hear no more of this ridiculous theory with relation to the vicar of St. Giles's."

"For your sake, Chief Inspector, and for Norris's, I fervently hope so," said Warren, concluding the meeting by standing and ushering the two men from his office. As they went out of the door, he paused only long enough to say, "Good morning to you both, gentlemen. Please pay heed to my words, Madden. I wish to hear no more of the persecution of a man of God by one of my officers."

"Sir Charles, I give you my word. Norris has left that theory far behind and is now diligently following new lines of inquiry."

The meeting over, Morrow and Madden returned to their duties, each man pleased to have escaped relatively unscathed from their confrontation with the commissioner.

Joshua Madden, however, experienced a certain sense of trepidation. A nagging voice in the deepest recesses of his mind couldn't help wondering just where Albert Norris was at that moment, and exactly what he was doing.

Chapter 17
A Matter of Identity

Weary grey clouds scudded slowly across a sullen sky, driven by a gentle but rising wind, as Norris and Hillman alighted from their cab at the steps of St. Giles's church. The air felt leaden, as though the trials and tribulations of the world had gathered and now hung heavy over the church, as the detectives made their way up the steps and through the thick oak doors, in search of Martin Bowker.

As the two men made their way up the aisle, they could hear the vicar's voice, coming from somewhere beyond their line of sight. As they approached the font, they saw a door a few yards to the left, from where the voice, and that of another, a woman, could be heard in conversation.

"They're in the vestry," said Norris. He and Hillman walked quickly to the door and the inspector knocked loudly, then pushed the door open without waiting for an answer from within.

In the small sacristy, which held the priestly vestments and sacred vessels for use during church services, the Reverend Martin Bowker stood facing a woman of around twenty-five years of age. Norris immediately noted the wedding ring on her finger, an item distinctly absent from the two victims of the railway killer.

"Reverend Bowker, good morning to you," said Norris, attempting to sound cheerful and light-hearted, not wanting to betray any hint of the reason for his visit.

Though obviously surprised at the sudden intrusion, Bowker replied in equal humour, "And good morning to you, Inspector, and you Sergeant. Mrs. Pendle, may I introduce you to Detective Inspector Norris and Sergeant Hillman."

"Good morning, gentlemen. I shall not pry into your business with the good reverend, but pray tell me, are the police any nearer to catching the vile beast who is so terrorising the streets of Whitechapel?"

"Though that is not my case, let us simply say we are hopeful of an early resolution, Mrs. Pendle," Norris replied.

Mrs. Pendle nodded but said no more on the subject. She was astute enough to recognise a prudent moment to depart.

"I was just here to discuss arrangements for the christening of my son, so perhaps, if you would like to speak with Reverend Bowker privately, I could return later?"

"That would be a help, Mrs. Pendle," said Norris, grateful for the woman's tact and circumspect attitude.

"If you could see me this afternoon, Reverend, around 4 p.m.?" she asked.

"Of course. I do apologise for the unexpected interruption," said Bowker, obviously irritated to have his work interrupted by the police officers.

"Our apologies, too, Mrs. Pendle. I hope all goes well with the christening."

"Thank you, Inspector. So nice to have met you," said Beryl Pendle, as she bustled her way out of the vestry, leaving the three men to their business.

As soon as she'd gone, closing the door behind her, Norris wasted no time.

"Reverend Bowker, we must speak on a matter of great importance."

"I certainly hope it is important, Inspector, as it seems to have interrupted the business of the church," Bowker replied.

"Do you have it, Dylan?" said Norris. He turned to Hillman, who reached inside his coat pocket and removed a hastily produced mortuary photograph of the second victim, which he passed directly to the inspector.

"I must ask you if you have any idea as to the identity of this woman," said Norris, looking into the eyes of Bowker as he took the proffered photograph from the hand of the policeman. Norris didn't need to be a great detective to see the look of shock that registered in the vicar's eyes.

"Why, yes, Inspector. This is Ann Cullen. She's a book-keeper for Andrews and Wright, the solicitors on Whitechapel High Street."

"And a member of your congregation?"

"Yes, she is."

"And also a member of your ladies' Bible Study class?"

"Yes again, Inspector. But tell me, please, what does this have to with Clara Forshaw?"

"Please look a little closer at that picture. Does something about it not strike you as odd?"

Bowker did as instructed, and then looked gravely back at Norris. "I thought at first she was sleeping, but, on closer examination, she looks. . . "

"Dead, Mr. Bowker, exactly! Her body was discovered in a tunnel at Moorgate Underground Railway station a few hours ago."

"But, this is a tragedy upon a tragedy!" the vicar replied, horror written on his face.

"Exactly what we think, too, Mr. Bowker. The odd thing is, we have to ask ourselves how two members of your congregation and more specifically, your Bible Study class, have managed to meet with such violent ends in a short space of time."

"Indeed, it is a mystery to me, Inspector. I don't know who would contemplate doing such harm to two young ladies of good character."

"Regardless of their character, they are both dead, and my job is to bring their killer to justice."

"I understand that all too well, Inspector. But tell me, why are you here, and why do you think I can help in this matter?"

"First of all, the sergeant and I came here to see if you could assist us in identifying the victim. You've done that, and we're grateful to you. Secondly, as this is perhaps more than an unfortunate coincidence, a word I don't hold much truck with, I must say, we must ask you to accompany us to New Street Police Station and give us a complete statement with regard to your relationship with these two unfortunate young ladies."

"The police station? My relationship with them? What relationships are you suggesting, Inspector? I had nothing but a professional and spiritual 'relationship' with those poor girls. You can't possibly be suggesting otherwise, surely? I hope you're not suggesting that I had anything to do with their deaths."

Bowker certainly wasn't stupid, and he had detected an air of menace in Norris's 'invitation' to the police station.

Norris was not put out by the vicar's protests, however.

"Reverend Bowker, in any murder investigation, the time comes when those involved, even those on the periphery, are required to make formal statements to the police about their possible connections with the crime, innocent or otherwise. You have so far co-operated with us in our preliminary inquiries and, I believe, you have kept close counsel with regard to Clara Forshaw's death..."

"How could I do otherwise?" the vicar interrupted. "Your Special Branch people visited my bishop, who made it clear to me that something called 'national security' may be involved. I've kept my silence under threat of some vaguely hinted at measures to be taken against me if I speak in public on the matter."

Norris smiled. He could imagine the pressure being placed on the church authorities and eventually on Bowker, by the bishop and instead of responding directly to Bowker, he continued where he had left off.

"Yes, now, as I was saying, so far you've been very co-operative. Surely you can see that matters have now taken a very definite turn for the worse. A second member of your congregation has met with a violent death, and we must begin to take serious statements from everyone, and I repeat, *everyone*, who had any kind of close contact with both victims. So far, Reverend Bowker, you are the only person we are aware of who knew them both, so you must see it is logical for us to begin with you. After all, I would think you'd want to see their murderer brought to justice?"

"Why, yes, of course I do. I never meant to suggest otherwise. I merely wished to make it plain that I have no intention of allowing you to treat me as some kind of suspect in these terrible crimes and. . ."

"Everyone who knew the women is equally regarded as suspect and innocent," said Norris. "We will establish your innocence just as soon as we have all the facts in place and can eliminate you from our inquiry. Is that not to your advantage, Reverend?"

He'd successfully backed the vicar into a corner and there remained nothing Bowker could do to wriggle out of the proposed visit to the police station.

"Very well, Inspector. I shall go with you, but please, allow me to leave a message on the church doors to indicate I that am away on business for a few hours."

That done, Norris and Hillman escorted Bowker to their waiting cab. Twenty minutes later, they arrived at New Street, where the vicar was led into Norris's office, given a hard, straight-backed wooden chair in which to sit, opposite the detectives, and Norris began what he hoped would be a fruitful and possibly conclusive interview with the man he continued to regard as his chief suspect.

Bowker, however, was not to be so easily broken. Thirty minutes of intense questioning produced not one hint of a confession, or even an admittance of any connection, other than a professional one, with the two dead women.

"For the last time, Inspector Norris, I had nothing to do with the deaths of those two women. I am a man of God, sir, and murder, as you know, is specifically covered by God's own commandments. I knew them both, yes, I had reason to minister to them in my capacity as parish priest, yes, and they were both members of my Bible Study class, yes, but that is all. I did not, at any time, have a relationship that could be construed as improper with either woman, and I certainly never met them outside of my capacity as their minister. Have I managed to make that clear?"

"Very much so," said an exasperated Albert Norris. Neither he, nor Dylan Hillman, could find a way through the vicar's defences, and, despite Norris's belief that Bowker knew far more about the case than he was divulging, he knew he was fast approaching the point where would have to release the man; at least until he could find some shred of evidence to support an arrest. He did, however, have one last card to play.

"Reverend Bowker, I apologise if you've felt I've been hard on you, but please understand, as I told you earlier, it is just as important for us to eliminate certain people from our inquiry, yourself included, so that we may concentrate on other avenues of investigation. I appreciate you having taken the time to come in and help us by answering my questions, and now, the sergeant and I have another call to make. As it will take us in the direction of St. Giles's, I insist you share our cab. We'll drop you off after making one short stop along the way."

So, once again, Martin Bowker found himself sharing a cab with the two policemen as it rattled through the streets of London, though he had no idea where Norris intended to stop before arriving at his church. When the cab eventually came to a halt, Norris alighted and Hillman assisted the vicar to exit the cab after the inspector.

"Where is this place?" asked Bowker, as they stood before a plain, drab, stone-coloured building with a low roof and no visible identifying signs on the wall with which to define its purpose or identity. Norris pushed his way through a painted green door and Hillman ushered Bowker in behind the inspector.

"Won't be long, Reverend," said Norris. "Perhaps you'll join me. There's something I'd like you to take a look at."

"Yes, of course, but where are we?"

"All in good time, Mr. Bowker. This way, please."

Another door stood at the end of a short corridor and Norris quietly pushed it open and beckoned the others to follow him. As soon as they entered the room, Hillman closed the door behind them and Martin Bowker instantly realised exactly where he was.

"This is the mortuary, Inspector Norris. Why on earth have you brought me to this place?"

In the centre of the almost bare, white-walled room stood the autopsy table, where, in accordance with Norris's pre-arranged plan, a mortuary attendant had placed the body of the now identified Ann Cullen under a plain white cotton sheet. Hillman guided the vicar by the elbow until the three men stood adjacent to the table.

"I just want you to confirm the identification you provided us with earlier, Reverend. It's so much better to have a positive identification from 'real life', so to speak, rather than from a poorly taken, grainy photographic image."

Before the vicar could protest, Norris pulled the sheet back, to reveal the cold, naked corpse of Ann Cullen, the stab wound in her chest visible to the left side of the large V-shaped incision in her torso that Doctor Roebuck had inflicted in order to carry out his internal examination of the dead woman's organs.

If Norris had hoped that his shock tactic might elicit a confession from the vicar, he was to be disappointed. Instead, he and Hillman watched as the vicar blanched, his face a mask of shock and horror, and then the churchman turned from the table and, recognising the distinctive gurgling sound from past experiences, Hillman quickly guided him to a basin at the side of the room as the Reverend Martin Bowker was most horribly sick. The vomiting continued for over a minute and both police officers could swear the man's face had a distinctly green pallor when he eventually ceased heaving and retching and pulled himself up straight once more.

By then, Norris had covered the corpse and now stood quietly waiting as the vicar composed himself.

"Well, Reverend Bowker, is that Ann Cullen, as you suspected?"

"Damn you, Norris. You knew damn well it was. I told you that when you showed me the mortuary photograph. That was unnecessary, and you know it. What do you expect to achieve by showing me the poor woman in such a state? Ah, I think I see. You still believe I had something to do with her death and thought to shock me into some kind of confession, is that it?"

"Of course not. I just wished you to confirm your initial thoughts as to her identity, as I said. Nothing wrong with that, surely, vicar? You did say you wanted to assist us, after all."

Bowker was now furious, realising he'd been duped into this terrible visit.

"You haven't heard the last of this, Inspector Norris. I shall see that your superiors are made aware of your appalling conduct in this matter. I'm leaving now, with or without your permission. Forget the cab. I shall make my own way from here, unless of course, you wish to arrest me for throwing up in a public building?"

Hillman moved to stop the man as he began to walk towards the door, but Norris gestured to him to let the man go. As Bowker departed, the room fell silent for a few seconds, though even the silence of the mortuary room felt as though it carried its own unique echo, which bounced from one wall to another, unnervingly.

Hillman stood and looked at Norris, waiting for him to speak. When he did, it was to say, simply, "Well, Dylan, old chum, I think we can safely say that I've managed to completely bugger things up good and proper."

Chapter 18
A Sprained Ankle?

"Have you completely lost your mind, man? What one earth possessed you to bring Martin Bowker in, subject him to a full inter-
rogation and then take him to the morgue and show him the body
of the latest victim in such melodramatic fashion? The Bishop is
totally furious and has accused the police of attempting to place
the blame for these crimes on Bowker simply because we have
no other suspect available and because you've taken a personal
dislike to the man. Can you give me one good reason why I
shouldn't have you suspended from duty, and removed from the
case for good, right now?"

"But, sir..."

"No buts, if you please, Inspector Norris. I demand an explanation for your reprehensible neglect of my previous instructions."

Joshua Madden had summoned Norris to his office as soon
as the virtually apoplectic Bishop, the Right Reverend Charles
Villiers, had left his office. His face was now a mask of uncon-
cealed rage and his fists were tightly closed as he thumped the
desk repeatedly to reinforce his anger. Now, he waited as Norris
attempted to compose himself in the face of his superior officer's
verbal onslaught.

"Very well, sir. As soon as it became clear, from my own personal
recollection of seeing the second victim in church, and on finding
that the second victim, Ann Cullen, was, like Clara Forshaw, a
member of Bowker's congregation, and, more specifically, his
Bible Study class for ladies, I deemed it wise to bring him in for

questioning. So far, he's the only man we know who has admitted to contact with both murder victims."

"But I thought you were going to question the staff at the railway station?"

"I was, sir, but this seemed to take precedence, to my way of thinking."

"Do you not remember our previous talk?"

"I do, sir, but this development altered everything, as far as I was concerned."

"I hope you realise what a difficult position you've placed me in, Norris?"

"I do, and I apologise, sir, but I do believe I was correct to follow the course of action I took."

Madden sat back in his chair, his hands no longer drumming the desk, but instead, placed in a 'V' below his chin as he rested his head on them, contemplating his next words carefully. At length, he leaned back in his chair and sighed heavily. He knew that word of Norris's actions would reach Sir Charles Warren, who would demand to know exactly what was going on in New street Police Station, and yet. . .

"As it happens, Bert, I understand your reasoning, and to some extent, can follow the logic of your suspicion, if not your means of pursuing it. For the next three days, you will stay at home, on sick leave. We'll say you have a sprained ankle or some such injury, and Hillman can continue to work the case, and will liaise with Inspector Hall at Moorgate Street in your absence."

"But, sir. . ."

"No buts, Bert, remember? What was due to be your next line of inquiry?"

"To seek out Miss Cullen's family, sir, and also to speak to the staff at Aldgate Underground station once more, as well as those at Moorgate Street, of course."

"Very well. I'll brief Hillman myself. He can have the use of two uniformed sergeants to assist him and he will report directly to me until your return. Be assured he will be able to bring you up to date when you come back to duty."

"Sir, three days away from the case is too long. I. . . "

"Listen to me, Bert. You already know the sensitivities behind this case as it is. I have to be seen to be doing something to curb your excessive zeal and possible persecution of a man against whom we have no real evidence as yet. Bowker may have known both women, but so did others at his church, surely? Until you can prove a personal connection, we can do no more without antagonizing the church establishment and also the bloody Commissioner of the Metropolitan Police. We can do without either of those men becoming our enemies, if we are to solve this case. Do you understand me?"

"Yes, sir, I think so."

"Good. Then go home, Bert. Take your dog for a walk, enjoy some time with your wife, and stay away from the station and from Hillman until the three days is up. I'll make sure the Chief Superintendent and the Commissioner are aware that I've taken what I consider to be relevant action against you if the pressure comes down from above, as I'm certain it will. You can thank your lucky stars that the force is so stretched with the bloody murders in Whitechapel, and that every man is vital to us at present, or you could have been facing an even longer lay-off. Now, please, just go away and do as I say."

Norris had been on the force long enough to know when enough was enough, and when the time had come to keep silent. He instinctively knew that Madden was doing his best to protect him from potentially greater sanctions and, after all, three days wasn't so long.

"Yes, sir," he replied. Stepping backwards towards the office door, keeping his eyes on Madden, he placed a hand on the door handle and added, quietly, "Thank you. I appreciate what you're doing."

"I'm glad you do, Bert. Now, bloody disappear, man, before I have the Commissioner, the bishop and probably the Home Secretary himself banging on my door, seeking your head on a platter."

Norris was out of the office seconds later, and as he walked along the familiar corridor towards the exit, Hillman came bustling towards him.

"What happened, Bert? Are you. . . "

"Sorry, old chum. I'm not allowed to talk to you or anyone else. I've been sent on sick leave for three days, until things calm down. Seems I've got a sprained ankle."

"What? But you haven't. . . oh, I see," said Hillman, as he realised exactly what must have taken place in the Chief Inspector's office.

"You're in charge until I get back, Dylan. You're to liaise with Thomas Hall as well. Try to keep out of trouble, eh?"

"I won't let you down, Bert."

"I know you won't. Just follow up on what we were already going to do. You don't need me to tell you anything else."

"I'll make sure I cover every inch of ground I can. I'll find the new victim's family, and see if they know of anyone with reason to murder their daughter, and then I'll go back to Aldgate as we'd arranged, and then. . . "

Before Hillman could finish, the door to Madden's office swung open and the Chief Inspector stepped into the corridor. Seeing Norris and Hillman conferring closely, he strode purposefully towards them.

"Inspector Norris! Does nothing I say ever get through to you without me having to say it at least twice?"

"Yes, sir, of course it does. I was just on my way out of the building, right now."

"I'm relieved to hear it," said Madden, a hint of sarcasm evident in his tone of voice. "Now, for the sake of your career, my career and any future Sergeant Hillman might have with the force, please *go*, Inspector!"

"Consider me nothing more than a ghost, sir," Norris replied, as he turned and swept down the corridor and headed for the street.

"As for you, Sergeant," Madden said, as soon as Norris had disappeared. "I'd like a word in my office, if you please. I need to brief you on the situation."

"Yes, sir," Hillman replied, following Madden along the corridor.

He emerged ten minutes later, breathing a sigh of relief at having personally escaped the wrath of the Chief Inspector. Instead, Madden had placed a great deal of faith in the sergeant, knowing that he could be relied upon to advance the investigation as though nothing had changed. Madden was only too aware of the close nature of the working relationship between Norris and Hillman, and though Norris would be absent in person, his spirit and his methods would continue through the efforts of Hillman, of that, Madden was certain.

"But remember, Sergeant," he'd said, as their brief meeting came to a close, "under no circumstances are you, or any of the men under your command, to go anywhere near Martin Bowker. Clear?"

"Very clear, sir. But, what if we unearth evidence that implicates Bowker?"

"In that case, Sergeant, you will bring any such evidence to me, and I will decide how you are to proceed."

"Right, sir. I'll be getting on with it then."

"Very well, Hillman. And Sergeant?"

"Sir?"

"Inspector Norris will be back before you know it. Let's try and give him something to go on when he comes back to us, eh?"

"Yes, sir," said Hillman, suddenly realising that Chief Inspector Joshua Madden wasn't such an ogre as he at first appeared. *My God*, thought the sergeant. *He's actually on Norris's side!*

* * *

Betty Norris was more than a little surprised when her husband walked through the door of their home a short time later. The inspector's wife had the sleeves of her dress rolled up and her bare arms were immersed in the metal wash tub as she scrubbed at Norris's shirt collars, one after the other, with a large bar of carbolic. Norris always tried to look his best when at work, and insisted on attaching a clean collar to his shirt each day, before reporting for duty. Betty would wash and iron his collars daily; any of his white work shirts in need of laundering, she'd wash every other day. It was hard, back-breaking work at times, bending over the low tub, scrubbing and wringing out the garments, and then rinsing and wringing again.

"Bert, what on earth are you doing home at this hour?" she asked, and then, as she caught sight of the sheepish look on her husband's face, Betty knew something was amiss. "What's wrong, Bert? What's happened?"

Ten minutes later, as Norris completed his explanation of recent events, leaving out only the name of the Reverend Bowker, Betty placed a still damp arm around her husband's shoulder in consolation.

"Now, you listen to me, Albert Norris. You've done nothing wrong, and I'm proud of you for following your instincts. You're a good copper, Bert, and Madden knows it, otherwise you'd be on official suspension by now. You'll be back on the case in no time, and in the meantime, Dylan will keep the pot boiling for you, you know he will. He's a good man, and he won't let you down. You can't sit here chafing at the bit, so you must make the best of the time. I've always said we could do with more time together. Listen, why don't I get cleaned up and we can take a stroll in the park together? Seems like ages since we did that, Bert. We can take that reprobate of a dog with us, too, if you like."

"Speaking of Billy, where is he?"

"I had to tie him up in the garden while I was working. I caught him trying to dig up your cabbage plants."

Norris laughed for the first time that day, strode out the back door and found Billy, tied to a clothes pole, dancing up and down with joy at the sight of his master.

"Come on, monster," laughed Norris, as he untied the terrier. Billy instantly jumped into Norris's arms and licked his face repeatedly, until Norris replaced the dog on the ground. Norris tied a shorter length of rope to the dog's collar and led him back into the house, where man and dog waited five minutes for Betty to prepare herself for their unexpected mid-afternoon promenade in the park.

Later, as the couple sat on a park bench, watching a small flotilla of ducks paddling back and forth on the small lake that formed the centrepiece of the landscaped area, while Billy ran up and down a small embankment, playing tag with another small dog of unknown ownership, Norris found his mind reflecting on the past. Betty, knowing him better than anyone, could easily read his thoughts and knew just where his mind had wandered to.

"You're back on the bridge again, aren't you, Bert?"

"Ha, you know me too well, my girl. Yes, I still have nightmares about it. You know that, don't you, Betty?"

"Of course I know, you silly man. I wouldn't be much of a wife if I didn't know when my old man's having a bad dream, now would I?"

* * *

Norris smiled a wry smile and his mind took him back again to the time when, as a Scotland Yard inspector, he'd replied to the shrill blast of a constable's whistle as he walked along Victoria Street. A wealthy member of parliament had been attacked and robbed of his wallet and pocket watch as he'd strolled through St. James's Park one autumn evening, just as dusk was about to turn into night. As Norris approached Westminster Bridge, he saw the constable in hot pursuit of the thief, a rough-looking young man who was, Norris thought, no more than about twenty years of age. Norris joined the constable in the chase and the three men crossed Westminster Bridge, the thief then turning left and heading in the direction of Waterloo Station.

The two police officers closed on the man as he reached the entrance to Waterloo, both men repeatedly shouting "*Stop, thief!*" as the chase continued. The few members of the public who were around at the time scattered as the three men hurtled along, until the thief eventually ducked down a small, tight alleyway that ran parallel to the station buildings. It was a dead end. Norris and Constable Peter Vane had the man trapped, or so it seemed.

As the young thief reached the end of the alley, and his precarious situation became apparent to him, he crouched low, ready, it appeared, to attempt to fight his way past the two police officers.

"*The game's up,*" said Norris. "*I'm a detective inspector with Scotland Yard and I suggest you come along quietly. There's nowhere for you to run.*"

"*Looks like you're right, copper,*" the man replied, straightening up and standing to his full height. "*Maybe I'd better do as you say and go along quiet, like, with you.*"

"*Very wise, my friend,*" Norris had replied. "*I think you can put the cuffs on him now, if you please, Constable.*"

As Constable Vane moved towards the thief, in the gloom of the gathering darkness neither officer saw the man reach into the right hand pocket of his coat. Before either officer realised what was happening, the gun appeared and the thief levelled it at Vane and fired in one swift movement. As the constable hit the ground, mortally wounded, a second shot rang out, this time catching Norris high on the right shoulder. The young inspector sagged to his knees, at which point the thief ran for his life, brushing Norris aside and knocking him to the ground as he raced, leaving the inspector lying beside the dying constable. Before pain caused him to black out, Norris had managed to reach across and grab Vane's whistle, on which he managed to sound three long blasts, and then the blackness of unconsciousness engulfed him. When police officers responded to the whistle, they found Vane dead and Norris unconscious and suffering from severe blood loss, though he would soon recover.

At a subsequent internal inquiry, held after Norris's release from hospital, the young inspector was cleared of direct negligence, but was heavily censured for failing to ensure that the thief was unarmed before sending Vane in to handcuff the man. After a period of six weeks' sick leave, Norris was quietly transferred out of his post at Scotland Yard, and ended up at New Street Police Station, where he'd languished in the rank of inspector from that day onwards. Thanks to the private nature of the inquiry, the censure was never made public; and so, though many knew that a cloud had once been cast over the career of Albert Norris, none, apart from those in authority who maintained a strict confidentiality, could testify to the truth of what had taken place. The thief-turned-murderer of Police Constable Vane was never apprehended, making Norris's personal pain over the affair even deeper, and that pain grew greater year after year, adding further anguish to the nightmares that continued to plague him.

* * *

"It wasn't your fault, Bert. You were young and inexperienced, and it all happened so fast."

"Not so young, and not so inexperienced, Betty," Norris replied, still ready to reproach himself after all this time. I was an inspector with Scotland Yard, twelve years a police officer. I was wrong, damn it. I should have made him come to us with his hands in the air, or made him lie on the ground until we'd got him in the cuffs, but I didn't. I thought it was an easy arrest, and a young man paid with his life."

"But, if you were so wrong, my dear, they would have suspended you, or worse still, forced you to resign, and yet, they did not."

"Because they only had my account of events on which to rely. If there had been witnesses, perhaps I would not have been so lucky in the aftermath."

"You're too hard on yourself, Albert. And it was so long ago. No one can hold it against you, surely? Not after all this time. Has not Joshua Madden done his best for you in this instance, for example?"

"I suppose you're right, on both counts, Betty. Perhaps 'tis my own conscience with which I must constantly battle, in order to attempt to find an absolution for the death of that young constable."

"Then, once and for all, you must absolve yourself, husband. Only then can you go on and find the peace of mind that goes with doing your best to protect the people of this great city, each and every day, as you do so well."

Betty Norris took hold of her husband's hand and squeezed it tightly, a sign of the deep affection between the pair.

"I loved you and believed in you then, Albert Norris, and I do so to this very day. You are a good man, and always were, and will be in days to come."

"You are a true rock, Betty, on which I cast my life so many years ago, and you have proved to be the foundation for all that is good in my life. I love you too, and must shake myself from this lethargy of the past, as you say, and look to the future, our future. Let us go now, and make the most of this time we've been granted to spend together. Now, where is that dog? Billy, come here, boy!"

The little black terrier appeared as if by magic at Norris's side, panting, his tongue lolling out. He had been playing energetically with his new canine friend, who trotted up behind him and appeared to wait expectantly for some sign of recognition from Norris, or from Betty.

"She looks like a stray," said Norris, noticing the dog bore no collar, no means of identifying her or her owner. "Maybe we should take her home with us and place an advertisement in the newspaper, in case her owner is searching for her."

"And if no owner appears, Bert?"

"Well, I'm sure we can find room for another waif and stray, eh, Billy? After all, they do seem to be getting on well together."

"Bert Norris, you're incorrigible," said Betty, patting the little bitch on the head and stroking her back. The black and white terrier wagged her tail, and, as the couple walked home, with Billy by Norris's side as usual, the new addition walked happily beside Betty, and within minutes of arriving at their home, the two dogs were playing together in the back garden. Betty could see the new dog had brought a little joy into Norris's day and she hoped any advertisement they placed would go unanswered. She'd also taken an instant liking to the new 'lady' in Billy the terrier's life. Maybe, she thought, the next couple of days would bring about a new beginning for her husband, and for the new little dog, in more ways than one.

Chapter 19
Stagnation

In the absence of his inspector, Dylan Hillman was determined not to let the investigation into the double murder lapse into stagnation. Madden had assigned Detective Sergeant Dove and Sergeant Lee to the investigative team and Constable Fry had been added as an additional pair of hands and eyes to assist Hillman. Over at Moorgate Street, Inspector Hall and Sergeant Willis would continue their own inquiries and would report any findings to Madden, who could then dovetail the two sides of the investigation together.

While Dove and Lee took on the task of re-interviewing the employees at Aldgate Underground station, Hillman took it upon himself to visit the parents of the unfortunate Ann Cullen, her address having been provided from church records by the Reverend Bowker. Hillman intended to speak to them first, hating, as always, the onerous duty of informing next of kin of the violent death of a loved one, and would then visit and speak to her employers.

Ann Cullen's mother opened the front door of her neat terraced home to find Dylan Hillman and the uniformed Constable Fry standing, grim-faced, on her doorstep. The fact that her daughter had failed to return home the previous night had perhaps steeled her for bad news, but even so, the tears that flowed after she'd escorted the men into her small, tidy living room, and Hillman had broken the bad news, could scarcely be abated after five minutes of sobbing.

"Your husband, Mrs. Cullen. Where is he? He should be with you." Hillman didn't want to leave the woman alone in such a distressed state. He would send Fry to fetch Mr. Cullen from wherever he might be.

"At work, Sergeant," she sobbed. "He's a carpenter at Ledger's, the furniture makers on Barrow Road. This news will destroy him, I know it. My poor Ann."

It's done a pretty good job of destroying you, too, you poor woman, thought Hillman, quickly despatching Fry to Ledger's with orders to break the news as gently as possible to the father, and then to secure permission from his employer to allow the man to return home to comfort his wife. Fry returned with the distraught man less than twenty minutes later, the factory being only two streets away from the Cullen's home.

Through their grief, it quickly became apparent to Hillman that Sheldon and Maria Cullen could tell them little that might help find Ann's killer. Ann Cullen had been a good daughter, so they said, with no great friends outside the home, and she was a diligent worker, well respected by her employer. She was always telling her parents of the praise she'd received from her immediate superior, Mr. Hargreaves, and they could think of no one who might wish to do their daughter any harm whatsoever.

Not wishing to intrude upon their grief for too long, Hillman and Fry left the house of sadness and made their way to Whitechapel High Street, where they soon found the offices of Andrews and Wright, Solicitors at Law. Hillman couldn't help noticing the newspaper billboards as they walked along, all announcing in bold black type the latest atrocities committed by the Whitechapel Murderer. No such publicity accompanied the case Hillman was investigating. The latest murder had been pushed to page ten of The Star the previous afternoon and written up as a potential suicide, a woman's body having been discovered beside the tracks of the underground railway at Moorgate Street, perhaps as a result of throwing herself from a train. That was it; nothing more nor less.

On arriving at the solicitors' office and announcing themselves to a middle-aged, maidenly secretary seated at a desk in the entrance hall, they were shown by a uniformed commissionaire to the office of the chief clerk, Harrison Hargreaves.

As Hargreaves rose from behind his desk to greet his visitors, Hillman decided that here stood a man he found easy to dislike on sight. Hargreaves was short, rotund and bald, with narrow, slanted eyes that gave him an almost oriental look. His thick, podgy fingers reached out to shake the hand of the policeman and when Hargreaves spoke for the first time, his high, squeaky voice added to the feelings of aversion Hillman had already formed.

"Gentlemen. Miss Threadneedle informs me you wish to speak to me on a delicate matter?"

Hillman could have laughed out loud. If ever a name suited someone, then 'Threadneedle' was the ideal appellation for the woman who'd greeted them a couple of minutes earlier. Somehow, he could picture the receptionist sitting at home, needle and thread in her hand as she worked on some delicate lace tracery or some such fine embroidery. Instead, managing to maintain a professional air, he replied, "Yes, Mr. Hargreaves. I'm afraid we have some sad news to convey to you."

On being informed of Ann Cullen's death, Hargreaves' face collapsed into a mask of tears, surprising Hillman, who hadn't expected quite such an emotional reaction.

"Oh, do tell me this isn't so," he wept.

"Were you close to Miss Cullen?" asked the sergeant.

"In as much as we worshipped at the same church, Sergeant, yes. We enjoyed many discussions about the work of The Lord. I even suggested she attend study classes with the vicar of St. Giles's church. She was very keen to broaden her knowledge of the word of God. I have myself attended the church for many years, and hoped that Ann would grow to see it as her spiritual home, as I do."

"You must know the vicar well, then, Mr. Hargreaves?"

"Oh yes, a fine man. Martin Bowker is his name. I'm sure he, too, will be devastated to hear such tragic news."

Hillman said nothing to indicate he knew Bowker, or that the vicar already knew of the murder.

"Did Miss Cullen have any close friends here at the office, Mr. Hargreaves?"

"Oh, no. She was a very private person. I believe she enjoyed visiting museums and art galleries in her spare time, but as far as I'm aware, she undertook such pursuits alone."

"If your relationship with her was a purely spiritual one, perhaps you might not have been aware of any such friendships. Would Miss Threadneedle perhaps know if she had any close friends, male friends, in particular?"

Hargreaves laughed, a high-pitched chortle that appeared at odds with his display of grief, but which suited the man's distasteful personality as far as Hillman was concerned.

"Really, Sergeant! Arabella Threadneedle has worked here for so many years, you'd think she would be aware of every matter pertaining to the staff's private lives, and yet, the woman hardly speaks to anyone, staff or partners, unless it concerns a legal matter or some other business connected with the firm. Ask her if you like, but I know what answer you will receive."

And so it proved. Hillman and Fry jointly spoke to Arabella Threadneedle and the two partners of the firm, neither of whom confessed to having had more than a few desultory conversations with the girl, and the other clerks all confirmed Hargreaves' description of Ann Cullen as being a loner, of good character and a God-fearing churchgoer with little time for the frivolous side of life.

"That didn't get us very far, did it, Sergeant?" asked Fry, as the two men walked slowly back towards the police station.

"No, Fry, it didn't. Ann Cullen sounds almost like a carbon copy of Clara Forshaw, a simple, studious and religious woman with little or no outside influences to interfere in her life, unless you count looking at museum exhibits as an outside influence."

"Could she have met someone at a museum, perhaps, and continued to meet him secretly?"

"She could have, but how would that connect with Clara Forshaw? Doctor Roebuck is certain the two women were killed by the same man."

"I understand, from the briefing we received, that news of the murder is to be kept as quiet as possible, Sergeant. What if the people at Andrews and Wright talk to outsiders?"

"Don't worry, Fry. Special Branch will probably have already sent someone over there, and to Moorgate Street Underground Station. Don't ask me how or why, but so far the powers-that-be are doing a very good job of keeping the lid on these murders. God alone knows what threats they're levelling at people, but of course, the Special Powers Act gives them the leverage they need to ensure everyone's silence, and if they can gag the press, then private individuals must seem like easy prey to them."

Fry said no more and, on arrival at New Street, Hillman was surprised to find Inspector Thomas Hall waiting for him in Norris's office. Hillman despatched Fry to write up a report on their visit to the solicitors' office and closed the door to allow himself and Hall some privacy.

"Hello, Sergeant."

"Inspector Hall."

"I thought I'd come over and let you know how we're progressing at Moorgate Street. Shame about Norris, by the way."

"Eh?"

"His ankle. Sprained it, I understand."

"Oh, yes, sir. He'll be back soon."

"So I heard," said Hall, and Hillman couldn't be sure whether the inspector knew the truth of the matter or not, but decided to play along with the charade of Norris's 'sick leave', just to be on the safe side.

"Anyway," Hall went on, "the Underground Railways employees at Moorgate Street seem to know nothing at all. No one saw or heard anything unusual at the time of the train's arrival last night. No suspicious characters were seen to alight from the carriages – but then, the staff don't usually take much notice of the people who enter and leave the trains when they stop at the platform. They don't expect to have to be on their guard in case a murderer with blood on his hands walks along the platform and disappears up to street level."

"I don't suppose they do, sir. Which leaves us right at the beginning again, doesn't it?"

"In a way, yes. How did your interviews with the parents and employers go?"

"A bit like your inquiry, sir. She was a good girl, a churchgoer and a home bird with few outside interests and no particular male friends, as far as we can discover."

"So, unless your men at Aldgate can coax some forgotten intelligence from the railway staff there, we can probably write off today as a waste of police time and resources."

"I'm afraid so, sir, and it certainly doesn't bring us any closer to finding out the motive for the killings, never mind who the killer is, does it?"

"You're right, Sergeant, and this time, the girl wasn't pregnant, so Inspector Norris's theory of a lover in the background can't be applied to the second killing, can it?"

At that point, Hillman became sure that Hall had been fully briefed by Madden and knew exactly why Norris was absent from the investigation. He said nothing on that subject, however, and instead simply spoke for Norris in terms of the investigation.

"Inspector Norris had good reason to believe in his theory, sir."

"I'm sure he did, Sergeant. For now, though, we need to look at other avenues, or we could find our investigation rapidly stagnating."

Despite Hall's positive idea of looking for 'other avenues,' the stagnation he feared began to leak slowly into every aspect of the case. Sergeants Dove and Lee returned from Aldgate with no new information. As at Moorgate Street, the staff employed by the Metropolitan Railway could provide no further information in relation to the death of Clara Forshaw. An air of depression fell over the officers involved in the case, and a cloud of defeatism began to gather in the minds of each man, as the murderer of Clara Forshaw and Ann Cullen appeared to be a wraith who somehow appeared and disappeared at will, in the dark of the night, on the carriages of the underground railway. As Hillman said, "A bloody motive might go some way to giving us a clue as to what sort of blighter we're after."

His words could just as easily be applied to the case of the Whitechapel Murderer, now known to the world as *Jack the Ripper*, thanks to the infamous *Dear Boss* letter, printed in the Daily News on the morning of October 1st, just as Norris and Hillman had begun their inquiry into the death of Ann Cullen. The other newspapers of the capital soon jumped on the sensationalist bandwagon, and within hours, the cries of '*Jack the Ripper stalks the streets of Whitechapel,*' '*Jack the Ripper taunts police*' and others of similar ilk were being shouted by newspaper sellers on every street corner of the capital.

Despite the letter and the new name appended to the Whitechapel Murderer, the Ripper investigation was also stagnating and proving a thorn in the side of the investigating officers, and of course, they were many and varied when compared with Norris and Hillman's case. As public condemnation of the police grew in the Ripper case, and confidence in their ability sagged to an all-time low, so the men at New Street found their own confidence waning in the light of a veritable brick wall of no information or clues in respect of their own case.

If the public had been given full access to the facts of the Underground Railway murders, they would have truly had cause to vent even more fury at the unfortunate members of the constabulary. Two cases of multiple murder, with not one suspect and not one clue? No wonder Hillman now felt something close to relief at the actions of those in power, who had taken steps to keep the underground railway murders as closely guarded from the public as possible.

He'd let *Jack the Ripper* hog the headlines any time, leave Abberline and his men to take the public's fury on the chin, for that would allow him and the men under his command, and Norris on his return, to get on with their own case, out of the glare of public scrutiny. But of course, as Hillman knew all too well, Norris would not be pleased if he returned to find very little progress had been made.

The day of Clara Forshaw's funeral arrived, coinciding with Norris's final day of sick leave. The service, conducted by Martin Bowker, with a tearful eulogy delivered by her father, was attended by all the members of the Bellhaven household, and a large majority of the regular congregation of St. Giles's church. No mention was made of the manner of Clara's death, Bowker merely referring to 'a young life cut short by these tragic events'.

Hillman attended also, sitting at the rear of the church, and standing well away from the main body of mourners at the subsequent interment. Norris had stayed away, keeping to his instructions from Madden. Hillman hoped he might learn something by observing the mourners, though exactly what, he couldn't define, even in his own mind. He simply felt he had to be there. He discerned nothing from his attendance, except the feeling of sadness and depression that accompanies such events.

So, as Norris's enforced sabbatical drew to a close, Dylan Hillman redoubled his efforts to move the case forward. His thoughts turned to the one place connected closely with the case that he hadn't gone over a second time. In the afternoon of the last day before Norris's expected return, with thoughts of the funeral lying heavy on his mind, Hillman, accompanied by Detective Sergeant Dove, set off for the home of Laurence Bellhaven. Maybe, just maybe, there was more to find there.

Chapter 20
Norris Returns

Albert Norris walked back into New Street Police Station with a spring in his stride. He felt surprisingly refreshed following his three days away from the job. It had been a long time since he and Betty had spent such a long, uninterrupted period of days together and in truth, it had benefited him greatly. In addition to a couple of enjoyable walks in the park, they'd attended a performance at the local music hall, where Norris had found himself entranced and entertained by the singers, the comedians and the acrobats who'd trodden the boards for their entertainment. After the performance, they'd strolled home, arm in arm, like a pair of star-kissed lovers, and Norris had paused under a streetlamp, looked deep into his wife's eyes, and kissed Betty in a way she hadn't felt for far too many years. The couple had taken the new dog to their hearts, too, naming her Lillie, after the great actress of the day, Lillie Langtry. She'd made a great companion for their own terrier, Billy, and had even succeeded in calming his over-exuberance down a little.

All in all, Norris considered that Chief Inspector Joshua Madden had done him a great kindness in forcing him to spend the three days away from the case. But now he was back, and ready to take up the mantle of public watchdog and protector once again. First of all, he reported to Madden's office, for an update on the case.

"Good to have you back, Bert," said Madden, much to Norris's surprise. "I have to admit that there has been little progress in your absence. So far, every avenue Hillman has explored has proved fruitless, though not through any fault of the sergeant's, I'd say. Inspector Hall has also found nothing that helps us advance the case. Hillman did visit the Bellhaven home again yesterday, I believe, but I've heard nothing from him on the results of that inquiry yet, though I suspect he'd have been battering my door down if he'd discovered anything relevant. So, how was your brief time away from us?"

"Surprisingly restful, sir. I have to thank you, really, for forcing me to spend some time away from the job. It's allowed me to see things in a different light, both in relation to the past and the present. My wife was also pleased to have some time alone with me for once, without the job interfering in our lives."

"Then it sounds as if the break was just the ticket, Bert. I presume you're ready to get right back into the thick of things?"

"Of course."

"Good. Then I think you'll find Sergeant Hillman in your office, anxiously awaiting your return."

Hillman was indeed delighted to welcome his inspector back to duty, though a little disappointed to have little progress to report.

"Never mind, old chum," said Norris, cheerfully. "Let's have a look at these reports you and Fry have prepared while I've been away."

Norris spent the next few minutes reading through the reports, muttering to himself under his breath from time to time, his eyebrows raising and lowering as he read points of particular interest. At last, satisfied, he turned to Hillman.

"This Harrison Hargreaves character, Dylan. Did you ask him if he knew Clara Forshaw?"

"I thought you'd ask me that. I may have been wrong, but, no, I didn't. I thought, what with the delicacies of the case and all, I ought not to alert him to a connection between them, especially as he may not be aware of the first murder. I didn't want Madden or anyone else accusing me of giving information away to a member of the public without good cause."

"I can understand that, Dylan, but you do see, don't you, that Hargreaves, through his church connection, must have known Clara, at least in passing?"

"It's a fairly large church, Bert, with a large congregation. We can't know that for sure."

"Maybe not, but I intend to find out. Don't you see that, apart from Bowker, Hargreaves is the only man we've found so far who has a connection to both girls, however tenuous the link to Clara might seem?"

"I have to admit I found him a particularly odious little man. He's what I'd call an oily character, not my cup of tea at all."

"All the more reason to go and have another word with him then, Dylan, old chum, and this time, I'll do the talking, eh?"

"Whatever you say, you're the boss."

"Good," said Norris, picking up another of the reports. "Now, I see that you and Dove carried out my proposed visit to the Bellhaven household."

Hillman nodded.

"According to this, no one had anything important to add, but, as I read this, Dylan, there is one important fact here that we were in ignorance of previously."

"There is?"

"Yes. Look what Dove says here. According to the butler, the Bellhavens had recently taken to attending church on a regular basis, rather than merely on sporadic occasions, as previously. Not only that, but he says they worshipped at the same church as Clara Forshaw, as she'd convinced them of the wonderful spirituality to be found in the sermons delivered by the Reverend Bowker. So, Dylan, we have another connection to St. Giles's."

"How did I miss that?" asked Hillman, feeling a little angry with himself.

"When did Dove write this up?"

"Just before we left last night."

"And did you read it, or did he tell you what the butler had told him?"

"No, but..."

"No buts, Dylan. You weren't to know, and Dove wouldn't have seen the significance in the butler's words, as he was only there to take statements and isn't privy to the full facts of the case as you and I know them."

"But all this is leading us back to Bowker, Bert, and you know what Madden said about that! It's what got you booted off on sick leave in the first place."

"Which is precisely why you and I are going to see Chief Inspector Madden right now, old chum. I want him to be aware of the connections we've established and give us the go-ahead to investigate further. This isn't a direct accusation against Bowker, after all, but every road seems to be leading us to St. Giles's right now, Dylan, and even Madden can't ignore that fact."

As Norris and Hillman walked towards Madden's office, the door opened and a man dressed in a brown suit walked out of the office and passed them in the corridor without giving them a second glance.

"Special Branch," said Norris. "I can smell 'em a mile off."

"Wonder what he was doing in there, Bert?"

"Maybe we'll find out soon enough," said Norris. He rapped on the door and, on hearing a gruff, "Come" from within, he and Hillman entered the Chief Inspector's inner sanctum once again.

Madden appeared worried as he glanced up at the two detectives. Hillman closed the door quietly behind him.

"Bert, Sergeant Hillman, sit down, will you? I've just had a visit from Special Branch, and have something here that was delivered to Sir Charles Warren this morning and which may cast a whole new light on our case."

Norris gave Hillman a look that said, *I told you so*, before replying to Madden.

"Yes, sir. I guessed that was Special Branch just leaving as we arrived. As matter of fact, we have something to tell you, too."

"It can wait a minute or two, Inspector. Here, read this."

Madden passed a sheet of paper across his desk, which Norris picked up, read, and then passed to Dylan Hillman.

"Oh, bugger it, Dylan," said Norris. "This is a real turn-up for the books."

"Isn't it just?" said Madden.

"Only trouble is, it doesn't really fit with what we've just added together and come to talk to you about, sir."

"Well, Bert, whatever you've got, you'd better fill me in, and then we'd better get to work on trying to find out just who the hell's responsible for *that*," said Madden, pointing at the paper in Dylan's hand.

Chapter 21
The Letter

Norris relieved Hillman of the sheet of paper, written in neat copperplate, and read aloud:

"*Believe in me, for I am the word. As the beasts that engineer Satan's cause and tunnel their way beneath, and those who serve the beast destroy the homes and the lives of those of the poor who exist above, so they who are carried in the belly of the beast, those whores of Satan's womb, shall line the tunnels of the underworld with their souls.* **WORTHY IS THE LAMB THAT WAS SLAIN TO RECEIVE POWER, AND RICHES, AND WISDOM, AND STRENGTH, AND HONOUR, AND GLORY, AND BLESSING.** *So sayeth The Lord. They shall die to receive purity in the eyes of The Father. I shall not stop, yea, not so long as Satan's followers destroy the land and send men to dwell in the underworld. Cease, and I shall cease, persist and I shall persist. An end to this, I say. To the worshippers of Satan, the Metropolitan Railway, go, now, before it is too late. I shall spill the blood of the innocents for now until forever, lest ye desist. In the name of the Father, and of the Son, and of The Holy Spirit, Amen.*

"Bloody hell, sir, this kind of blows our news out of the water slightly, I'd say," said Norris.

"The thing is, Bert, do we believe it? Is it from our killer, or just a crank jumping on the bandwagon after seeing the Jack the Ripper letter in the press?"

"But sir, we've allowed little or no news of these killings to be reported. How does the writer know about them unless this is indeed his hand?"

Madden nodded, solemnly. Norris had a point.

"This has to be a religious freak, sir, surely?" said Hillman.

"I know where your mind is leading, Sergeant," Madden replied, "but it may also be someone merely trying to lead us to believe in a religious connection."

"But it is tempting to look in the obvious place when we start to receive messages of a Biblical nature, is it not, sir?" asked Norris of the Chief Inspector.

"Bert, if Martin Bowker really is the killer, do you think he'd be so stupid as to send something like this, which smacks of religious fervour from start to finish?"

"If he's as fanatical as I believe him to be, then yes, I think it's exactly what he'd do, sir. It could even be a way of appearing to make it so obvious it must be him, that we are forced to believe otherwise."

"A complex way of looking at it, Bert," said Madden.

"I don't see any other way of looking at it. So far, we have virtually nothing to go on. You've decried my theory regarding Bowker, though I don't consider him out of the frame yet, and now we have this note to contend with. I know we've kept a lid on things to a point, sir, but is it possible that someone has got wind of the investigation and has decided to play a very sick joke on us by sending it? This also sounds as if someone is trying to stop the expansion of the underground railway, and surely, no one in their right mind would dream that anyone would give in to such actions. Also, any such perpetrator would make sure, press or no press, that his actions were made loudly public."

"I'm not saying Bowker's out of bounds totally, Bert, but you must be a little more circumspect in your dealings with him. I've managed to placate the Commissioner and the bishop by sending you off home for three days, but now, you need to tread carefully. No more harassment of Bowker unless we have something definite to pin on him, agreed?"

"Agreed, sir. Now, as for this letter. . . "

"Yes, you're right again. It does appear odd that someone would go to the lengths of killing passengers in order to try and forestall future development, without making damned sure his actions were known, in order to stir up public opinion against the railway. Of course, this is precisely what the commissioner and the railway board feared may happen, in the beginning."

"But there must be better ways to stir up public unrest, sir, other than random killings on the railway. No one can believe that the railway is so unsafe, just because a madman appears to be on the loose in the tunnels. How can he hope to stop progress in such a way?"

"And why is that line in the middle in capital letters, sir?" asked Hillman.

"I think you'll find that the words of that line are a direct Biblical quote, Sergeant," Madden replied. "If I'm not mistaken, those words are to be found in the Book of Revelation."

"We could always ask Reverend Bowker," added Norris.

"Inspector Norris!" said Madden sternly.

"Just my idea of a small joke, sir. I suppose we should look it up and confirm your theory."

"Good idea, here's a Bible."

Madden passed a heavy, leather-bound Bible across the desk and Norris in turn passed it to Hillman, who began leafing through the pages of The Book of Revelation in the hunt for the words on the paper. As he searched, Norris asked Madden a question.

"Was this delivered in an envelope, sir, through the usual postal service, or was it delivered by hand to Scotland Yard?"

"It was posted at King's Cross yesterday morning. The envelope was in the same handwriting, and is still at Scotland Yard."

"And King's Cross, of course, stand neatly on the Metropolitan Railway, does it not, sir?"

"Meaning?"

"Whoever sent it could have travelled there on the railway, and then scurried back to wherever it is he really came from. We've no guarantee that he lives anywhere near the place where he posted it."

"You're right, of course. We're no nearer finding our man, just because we know where he sent this crazy epistle from."

"Got it," said Hillman, suddenly. "The Book of Revelation, Chapter 4, verse 12. Reading around it, none of the text seems to have any relevance to our case. I'd say he picked the words at random, because they fitted in with his scheme."

"Which indicates some knowledge of the Bible, I'd say," said Norris. "He probably knew where to look for the exact words he wanted."

"I can see you're still leaning heavily in the direction of the vicar, Bert," said Madden.

"I can't help it, sir. So far, despite there being no evidence to really link anyone directly with the murders, everything we've learned is pointing us in the direction of St. Giles's church, and Reverend Bowker in particular."

"Look, you know what I think, and you know how heavily I'm being leaned on from above. Go about the investigation as you would any other, Bert, but please, for your own sake, do it quietly, understood?"

"I understand, sir. We'll give this letter every attention, but it may simply be a blind to lead us off in the wrong direction, as we all know."

"Of course, I agree," said Madden. "Now, do tell me what it was you were going to tell me when you first came in. You looked as though you might have something important on your mind."

Norris soon gave Madden the information concerning the Bellhaven family worshipping at St. Giles's and, after expressing a low groan at yet another connection to Martin Bowker's church, he turned to the two men and spoke solemnly.

"You men had better go about your business. Take this investigation as far as it will go, Bert, but, if you find any proof that Martin Bowker is in any way even remotely connected to the murders, you bring it to me first. If a man like Bowker is found to be involved in the killings, then our Evangelical Commissioner of Police is going to have a bloody heart attack, I'll swear to it. We must be certain, leave no stone unturned, but don't let Bowker know you're targeting him. By all means speak to other church members. He can't deny us that right, as we have so many connections to St. Giles's rearing up before our eyes, but do not, under any circumstances, allow him to think you're investigating him directly, got it?"

"Clear as crystal, sir," said Norris, as he slowly moved towards the door, beckoning Hillman to follow him. "We'll be getting along then, sir. As you say, we've a great deal of work to do."

Madden half rose from his chair – almost a mark of respect, thought Norris – and, as he and Hillman were walking out of the door, the chief inspector said, "Oh, Inspector Norris?"

"Sir?"

"I think I may have said as much already, but anyway, welcome back."

Chapter 22
Back To The Beginning

Unfortunately for Albert Norris and his team, the following days produced nothing but a frustrating menagerie of false hopes and bitter disappointment. First, Norris had the idea that a comparison of the newly received letter with those already on file, and shown to him weeks earlier by Madden, might bring some reward. If they could find a similarity in the handwriting to any of the earlier threatening letters, it might indicate a definite threat against the Metropolitan Railway. No such similarity could be found, however, despite painstaking examination of the earlier correspondence.

Next, the idea of interviewing the congregation of St. Giles's Church also presented its own set of difficulties. Services in the Anglican Church were, of course, open to all, and though many of the congregation of Bowker's church were regular attendees, just as many were infrequent or casual worshippers. The thought of standing outside the church on a Sunday morning, trying to interview so many people, without raising a hue and cry from the vicar and probably most of the churchgoers, didn't bear thinking about, bearing in mind the politics of the case.

That left the Bible Study Class, and Norris knew that would also be a thorny issue, as all the members of the class were female and the only way he would be able to gain access to the inner sanctum of the class would be with the permission of the vicar himself. Norris thought it highly unlikely that Martin Bowker would be happy to cooperate, and yet, to deny the police access to the ladies of the Bible Study could also be seen as obstructing a police inquiry, and so, the inspector decided to approach the vicar in as amicable a manner as he could.

Hillman suggested, and Norris agreed, that perhaps he should approach Bowker so that so any chance of personal hostility towards Norris from Bowker would be eliminated. Hillman was pleased to report later that Bowker had agreed to the detectives visiting the church hall on the night of the next meeting, five days hence. Though frustrated at the delay, Norris realised it would be the only way of seeing the whole class in one go, and reluctantly agreed with Hillman that the wait would probably be worth it.

Norris continued to baulk at the restrictions placed on his investigation. He firmly believed that press exposure would have raised the possibility of witnesses, so far non-existent, coming forward in at least one of the two cases. He was a firm believer in the '*someone must have seen something*' theory, and yet, for reasons that he still believed stupid and unreasonable, he was prevented from utilising the power of the press.

Even the families of Clara Forshaw and Ann Cullen, despite being warned of the need for circumspection by the men from Special Branch, were beginning to visit the police station every day in hopes of news regarding the deaths of their daughters. Norris felt a powder keg brewing under the case. He thought it only a matter of time, and maybe not too long at that, before the lid blew and the families, or someone else connected to the case, blew the whole thing wide open to the public gaze.

In a move that smacked more of desperation than hope, Chief Inspector Madden had even invited officers from the Ripper investigation to visit New Street, and Detective Inspector Frederick Abberline and Detective Sergeant George Godley duly arrived, armed with the so-called Ripper letter, plus another communication, a postcard, reputedly from Jack the Ripper. Madden thought the letters may all have originated from the same source, a complex and cruel hoaxer being responsible, and that they could thus all be consigned to the 'hoax' files, but again, no similarities could be ascertained.

As Norris and Hillman sat in the inspector's small office, sipping tea from tin mugs and ruminating on the case, almost in despair at the lack of tangible progress they'd so far achieved, Norris came up with his latest idea.

"Listen, Dylan, old chum, I don't care what anyone says, including Madden. This case began with Clara Forshaw and, unless I'm mistaken, I think if we dig deep enough, we'll find that the root to the solution of this bloody case lies somewhere in her life. She was the first victim, after all, and there has to be a reason for that."

"Unless the victims really are being chosen at random," Hillman cautioned.

"And do you actually believe that, given the connections to the church we've discovered? And don't forget, the butler let slip that the Bellhavens attend St. Giles's, too. Laurence Bellhaven didn't volunteer that information, and neither did his wife."

"You don't really think the Bellhavens have anything to do with it, do you, Bert?"

"I'm not saying that at all, Dylan. What I am saying is that Clara worked for Laurence Bellhaven; she went to the same church as they did, and she lived under the same roof as her employer. The servants were all very right and proper in our interviews with them and Mr. and Mrs. Bellhaven were very helpful, but, let's face it, no one has done anything more than scratch the surface of Clara's life. Everyone professes shock when we tell them she was pregnant, but no one appears to know anything about her mysterious lover. For God's sake, man, she wasn't exactly a wealthy society lady, with good reasons to keep a liaison such a closely guarded secret, unless, as we previously surmised, her lover is a married man. And, she was very much a private person, with few outside interests, just like Ann Cullen, victim number two.

"I have a gut feeling here, old chum, and it's telling me to go back to the Bellhaven house and to try and jangle a few bells, pull a few strings, rattle some cages, and let's see who jumps. Maybe someone there is protecting this mystery lover to help save his marriage. It may not be someone in the household, but someone in that house has to know something, Dylan. It's almost inconceivable that no one in the house knew anything about her private life. It's time that house on Lewisham Place gave up its secrets."

"If it holds any, Bert."

"Yes, right, of course, if it holds any, old chum."

* * *

Norris and Hillman were ushered into the drawing room at Lewisham Place by the butler, Roland Soames, who, in the true tradition of his calling, expressed neither surprise nor any other emotion on opening the door to find the two policemen once again wishing to speak with his employer. Soames had merely left them in the marble-tiled hallway for a minute whilst announcing their arrival to Laurence Bellhaven and now, his duty fulfilled, the man retreated from the room, leaving them with the master of the house.

"Detective Inspector, Sergeant, good day to you. How may I be of assistance? Or do you have news for us regarding poor Clara's death?"

"We have no new developments to report, I'm afraid, Mr. Bellhaven," Norris replied. "However, I must trouble you with a few more questions, if I may?"

"Of course, Inspector, ask away. I'm happy to do all I can if it will help bring Clara's killer to justice."

"I'm sure you're also aware of the second murder, sir? It can't have failed to have been reported to you as a member of the railway's board of directors."

"But of course, and it surely goes some way towards building on the theory that we are dealing with a maniac who intends to ruin the Metropolitan Railway, by making it appear we cannot ensure the safety of those who travel with us."

"Maybe, and then again, maybe not, sir. We still can't eliminate other motives from our inquiry. For example, both women attended the same church, as, I now understand, you and your wife did as well."

"Why yes, Inspector, we did, though I hardly think it pertinent to the inquiry into Clara's death. How can the fact that she suggested my wife and I might enjoy the services conducted by Mr. Bowker have any bearing on the case?"

"I'm not saying it does, at least not directly, but it does seem odd, don't you think, that everything to do with Clara's death, and that of Miss Cullen, the second victim, leads us back to St. Giles's Church?"

"I see. Are you then suggesting that the Reverend Bowker has something to do with the deaths?"

"I'm suggesting nothing, sir, apart from the fact that the deaths seem inextricably linked to something, or someone, at the church."

Bellhaven paused for a few seconds, his mind obviously taking in the information Norris had just imparted. He then took up the conversation once more.

"Ah, I believe I see. You are thinking, are you not, that the man who made Clara pregnant is, in all probability, a member of the congregation of St. Giles's? She spent a lot of time there, and it was of course, quite possible for her to meet someone and carry on a clandestine relationship under the guise of attending church, or church functions."

"Quite correct, sir. You follow my line of reasoning very well. For that reason, I wish to probe a little deeper into Clara's private life, beginning, I'm afraid with a rather more intense round of questioning of your household – with your permission, of course."

"We are at your disposal, Inspector," said Bellhaven, his hands reaching out expansively as though to encompass the room. "I shall summon Soames and instruct him to have the staff ready to speak with you whenever you wish. Luckily, they are all here today, so you have called at an opportune time."

"I appreciate your cooperation, sir," said Norris, as Laurence Bellhaven walked to the wall and depressed the bell-push in order to summon Soames. The butler appeared in a matter of seconds, and Hillman couldn't help wondering if the man had been listening outside the door, so fast was his response to the summons.

Bellhaven quickly gave instructions that the staff were to make themselves available once again for police interviews and Soames departed, assuring his employer that he'd have everyone ready to take their turn as soon as the officers were ready for them. Bellhaven ordered the butler to show Norris and Hillman to the now familiar kitchen, which once again would serve as the interview room.

Soames led the way, and appeared surprised when Norris informed him that he'd like to speak with him before interviewing any of the under-staff.

"Oh, very well, sir, if you wish. I'll inform the staff first and then join you in the kitchen, if that will be acceptable."

"That'll do nicely, Mr. Soames," said Norris and he and Hillman were left in the kitchen as Soames went off to give their orders to the staff.

"Do you think he knows more than he's told us so far?" Hillman asked, as soon as the kitchen door closed, leaving the detectives in private for a few minutes.

"He's the butler, Dylan. If anyone in this house knows anything about anything, it's Soames, you mark my words. I don't know if he's keeping anything from us, but I aim to find out in the next few minutes. I'm bloody fed up with pussyfooting around with this case. It's time to get a bit nasty, if we have to."

"I've not seen your nasty side for a while." Hillman smiled.

"Well, sit back and watch, old chum. You might see it again very soon, depending on how Soames reacts to my questions."

A knock on the door broke into their conversation. "Enter," Norris called, and Soames walked into the room and, at Hillman's request, seated himself opposite the detectives at the large, solid oak kitchen table.

"At your service, sir," the butler said as he waited for Norris to begin.

Hillman held his breath. Maybe things were about to become interesting.

Chapter 23
What the Butler Saw
(And Heard)

"Mr. Soames," Norris began, "I know you are a loyal and faithful employee of Mr. Bellhaven, but, as I'm sure you understand, in the case of a murder investigation, such loyalties must be relegated to a lower priority in the name of justice."

Norris had begun as he meant to go on; giving Soames the impression he was aware that there were hidden secrets within the house, even though he had no proof of any such thing. It was a tactic he'd used often, aimed at knocking the interviewee off their guard. He hoped it would have the desired effect on the butler.

"I'm not sure what you mean, Inspector," Soames replied, obviously not ready to be caught out by Norris's ploy; at least, not yet.

"What I mean is that, as the butler in this household, there must be very little that happens within these four walls that escapes your attention, and your knowledge. If you have any information, no matter how trivial it may seem to you, that may have pertinence to my inquiry, then it is your duty to reveal it to me and the sergeant, here and now."

Soames' brow knotted into a furrow, the man appearing perplexed and unable to grasp Norris's meaning.

"I'm aware of the fact that you are investigating the death of poor Clara, Inspector, but what that has to do with Mr. Bellhaven and this household, I fail to see."

"Let me give you an example, Soames," said Norris, dropping the *Mister* deliberately as he switched to a firmer tone. "During the most recent visit by Sergeants Dove and Lee, you volunteered the information that Mr. and Mrs. Bellhaven had recently begun accompanying Miss Forshaw to St. Giles's Church. That information could prove useful, as it tells us that Miss Forshaw perhaps held some influence over her employer, at least in spiritual matters. It also places your employer in the victim's company rather more than was first intimated to us."

"Really, Inspector, I must protest! Just because the master and mistress accompanied Clara to church hardly constitutes reasons for suspicion, surely?"

"No, it doesn't. No one is saying there is any suspicion attached to your employer. I'm merely pointing out that there are many things you could tell us that might shed light on our inquiry – things that you may dismiss as inconsequential, but which we may find useful in building a better picture of Miss Forshaw's life."

"I see. But what kind of things are you referring to?"

"That's for you to tell us, Soames. Let's start by you telling me what church the Bellhavens attended prior to their joining Miss Forshaw at St. Giles's."

"Of course. They used to attend Christ Church, about half a mile away, as you probably know. They used to enjoy a leisurely walk to the church on Sunday, unless, of course, the weather was inclement, in which case they'd use the carriage."

"Ah, the carriage. Do you know why Mr. Bellhaven doesn't employ a driver for the carriage, or a groom for the horse?"

"It's rarely used, Inspector. Mr. Bellhaven drives himself on the rare occasions they use it. He's quite a good driver and has taken part in carriage races in his younger days. As for grooming, I was once in the Royal Horse Artillery and it gives me great pleasure to attend to Firefly on Mr. Bellhaven's behalf, in my spare time of course."

"Firefly?"

"Mr. Bellhaven's horse, sir, she's stabled at the rear of the house."

"I see, and the carriage is also kept there, I presume?"

Soames nodded.

"When did he last use it?" asked Hillman, breaking his silence.

"I believe the master took it out a few evenings ago, on Sunday night, just to give the horse some exercise, of course."

"Of course," said Norris, looking at Hillman as he spoke. "Now, can you tell me if you ever saw any signs of a disagreement between the Bellhavens and Miss Forshaw?"

"Oh no, sir, nothing like that. Relations between them were always most cordial, apart from. . . " Soames hesitated.

"Go on, Soames, apart from what?" Norris's interest had just risen markedly. Perhaps there was something here, after all.

"It's nothing really, Inspector. I shouldn't have even hinted at anything."

"Soames," said Norris, his voice taking on a harder edge, "I need hardly remind you that this is a murder inquiry. If I feel you're withholding information, I'll have you down at the station in no time and we'll see what effect a few hours in a cell has on your reluctance to cooperate."

Soames looked horrified at the prospect.

"Well, Inspector, when you put it like that, I have to say that it isn't much, but. . . "

"I'll be the judge of that, Soames. Do go on."

"One day, I was passing the Master's study when I heard the sound of raised voices from within. I recognised Clara's voice and Mr. Bellhaven's, of course. I heard Miss Forshaw say something about Mr. Bellhaven having made certain promises that he hadn't adhered to, and the Master bellowed quite loudly that he needed time to attend to the matter. I admit, it was the only time I've ever heard the Master raise his voice in such a fashion. Clara was a lovely young lady, Inspector, and I wished to spare her from the Master's wrath, so I quickly gathered up the morning post and placed it on a silver salver and returned to the study, where all appeared quiet, at least from outside the door. I knocked and entered and found Miss Forshaw seated in her usual secretarial chair opposite Mr. Bellhaven, who was behind his desk. Whatever disagreement had taken place had obviously been resolved, because all appeared amicable between them. I passed the mail to Clara, as was usual. She thanked me and I withdrew from the study. Mr. Bellhaven didn't speak to me, which was usual at such times, as he was busy perusing some paperwork. That's all there was to it, Inspector."

"And you simply left it that?" asked Norris, suspecting that the butler was holding something back.

"Well. . ."

"Come on, man, out with it. There's more, I know it and you know it."

"Only that I spoke with Clara a little later, wanting to know if everything was all right. I asked her about the altercation, and she told me she was sorry I'd overheard it, and that it was simply a matter of money, something to do with her contract as the master's secretary, and that he didn't seem to value her highly enough. It had been quickly resolved, she assured me, and all was now harmonious between them once again. She appeared a little flustered and a little red-faced to discover I'd overheard them, which I put down to her being embarrassed at having to reveal matters pertaining to her finances to me. I assured her I would say nothing of the matter, and thought no more of it until now."

"And is there anything else, you can recall, Soames? Anything that might tell us more of what may have been in Clara's mind around the time of her death?"

"Honestly, Inspector, there's nothing else, I assure you. Nothing in this house could possibly have any bearing on Clara's murder, I'm sure of it."

Norris appeared satisfied and quickly dismissed the butler. Hillman was about to say something, but Norris cautioned him to silence, simply saying, "Later, old chum, later."

Once again, interviews with the remaining staff produced nothing of use. Before departing, Norris requested another brief meeting with Laurence Bellhaven, which Soames quickly arranged, guiding them this time into the study, where Bellhaven awaited them, seated behind his desk, a sheaf of papers piled in front of him, and a long, quill-handled pen in his hand.

"Ah, gentlemen, I trust your interviews with the servants have gone well, this time around?"

"Fairly well, sir," Norris replied. "Before we leave, there are just a couple of things I'd like to ask you, if I may?"

"But of course, Inspector, go ahead."

Norris wasn't about to beat about the bush and went right to the point.

"Can you please tell me the reason for an argument you were overheard to have been involved in with Clara Forshaw, some weeks before her death?"

Bellhaven appeared stunned by the question and the pen almost dropped from his hand.

"I... what... who on earth has told you such a thing, Inspector?"

"That's not important, sir. Please be kind enough to answer the question."

"If one of my staff has been eavesdropping on private conversations, I'll have them dismissed instantly."

"Sir, what were you arguing about?"

"In the name of God, Norris. Am I now to be treated as a suspect in the death of my own secretary? What business is it of yours, or anyone else's, if Clara and I had a minor disagreement?"

"So, you did have an argument with her, sir?" Hillman interjected into the conversation.

Caught out by his own indignation, Bellhaven was forced to admit to the altercation.

"Yes, damn it. I did have an argument with Clara, or rather, the other way round. She was unhappy with the terms I'd offered for an extension to her contract of employment as my personal secretary. She seemed to think the salary on offer for a further two years of service was too 'demeaning', as she put it, for the level of expertise she'd brought to the position. After some haggling and a few raised words at what I thought to be her ingratitude, bearing in mind her privileged position within my own household, I increased the terms of my offer and the matter was resolved."

"And did you feel anger towards her as a result of this argument?" asked Norris.

"Only at the time of the argument itself, Inspector. This was a matter of business, after all, and not worth permanently souring the amicable relationship I'd always sustained with Clara. Once the matter had been resolved, it was forgotten about, and we resumed working together as we always had done."

"I see, and please can you tell me why you also ceased worshipping at Christ Church and began to attend St. Giles's along with Clara?"

"Oh, really, Inspector, I hardly find that relevant to anything at all. Clara would often speak to my wife of the wonderful, spiritually uplifting services she attended at Martin Bowker's church. My wife, though not a lady of radical beliefs by any means, was finding the services at Christ Church a little staid and quite boring at times, and suggested to me that we might try St. Giles's. I was happy to accommodate her, as it gave me an opportunity to exercise my horse and my carriage-driving skills. I quite enjoyed driving my wife and Clara to church each week, Inspector."

"You drove Clara to church?"

"But of course. You don't think I would take my wife in the carriage and leave Clara to find her own way there?"

"I thought she travelled on the underground railway, that's all, sir."

"Ah, she used the Metropolitan Railway to attend her Bible Study classes, I believe, but on Sundays, she enjoyed travelling in a little style with Mrs. Bellhaven. My wife will, I'm sure, be happy to tell you of the pleasure she derived from the change of venue for her Sunday worship."

"I'm sure that won't be necessary, Mr. Bellhaven. I'll take your word for it. One last question, if I may?"

"Yes, Inspector?"

"During your visits to St. Giles's church, did you ever see anything that might lead you to believe that Martin Bowker might share any, shall we say, overly friendly relations with any of his congregation?"

"You mean female members of the congregation, I presume?"

"Yes, sir, I do."

"Far be it for me to cast aspersions on a member of the cloth, Inspector, but I have often thought Martin Bowker to be a little too 'personal' in his approach to certain young ladies within the church. I've often felt that he decided to make his Bible Study classes all-female for the express purpose of having exclusive rights to a room full of female company for a couple of hours at a time."

"And what led you to this 'feeling,' Mr. Bellhaven?"

"If you stand outside the church any Sunday morning at the close of service, Inspector, you'll see that Martin Bowker spends a great deal of time speaking to the ladies leaving church. Far more time than he affords the many gentlemen who grace his pews, and who greatly contribute to the coffers of St.Giles's through the collection plate, and through other means, I dare say. He has a tendency to shake the ladies' hands in a rather tender fashion, if I may be so bold as to express the opinion. It may not be anything more than a way of showing reverendly affection, but it just doesn't appear seemly or proper to me, Inspector Norris. There now, you've asked, and I've answered. I hope I haven't said anything out of turn."

"Not at all, sir. I appreciate your candour on the matter. I hope, on your next visit to St. Giles's, you will keep this interview strictly confidential?"

"But of course, Inspector, not a word shall pass my lips. Now, if there's nothing else?"

Laurence Bellhaven had a way of making sure that whoever he was speaking to knew when a conversation with him was at an end. Norris and Hillman rose and departed, before Soames could be summoned to show them out. On the street outside the house, with the all-white façade gleaming in a sudden burst of late afternoon sunshine, Hillman at last had the opportunity to voice his thoughts.

"Bloody hell, Bert, that was some interview with Soames, eh?"

"It definitely opens a few new doors, Dylan, old chum."

"When he told us old Bellhaven took his carriage out on Sunday night, I nearly fell off my chair. That was the night of Ann Cullen's murder."

"And the two Ripper murders, Dylan."

"So, Laurence Bellhaven could be our man, or Jack the Ripper, or both?"

"Or none of them of course, old chum. It may be just as Soames said. He was out exercising his horse, and taking a leisurely carriage drive through the streets of London. It's not much to base a suspicion on, not really, and certainly not enough to go to Madden with."

"But we will report it to him, won't we?"

"Oh yes, Dylan. We certainly will, along with Bellhaven's words on Martin Bowker."

"That was a surprise too, don't you think?"

"I do, and I also think Bellhaven was very quick to point the finger at Martin Bowker, as if he couldn't wait to tell us. Now, you tell me, Dylan, if he had such thoughts about the vicar, why didn't he tell us when we first spoke to him?"

"Perhaps he just didn't want to cast a shadow in the direction of a man of God?"

"Or perhaps he simply told us a load of old twaddle in order to deflect any suspicions we may be developing towards the vicar as opposed to himself."

"So, what next, Bert?"

"We go home, Dylan, that's what's next. Tomorrow, we see Madden, write up our reports on today's progress and then. . . well, for once, I'm not sure. We'll see what our wise chief inspector has to say before we make another move."

As the two men parted that late afternoon, Hillman reflected on the fact that the interview with Roland Soames, coupled with a certain reticence on the part of Laurence Bellhaven, followed by his ready declamation of Martin Bowker, had indeed made for an interesting piece of police work. Norris certainly knew how to get to the heart of matters, when it really counted. Hillman felt sure they were getting somewhere; though, like Albert Norris he wasn't quite sure where. At least, not yet.

Chapter 24
Closed Ranks

"You're not serious, Bert, surely?" asked Madden, following Norris's report on his visit to the Bellhaven home the following morning. "You expect me to believe that a man like Laurence Bellhaven could even be remotely suspected of being the railway murderer, or even worse, that maniac Jack the Ripper? I'm afraid that's even more fanciful than your theory about the Reverend Bowker. I'm beginning to believe that, in the absence of viable suspects or hard evidence, you've started clutching at straws now, Inspector."

Norris sighed. He'd spent the previous evening at home with Betty and the dogs and, though unable to tell her much without betraying the confidential nature of the case, he'd been able to reveal enough for her to concur with him that any hint of an upper class, well-respected man being a suspect was bound to meet with derision from his superiors. Norris had taken Billy and Lillie for a long walk around the park while Betty prepared their evening meal of fish and potatoes, and ran through the meeting with Bellhaven in his mind again and again as he watched the two little terriers playing together. Maybe Bellhaven wasn't the man they were looking for, he concluded, but something in that house and its connections with the church of St. Giles worried him enough to want to take his inquiry further and, in order to do so, he needed Madden's sanction, hence his full disclosure to his boss that morning.

"Look, sir, you wanted me to tell you everything we found in the course of the inquiry from now on, and I have. I can't help it if the news is potentially unpalatable or offends those in high office. I've thought about it through another bloody sleepless night and, though I can't give you proof, both me and Hillman felt that Bellhaven was first of all a little defensive when it came to the argument with Clara Forshaw, and also a little too quick to confirm the Reverend Bowker's alleged liking for the younger women attending his church."

"So, just because a gentleman of means is reluctant to reveal details of his personal financial arrangements with his secretary, and because he is cooperative enough to confirm your own feelings about Bowker, you now suspect him of some involvement in the murders, is that it?"

"Clara Forshaw is dead, sir. She was pregnant at the time of her death. She had an argument with Bellhaven, and we only have his word for it as to the subject matter of that argument. . ."

"And her own words to the butler, according to your report."

"That's true, sir, but what about Bellhaven's carriage ride on the night of the Ripper murders and the killing of Ann Cullen?"

"Oh, come now, Inspector. Do you have any idea how many carriages must have been out on the streets of London that night? To accuse a man like Bellhaven of such things, based on the fact that he took his carriage out, is surely preposterous. He'd hardly have been likely to confirm that event if he had something to hide."

"Ah, but he knew we'd been told of the carriage ride by one of his staff, so denying it would have been even more suspicious and he'd have realised that."

Madden fell silent for a few seconds, pondering Norris's words. When he spoke again, it was merely to confirm what Norris already expected him to say.

"I have to say I fail to see any reasoning in your theory, Bert. As in the case of Martin Bowker, you're basing your suspicions on a distinct lack of evidentiary proof, and on a whole load of suppositions and ifs and maybes. Don't lose sight of the fact that Laurence Bellhaven is a member of the board of directors of the Metropolitan Railway, and therefore one of the possible targets for a smear campaign, if the letter we received is genuinely from the killer. What better way to discredit the railway than to have a series of deaths occur, coupled with a senior employee of the company being made to appear responsible? And there's one other thing you appear to have overlooked."

"Sir?"

"Even if I hypothetically accept your theory about Bellhaven being involved in Clara Forshaw's death, which I don't, by the way, that still doesn't explain his connection with, or motive for, Ann Cullen's murder. Answer me that one, if you can, Inspector."

It was Norris's turn to fall silent as he pondered the chief inspector's words.

"I can't, sir," he eventually replied. "Yes, Bellhaven and Ann Cullen went to the same church, but I'm sure you're about to point out that so did many others, and until I know if any of them could have had a motive for the murders, then I'm to leave Laurence Bellhaven alone. Am I right?"

Joshua Madden smiled and nodded.

"Ah, at last, I see you're thinking along the same lines as me on this one, Bert. There's too much at stake for us to go making wrong decisions and chasing wild ideas around town when the real killer is probably out there, planning his next move, even as we speak. Go out and find him, Bert. Talk to as many people as you like, but get this bastard before he does it again, because I have a feeling he just might do that."

"I have the same feeling too, sir, which is why I'm trying all I can to advance the investigation. But I have to say I feel as though I'm being tied in knots by those in authority, yourself included, regarding the way I'm allowed to conduct the case."

"Be very careful, Inspector." Madden scowled. "You're coming very close to insubordination with that last remark. I've told you how things are, and why I don't want you going down certain avenues. That comes not just from me, but from the very highest level. Now, I'm sure you understand my position on the subject, and just how far the implications surrounding the case go. So, let's hear no more of such talk, eh, Bert."

Madden smiled, an attempt at placating his angry and frustrated-looking inspector. "Please, Bert, just do the best you can and, like I said, go bring the killer in, before he kills again."

Norris turned on his heel and walked to the office door, and left Madden with a final, parting shot.

"Yes, sir, as you say, I'll get out there and bring you in a killer. But, just tell me this. Do you want the *real* killer, or will anyone do?"

"Get out, Norris!" shouted the chief inspector, but Norris had already closed the door and was walking down the corridor as his boss's anger bounced off the walls of his office and fell on deaf ears.

Dylan Hillman stood in Norris's tiny office, a look of incredulity on his face as Norris apprised him of his meeting with Madden.

"He said what?"

"We're to drop it, Dylan, old chum. According to Madden, there's no way a man like Laurence Bellhaven could be involved in the murders. This whole thing is beginning to smell of an establishment cover-up. No Bowker, no Bellhaven, hands off, don't look there, Dylan, no suspect who might be connected with the establishment in any way whatsoever. Oh yes, Madden wants us to bring him a killer, but only so long as that killer comes from the bloody dregs of society. God forbid that anyone connected with the toffs and the nobs should be thought of as being a callous, murdering bastard. I'm afraid that's a job description reserved for the lower classes, old chum."

"But for God's sake, Bert, we might have found the killer, or even Jack the Bloody Ripper for all he knows, and we're told to go and look elsewhere?"

"I'm afraid so, Dylan."

"And is that what we're going to do?" asked Hillman, almost anticipating the answer he was about to receive.

"Oh yes, old chum. That's exactly what we're going to do. We'll send Dove, Lee and Constable Fry out onto the streets. We'll have them question anyone and everyone, in as quiet a way as they can, of course, and, in the meantime, Dylan, my friend, you and

I are going to dig, dig, dig, until we find something we can hang on somebody."

"Why did I know you were going to say something like that?" Hillman laughed.

"Maybe because you think the way I think, Dylan, and because, like me, you can't stand being messed around."

"Let's just hope Madden doesn't get wind of what we're up to, though, Bert, or we might both be looking for new jobs by this time next week."

"Well, Dylan, if we are, I can't think of anyone whose company I'd rather share in a job queue." Norris smiled wryly. "Now, I think we'd better prepare our tactics for our interviews with the ladies of the good reverend's Bible Study Class, don't you?"

Chapter 25
The Diarist

Slender, swirling tendrils of evening mist stretched like eerie tentacles of the coming night over the half-open sash of the window, creeping into the room and sending a chill shiver through the body of the writer who was sitting facing a mirrored desk, on which a small, black, leather-bound diary lay. Sensing the onrush of fast-approaching night, the writer rose and lit the two gas mantles that brought a soft, welcoming, creamy-yellow light into the room. Next, the window was closed, amputating the mist tendrils from the greater whole of their swirling forms that lingered outside in the open air.

The diary lay open and beside it was a small brass padlock, waiting to be clipped into place on the tiny hasp attached to the cover once the diarist was done for the day, sealing the secrets once more within its covers. Satisfied that the room was secure from the encroaching fingers of the night, the diarist returned once more to the waiting pages. Dipping pen in ink pot, the writer reached across to the page and began, in a confident hand:

> *Dear Diary,*
>
> *All appears well. The police continue to make their inept inquiries, so far without a modicum of success, as was to be expected. Detective Inspector Norris is a good man, diligent and determined, but even the most diligent man can only solve a crime if given the information and the clues that will lead him to the solution, and for*

Norris, no such clues are forthcoming, for none were left. A good man, yes, but one who can do little to solve the mystery I have woven. The police are easy to outsmart as they think along such narrow lines. Narrow lines? A good joke there, for the railway conspiracy believers. If anyone should care to delve into this affair in the future, after I am gone, then think not too harshly of me, for self-preservation is surely the most precious gift with which the Good Lord has imbued within our souls. Did God himself not condemn the sin of fornication? Does the Bible itself not tell us that we should not suffer a witch to live, and is it not a witch who so beguiles and takes advantage of those weak enough to fall into her wicked ways, and initiate a man's fall from grace? Clara is gone, and another, avoiding for ever any calamity to my family. The letter to the police should serve to cloud their thinking, and allow time for things to die down quietly, for the case to be consigned to the many unsolved files that must lie within their records. Let them chase the author, they shall not find me. I am neither crazed, nor unhinged; my mental capacity is undiminished by the deeds that had to be done. My diary shall speak for me, long after I have departed this mortal coil. Goodnight, sweet diary, and keep my secrets safe. I am for bed, now, until the next time.

The pen was soon returned to its resting place on the ink stand and the small padlock clicked and locked into place on the diary, which was securely placed in a drawer in the desk. Another key was turned to lock the drawer, before being returned to the wall safe that stood open and ready to receive it, and the diarist rose once more, turning out the gas lamps and standing by the door as they guttered into darkness; a darkness which enveloped the small dressing room and left a still quietness in the place of the soft light so recently evident within the room. Soon, the entire house fell quiet, and the mist of evening gave way to a rolling fog that swept up from the Thames, and London soon lay sleeping beneath the hush of the fog's chill, muffling grey blanket.

The diarist lay in bed, sleep an evasive wraith despite a tiredness that craved a few hours of restful oblivion. Downstairs, the sound of a grandfather clock chiming the midnight hour reached the ears of the restless figure. As the minutes ticked by, the sounds of the house as it settled for the night were heightened by a lack of sleep – a floorboard creaking, a rustling in the eaves outside the bedroom window and other unknown but familiar sounds as the night drew inexorably on towards the daylight hours. Eventually, as the grandfather clock's distant chimes announced the second hour of morning and most of London lay beneath the shroud of river fog, the diarist fell into the warm and welcoming arms of a deep sleep, a sleep that would last until the light of dawn once more wakened the house to life and with it, the veiled promise of new beginnings.

PART THREE

Chapter 26
Situation Report

"Got nothing, going nowhere, and our hands bloody well tied behind our back by officialdom. Just how do they expect us to conduct an investigation, Dylan, when we can't talk to people, can't haul anyone in for questioning without telling Madden first, and can't even suspect anyone, unless they happen to fit the damned Commissioner's idea of a murderer?"

"I think frustration is getting to you, Bert," said Hillman, as the two sat together in Norris's office, reviewing the case so far.

The meeting with Martin Bowker's Bible Study Class had brought no results. The vicar had been more cooperative than Norris had expected and had asked all the lady members to attend, and stay behind and allow the detectives to speak with them. Sadly, no one had been able to volunteer any information that Norris found helpful, apart from one young woman who said that she thought Ann Cullen and Clara Forshaw had been 'sort of friends and had sometimes spoken with each other as they left the church or the study meetings. In itself, that was nothing as far as evidence was concerned. An assumed friendship of sorts proved nothing, and Norris was only too aware that many of the ladies present would probably exchange pleasantries and smatterings of conversation after church services. The woman who'd provided that small snippet of tittle-tattle, Ruby Meadows, appeared to be a bit of a gossipmonger, and Norris felt unable to take her too seriously. In fact, he was inclined to believe she'd made the whole thing up, just to gain a little attention, in the lack of anyone having anything to give to the detectives.

"Too right I'm frustrated, old chum. I mean, all this time, and what have we got? Sod all! Come on, Dylan, you tell me what we've achieved so far, and let's see if I've missed anything out."

Hillman thought he might as well go along with Norris's request. There was nothing to lose from a swift recap of the case after all.

"Okay. First we had Clara Forshaw's murder, and the boss almost ordered you, us, to keep the whole thing quiet because the Commissioner or someone even higher up the chain of command thought it might have something to do with a terrorist or Fenian attack against the Underground Railway, which could have dire financial consequences for the city. Oh yes, we were also to keep things low key because the boss didn't want to start a panic on top of the Jack the Ripper murders already under investigation in Whitechapel."

Norris nodded. "Go on, Dylan."

"We put together a fairly strong case that put Martin Bowker in the frame for the murder, but then we get told to back off. Seems he's not a viable suspect because he's a vicar, and, according to the brass, vicars can't be murderers. We find out Clara was pregnant, but all our efforts to find out who the father might have been lead nowhere. Next, Ann Cullen's body turns up in the tunnel at Moorgate Street. It turns out that not only did she attend St. Giles's church, like Clara, but she was also a member of Bowker's Bible Study Class, too. Cue another meeting with the good reverend, who we bring in for questioning and then show him the body of Ann Cullen. He throws up and goes green and the next thing we get is a hauling over the coals from the chief inspector, because the Commissioner and the Bishop are up in arms over the way poor Bowker's been treated. You get suspended – er, sent on sick leave – and me and the boys wander around aimlessly chasing shadows for three days."

"Spot on so far, Dylan, old chum. Keep going."

"Right. You come back, we interview the Bellhaven family butler who gives us a hint that all wasn't well in the household. You speak to Bellhaven, who sort of confirms what the butler heard and said, and also hints at the Reverend Bowker's liking for young ladies. Something in what Bellhaven tells us gives us an idea he might be involved in some way, but Madden tells us to back off again, because nobody from the heady echelons of society, like Laurence Bellhaven, could possibly be involved in such barbaric bloody killings. So, we're back to square one and even though we may have stumbled upon the killer on more than one occasion, the political machinations of the case mean that we're blocked at every move, and you're told to bring the killer in whoever he is, as long as it isn't Bowker or Bellhaven. How's that for a short summary?"

"I'd say you're about spot on, Dylan. Half the force is assigned to searching for bloody Jack the Ripper, and we're left with just a couple of blokes to try and find this damned maniac on the railway. They get all the help from above, we get none. Even Thomas Hall was sent packing back to his own cases, so that not too many people would get too knowledgeable about what we're investigating."

"I wondered why he disappeared so soon after you got back."

"Madden wanted to make sure he had someone to cover the case while I was away and quickly got rid as soon as I was back. Shame, really. Thomas Hall is a good man and could have helped us a lot, I think."

"At least you got a new dog out of it all. How is she, anyway?"

"Ah, Lillie's fine, and Billy's enjoying her company. We placed an advertisement in the evening paper, in case her owner was looking for her, but we've heard nothing. To be honest, I hope nobody claims her because me and Betty have grown attached to the wee beast, and Billy certainly has."

"So, any good ideas as to where we look next for our killer, Bert?"

"Look, Dylan, old chum. I'm sure we've already met and talked to the killer. Trouble is, we've no real way of proving which of the people we've interviewed so far is the one with blood on his hands. We're going to have to keep digging away until something breaks. For a start, I want a watch kept on both Martin Bowker and Laurence Bellhaven. I also haven't discounted that weird solicitor's chief clerk, Harrison Hargreaves, at least not entirely. Did anyone do a follow-up on him – check out his background and so on?"

"I'm sorry, Bert. No one thought to do that while you were away, and since you got back he's kind of been forgotten."

"Never mind apologising, let's get him checked out as soon as we can. Find out where he comes from, if he has anything murky in his past, and what his tastes in women are, if possible. Get Dove on it. Tell him I want him to follow Hargreaves around for a day or two, just to see what he does after work."

"And what are *we* going to do?"

"Us, Dylan? Well, for a start, we're going to revisit the sites of the murders – or, I should say, where the bodies were found. I want to get a better feel for this case. I need to see if we can connect with the victims somehow, and also try and find out if we can get inside the head of the killer and try to think our way into 'seeing' what happened at Aldgate and Moorgate Street. The lack of defensive wounds on both women's hands makes me think both girls knew their killer. They trusted him enough to let him get close, Dylan, and that's when the bastard stabbed them."

"You seem to be leading us back to your original theory here, if you don't mind me saying so."

"If you mean I'm leaning in the direction of Martin Bowker, despite what the bigwigs at Scotland Yard and the Archdiocese of London say, then yes, you're correct, old chum. Whatever Madden says, we can't give up on him as a suspect just because the aristocrats in charge of the country tell us to. If he's guilty, Dylan, we're going to nail him, man of God or not. Now, I'm off to Aldgate. Are you coming?"

With that, Norris rose from his chair and walked briskly out of the office, closely followed by Dylan Hillman, glad at least to be doing something, instead of sitting around ruminating on a case that, to all intents and purposes, was heading straight for the 'unsolved' files as far as everyone around them was concerned. Hillman, however, knew that Albert Norris was not so easily beaten and could be every bit as tenacious as the terriers who shared his home, once he got his teeth into a case. Perhaps because of the obstructions and restrictions that he'd seen placed on his investigation, that tenacity had grown even stronger within the inspector, and Hillman felt that the time was drawing near when Norris would throw off the shackles of those restrictions in order to prove his case. Whether such action would solve the case and bring a killer to justice, or simply hasten the end of Norris's career as a police officer, only time would tell.

The date was November 8th and, as events in the very near future were to show, time was running out, not just for Norris and his case, but for others in far more vaunted positions.

Chapter 27
Goldstein's Information

Norris and Hillman emerged from Aldgate Underground Station, feeling slightly queasy and none the wiser for their two hours' work. Norris had decided to follow the journey undertaken by Clara Forshaw on the night of her murder. He had first caught the train that took them from Aldgate to Farringdon Street, the station nearest to St. Giles's, where she would have boarded the fateful train that carried her to her death; assuming, as they now did, that Clara had been murdered in the carriage in which her body had been discovered. The fumes, smoke and noise from the locomotive that had seeped into the carriage as they traveled, were enough to put both men off underground travel for some time to come, and when they next boarded a train that took them back from Farringdon Street, via Aldersgate Street, Moorgate Street and Bishopsgate stations, both spent most of the short journey longing for the fresh air of the streets above once more.

Norris gulped in large quantities of London air, heady with the smells of the street, but preferable by far to that of the tunnels. His actions were copied by Hillman, and it was a full thirty seconds after emerging into the daylight before either man spoke.

"Well, Dylan, old chum, that was pretty much a waste of time."

"We didn't learn much, did we?"

"I didn't really expect to, to be truthful. I was looking for inspiration and thought the ride Clara took might have helped. You know, it might have helped if we'd known how many people travelled on the train that night. Surely there must have been some who disembarked at the other stations before arriving at Aldgate? No one could have committed the murder if there were others in the carriage, so we have to assume she was alone in the carriage with her killer when the train left Bishopsgate. If anyone was in the carriage with them up to that point, we may yet have a witness who could identify the killer."

"But if we're not allowed to ask the press to help by publicising the need for witnesses, how the hell do we trace anyone who was on the train?"

"I know, Dylan, it's a sod of a problem. Maybe Madden will authorise a press release asking simply for anyone who travelled on the appropriate train to contact the police, without giving a reason."

"Do you really think he'll let us do that?"

"No, Dylan, I don't. They're all afraid of attracting publicity to the case and, if they allow us to do it, there's a chance that word may leak out if too many people come forward. After all, once we start asking them if they saw anyone in the carriage with Clara, some of them are bound to start putting two and two together. Madden will know that, too, so I doubt we'll get the chance to try."

"All right, so what about Ann Cullen, Bert? She had to have been killed between Farringdon Street and Moorgate Street, so there was only one stop in between. Whoever killed her and threw her from the train had to have worked fast, and again, she must have been alone with him."

"Good point, Dylan. So, whoever killed her was already either on the train when it pulled in to Farringdon Street, or boarded with her, or boarded at Aldersgate Street, which wouldn't have left much time to carry out a murder."

"If he did get on with her at Aldersgate, it narrows things down a bit. Maybe a member of the station staff saw someone board the train with her, or at least at the same time as she did, at Farringdon or Aldersgate."

"It's worth checking, Dylan. We're running out of ideas, and fast. If the killer doesn't strike again, and I hope he doesn't, of course, we may end up losing this one, old chum."

"So, where do you want to start?"

"Farringdon Street. It's a long shot and some of the people who were working that night may not even be on duty there in the daytime, but we have to start somewhere."

"You mean, right now?"

"Right now, Dylan."

"You mean we're going back down. . . "

"'Fraid so. Back into the smoky hole it is."

"But, we've just come back from Farringdon Street!"

"I know. We're getting to be regular underground travellers, eh?"

Hillman groaned as Norris led the way back down and onto the platform at Aldgate. They were soon rattling along the tracks once more, both holding their breath as much as they could as the smoke and fumes seeped into their carriage. The sulphurous stench assaulted the nostrils of every passenger, and Norris could easily see why so many people thought ill of the underground railway system. Fast, it may be, but surely injurious to health if used too often!

Sadly, Farringdon Street proved barren ground for their inquiry. Only three of the staff on duty had been working on the night of Ann Cullen's murder, and none of them had been on duty on the night of Clara Forshaw's demise. Not so at Aldersgate Street, however, where at last Norris received what he felt was a break, albeit a small one.

Forty-year-old Joseph Goldstein was a ticket inspector at Aldersgate, his job being to check the tickets of those leaving the train to ensure that no one was attempting to travel without having paid.

"I remember the night you speak of, Inspector, when that poor woman's body was found on the tracks a little way from here, near Moorgate Street. Word soon reached us here, though we were later told to keep anything to do with the case to ourselves, pending police investigations, which is why you're here now, I suppose?"

"Quite so, Mr. Goldstein."

"I saw her, you know."

"Ann Cullen?"

"Well, yes, if that was her name. I came down to the platform to meet the train. There weren't many people aboard, and it only took me a minute to check the tickets of those who alighted. There can't have been more than six, I think. Anyway, as I walked towards the steps at the end of the platform, I looked into the remaining carriages. The train was virtually deserted but there were a man and a woman in one of the carriages. No one else in it, you see. There were only men in the other carriages, so it had to be her, don't you think?"

"Yes, I do, Mr. Goldstein. What did you see, exactly? Can you describe the man?"

"I wasn't taking much notice, to be truthful. Why should I? It's not my job to spy on the passengers, after all. But, I did think the couple were having a bit of an argument. The woman was gesticulating at the man, pointing at him, and he was standing up, looking menacing – yes, that's the word, menacing. I'm sorry, but a description I cannot give you. He seemed well-dressed, in a black greatcoat, but as he had a hat on his head and a black muffler around the lower part of his face, there was little of him to see, and anyway, it was just a fleeting glance as I walked past. That's all I can tell you, Inspector."

"And did you not think to inform anyone of this earlier, Mr. Goldstein?" asked Hillman.

"No one asked me, Sergeant, and we were told not to discuss it with anyone while the police. . . "

". . . were conducting their inquiries." Norris finished the man's sentence, silently cursing the man from Special Branch who had, in all probability, put the fear of God into every one of the Metropolitan Railway's employees. Because of that, a piece of vital information had been denied to them for too long.

"I'm sorry, should I have spoken sooner?"

"It's not your fault, Mr. Goldstein," said Norris. "You were simply doing as you were told. We thank you for telling us now. Please be so good as to tell no one else what you've just imparted to us?"

"But of course, Inspector. Confidential information, yes?"

"Yes, that's it. We're really very grateful to you."

* * *

Back at the police station, Norris and Hillman finally felt they were getting somewhere.

"Right, Dylan. At least now we know it's a man. We might have thought it before, now we know for sure. We also know he was on the train when it passed through Aldersgate, so he must have boarded either before, or at Farringdon Street. It's my guess he boarded with Ann Cullen. They were arguing, so it's a reasonable assumption to make that they knew each other. Strangers rarely fall out in the short space of time it would have taken to travel between stations."

"Unless he was trying to force himself on the woman, Bert?"

"We've no evidence to suggest a sexual motive, have we? Neither woman was sexually assaulted. No, Dylan, she knew her killer, of that I'm sure. Now, all we need do is try to eliminate certain people from the list of suspects and narrow things down a bit. How's the inquiry into Harrison Hargreaves coming along?"

"I'll go and see if Sergeant Dove's in, and ask him."

"Good man. You know, I think we're about to get lucky, Dylan, old chum. Our killer might have made one mistake somewhere along the line, and we're just the men to sniff it out and bring him in, and believe me, that's just what we're going to do."

Hillman left the office and returned soon afterwards with Dove's written report on Harrison Hargreaves.

"He was just finishing it, Bert. Seems Hargreaves is almost whiter than white. No skeletons in his or his family's closet, apart from the fact that Dove tailed him to a rather seedy little opium den two nights ago, where Hargreaves appeared to be a regular, judging by the welcome he received at the door. Dove raided the place in daylight and the owner was only too happy to cooperate. Seems Hargreaves enjoys chasing the dragon so much that he visits the place every other night of the week, sometimes spending a few hours there, sometimes all night. The owner can't remember the night of Clara Forshaw's killing, but he gave Hargreaves an alibi for the night of Ann Cullen's murder. He was there all night, out of his head on the stuff."

"Hmm. Wonder if his employers know their chief clerk's an opium addict? Oh well, that's not our business, is it, Dylan? At least it puts him in the clear. I'm certain the same man killed both girls, so if Hargreaves is innocent of Ann's murder, then he's innocent of Clara's, too."

"I have an idea where your thoughts are leading us, Bert."

"I'm not saying a word, Dylan, old chum. At least, not yet. We could still be barking up the wrong tree, and I'm not going to do anything that drops us both in trouble with Madden and the Commissioner, or worse still, the bloody Home Secretary."

The thought of incurring the wrath of Henry Matthews, the staunch Roman Catholic Home Secretary, the first member of his religion to hold cabinet rank since the time of Queen Elizabeth, was enough to curb any thoughts of making rash moves that Hillman might have imagined. Appointed by the Prime Minister, Lord Salisbury, Matthews, despite being an able politician, was roundly disliked by Members of Parliament of all parties, and had recently refused entreaties to issue the offer of a reward for the apprehension of Jack the Ripper. As the man to whom the Commissioner of Police, Sir Charles Warren, was responsible, he was the last person Norris wished to feel coming down upon his investigation from a great height. Norris had no doubts that Matthews himself was the man responsible for the strictures placed on his investigation, so for now, the ploy was strictly *softly, softly.*

The inspector spent the next two hours formulating his new plan of action with Dylan Hillman. Then, as twilight began its inexorable encroachment upon the light of day, and the street lamps of London were lit, bathing the streets in their soft yellow glow, Norris sent his sergeant home with orders to get a good night's sleep, and to be ready to move fast with their plan the following day.

Unfortunately for Norris, Hillman, The Home Secretary, the Commissioner of the Metropolitan Police, and everyone concerned with not only the Underground Murders, but also the Jack the Ripper inquiry, events were about to take a number of ghastly turns, with dire and tragic consequences for many of those involved.

For now, though, Norris headed home, with the prospect of a good meal with Betty and a sound night's sleep ahead of him. He figured he'd earned at least that much. After all, he decided, things were beginning to come together.

Chapter 28
An Evening With The
Norris's

Crime, and the talent leading to its solution by the authorities, is, by the very nature of its commission, a dubious and unpredictable activity at the best of times. In the world in which we live today, police forces around the globe have managed to raise the detection rate of most crimes, including murder, to a level far more acceptable to society than was the case a hundred years and more ago. At the time of the Jack the Ripper killings and of the Underground Railway murders, however, the science of criminal detection relied almost as much on luck and the caprices of chance, as on the painstaking detective work carried out by the committed, though technologically bereft, members of the police force.

Without doubt, the longer a case remained unsolved, the less chance the police stood of arriving at a solution. In general terms, twelve weeks took the case into the realms of the unsolved, six months to the unsolvable and certainly, once a number of years passed with no resolution to a particular crime, the perpetrator could reasonably be considered to have got away with it – unless, of course, one of those odd caprices mentioned earlier should choose to rear its head.

Having enjoyed an evening meal of boiled beef, carrots and turnips, with lashings of gravy, Albert Norris had spent an hour walking the two dogs in the dark, keeping to the pathway that meandered around the small local park. Now, feeling better than he had for some time, both about himself and the case, he sat relaxing in his armchair by the fire, a small one lit by Betty, as the evenings were growing a little colder and she felt the glow and the warmth would add to the homeliness of their small parlour.

Norris decided to indulge himself in his one rare luxury, and filled and lit his pipe. As the smoke from the aromatic pipe tobacco favoured by Norris filled the small, cosy room, Betty took pleasure in the domesticity of the situation. It was rare for her husband to appear so at ease, and she was on her way to the kitchen to prepare a pot of tea for the couple to share when a knock sounded on the front door. Billy and Lillie barely stirred, and lay quietly across the front of the hearth, loving the warmth from the softly glowing embers of the fire.

"You stay there, Bert. You deserve a bit of peace. I'll see who's there, and unless someone's stolen the crown jewels, they can go away and leave you be."

Norris blew a mouthful of smoke into the air and nodded to Betty. Norris heard the muffled sound of voices coming from the direction of the front door and after about two minutes, a worried-looking Betty reappeared in the room. Seeing the look on his wife's face, and the obvious agitation in her manner, Norris stood up immediately, sensing a problem.

"Betty? What is it? What's wrong?" Norris placed an arm round her shoulder, feeling the tension in her muscles as he did so.

"There's a man at the door, Bert. I told him to wait. He looks a bit, well, rough, and he says Lillie's his dog. I don't like him. He says she ran away from him... called her a worthless, mangy little cur. I'll bet he beats her, Bert. You can't let her go back to him, please!" she begged.

"Now, now, Betty, calm down, my dear. I'll handle things. You wait here with those two," he said, glancing at the two dogs, who were snuggled together like peas in a pod.

Leaving a worried-looking Betty in the company of the terriers, Norris strode out of the room and up to the front door, which Betty had left on the latch. The caller was standing outside on the step. Norris pulled the door open and took in the appearance of the man standing on the threshold of his home. Around thirty years of age, he was dressed in the rough-looking clothes of a labourer, or worse. He looked in need of a wash and a shave, and his hair was matted and filthy with grime.

"'Allo, matey," said the man. "Me friend wot can read says you placed an advertisement in the newspaper, and that you've found me dog. Little bugger ran away when I sent her after a rat, ungrateful little bitch. I'll thank you to return her to me so as I can give 'er wot for, and get back to me rattin' and earn a few bob."

Norris stared at the man for a minute, saying nothing. He stared into the eyes of the stranger, and a long forgotten memory resurrected itself in the detective's mind.

"Ere, somfin' wrong, matey?" asked the stranger, on receiving no reply from Norris. "Cat got yer tongue or wot? How's abart me dog?"

Without a word, Norris suddenly sprang from the step and grabbed the man, quickly pulling him to the ground and pinioning his arms behind him. The man struggled and fought and shouted, "Oy! What's yer game, matey? I only came for me dog." But Norris refused to speak or to release his grip.

"Betty, fetch my handcuffs," Norris shouted at the top of his voice. "And my whistle."

Still the man struggled, and still Norris held onto his prisoner. Betty appeared in seconds, looking bemused, but carrying the handcuffs and Norris's police whistle as he'd requested. Norris released one hand from his grip on the man, and took the proffered handcuffs, which he quickly snapped in place, securing the man with his hands behind his back.

"Blow the whistle, Betty, as loud as you can," Norris instructed his wife, who did as her husband asked. The shrill blast of the police whistle rang out, and with it, a number of doors on the street opened and Norris's neighbours found themselves staring at an extremely odd sight. Even in the dark, they could see their policeman neighbour sitting astride a rough-looking man who lay face down on the pavement, his arms handcuffed behind him, and Norris's wife, Betty standing over the pair, police whistle in her hand.

The sound of running footsteps resounded from the end of the street, signalling the arrival of a constable, responding to the sound of the whistle, which in those days was a universal signal to all police officers that an officer was in need of assistance. As the uniformed officer drew closer, Norris rose to his feet, pulling his prisoner up with him, until the two men were standing, facing the oncoming constable. The man continued his feeble and futile attempts to struggle free from Norris's grip. Norris simply held on tight.

"Now then, what's all this?" asked the constable, who Norris quickly recognised as a man named Fellows, from New Street. "Oh, it's you, Inspector Norris. What on earth's happened, sir?"

"What's happened, Fellows, is that fortune has smiled on me tonight. After all my years on the force, I pride myself on never forgetting a face, certainly not one that has lived with me for as many years as I care to remember. I want you to take this specimen back to the station with you, where he's to be charged with the wilful murder of Police Constable Peter Vane."

The handcuffed man stared at Norris as he spoke and at last, recognition burned in his eyes.

"You!" he exclaimed. "You were the other bloody copper!"

"Yes, you filthy, murdering little wretch, I was. I've waited years to feel your collar, my lad. Now you'll swing for what you did, never doubt it for a second, you murdering bastard."

"Sir?" It was Fellows. "Police Constable Vane? I've never heard of him."

"Oh, it was a few years ago, Fellows, before your time, but this man gunned him down in cold blood and shot me, too. I thought he'd escaped justice, but chance put him into my hands this evening."

"Well then, that's good enough for me, sir. Come on, you," said Fellows, as he took charge of the vicious-looking but now slightly cowed figure. "What's your name?"

"My name's Drago, Ted Drago, for what it's worth to you, copper."

There was a sneering lilt to the man's voice, even though it was obvious to him that his future looked positively bleak.

"Well, Drago, you're coming with me. I presume you'll be coming down to the station to question him, sir?"

"I will, just as soon as I calm Mrs. Norris down and make sure all's secure here."

"Of course, sir. Well, I'll be getting along then, and we'll see you when you get there. Move, you!" He prodded Drago in the back. "We've got a nice comfy cell waiting for you at New Street."

Drago merely growled in response, and then found himself being shepherded along the street, past a small assembly of Norris's astonished neighbours, in the direction of the police station. Norris watched until Fellows and his prisoner disappeared around the corner at the end of the street before turning to Betty, who had never left his side throughout the mêlée that had taken place right on her own doorstep.

"Are you all right, Betty?"

"I'm fine, Bert, but you gave me a right turn there, I can tell you. I'd no idea what was going on when you shouted like that."

"Sorry, I hadn't time to explain."

"Of course not."

"Can you believe it, Betty? Poor Vane's murderer just walking up to my door, after all these years?"

"Seems like a miracle to me, Bert."

"You're not far wrong there, my dear. After all that time, he'd hardly changed. Ten years older, yes, but I always remembered the scowl on his face, and those eyes, Betty. I've dreamed about those piecing, menacing eyes of his, and waited and bided my time, hoping one day I'd come across him again."

"And you have, Bert, all thanks to little Lillie."

"Yes, indeed. All thanks to a tiny terrier and an advertisement in the paper. I always told you it was the best thing to do, the honest thing to do, to place that advertisement."

"And you were right, Bert, in more ways than one. You've caught Vane's killer after all this time, and hopefully laid the ghost of your own nightmares, and we've got little Lillie for keeps now, haven't we?"

"Oh yes, Betty. That little dog's going nowhere now. She stays with us, and that's final. Now, if you'll excuse me, I'd better make myself presentable and get along down to the station. I've got some serious questioning to do."

"Yes, Bert, you'd better do that."

Ten minutes later, having changed into his working suit, Albert Norris closed the front door of his home and strode purposefully towards the police station he'd left just a few hours earlier. As he walked, a feeling of closure rose from within, and Norris felt as though everything that had taken place all those years ago, the spectre that had haunted him for so long, was about to depart from his life. Somehow, Norris knew that from now on, life would be different, better, that a vindication could be in the offing, and with that, the mental cloud that had hung over him since that fateful night when Drago had killed Peter Vane, disappeared for ever.

When Detective Inspector Albert Norris walked back into New Street Police Station that night, not a man on duty failed to sense a change in the man. His voice, his stride, his straight back and proud bearing bore the marks of a man at peace with himself and one whose confidence suddenly seemed brimful.

"Where is he?" he asked of Constable Fellows, who had walked out of the back office to meet him upon his arrival.

"Cell four, sir. Shall I get him?"

"No, leave him there. I'll talk to him in the cell, make the little bastard feel more uncomfortable. Care to join me, Fellows?"

"Yes, sir," said the constable, eager to see and hear the inspector at work on the questioning of the murderer.

As the heavy iron door to cell number four opened and closed with the entry of the two policemen a minute later, Ted Drago looked up disconsolately from the hard, iron-framed bunk on which he sat. Norris and Fellows stood before him, looking menacing simply by virtue of their standing position, elevating them above his lowly place on the bunk. His bravado gone, the man looked at Norris, maybe hoping to see something he could exploit in the policeman, as he'd done once before, many years ago. This time, however, when he looked into the eyes of Albert Norris, all he saw was a man with steely determination and displaying little in the way of compassion. This time, Drago knew, there would be no easy way out of the situation. He'd had a good run, but now it was time for Norris and the law to extract their retribution for his actions ten years previously.

Chapter 29
9th November, 1888

Albert Norris emerged from cell number four an hour after making his entrance. Ted Drago, knowing the game was up, had eventually confessed to a number of lesser, petty crimes, almost out of sheer bravado, but, when faced with the prospect of a swift trial and the almost inevitable hanging that would follow soon afterwards, all sense of bluster eventually deserted him. The murder of a police officer in the execution of his duty was regarded as one of the most heinous of crimes, and the likelihood of a life sentence, as opposed to the death penalty, was extremely unlikely in his case, as Norris took great pains to point out to the man. He and Constable Fellows left Drago to ponder on his eventual fate, and Norris quickly made the arrangements for Drago's appearance before the magistrate, where he would be formally arraigned and committed for trial.

Never, in all the years that had passed since the murder of Peter Vane, had Norris expected to come face to face with the constable's killer, and the man who'd shot him in the shoulder. Now that one of those strange caprices of fate had brought the man right to his door and into his custody, Norris felt a lightness of mood he'd thought would forever be denied him. Despite the late hour, he felt alive, refreshed and rejuvenated. The heavy burden he'd carried around for ten years finally eased, and Norris walked home through the dark, virtually silent streets, ready to face whatever the following day might bring.

Betty Norris welcomed her husband home with a hug and a kiss. She'd sat up, waiting for her husband to return, sleep being the furthest thing from her mind after the events of the night. As the pair made their way to bed, Betty felt her husband had grown an inch or two since he'd left home earlier. That's when she realised the slightly hunched shoulders he'd developed since that awful day ten years ago had vanished, and her husband was walking tall once again. As she pulled her husband on top of her and felt the heat and strength of his manhood pressing into her, Betty revelled in the urgent and passionate intimacy that followed, as Norris allowed years of pent-up guilt and frustration to leach from his body as he indulged in a bout of lovemaking that Betty found exhilarating and thrilling beyond her dreams.

Sated at last, Norris rolled over and lay with his arms draped warmly around his wife as she rested her head on his shoulder.

"Bert?"

"Mmm?"

"You were wonderful."

"That's nice."

"Nice? Is that all you can say? You haven't been like that in a long while."

"Just felt right, Betty, that's all. Everything feels right again, after tonight."

She leaned across and kissed his cheek.

"If that's the case then, Albert Norris, you'd best get some sleep and set about solving those murders of yours in the morning."

Receiving no reply, Betty turned her head to look at her husband. Norris's eyes were tightly shut. He'd fallen fast asleep in seconds. Kissing him softly once again, Betty slowly and gently removed her head from his shoulder and rested back on her pillow. Norris's arms remained wrapped round her in a loving and comforting embrace, and it was merely a matter of minutes before she joined her husband in a peaceful repose that lasted until daylight began its inevitable intrusion into their bedroom at a little after six o'clock.

Breakfasted and refreshed, and sporting a clean shirt and tie, Norris walked to New Street that morning, feeling invigorated and ready for almost anything the world could throw at him. As he entered the muster room, he was surprised to be met by a round of applause and a chorus of 'Well dones' and 'Congratulations'. It appeared word had spread quickly about the events of the previous night, and, though few knew the hidden secret of Norris's past, the fact that he'd arrested the murderer of a fellow officer on his own doorstep had been sufficient for every officer in the station to want to join in the celebrations. Embarrassed by the attention, Norris merely nodded in acknowledgment of the universal praise and headed straight for his office, where Dylan Hillman was sitting waiting for him.

"So, that was a turn-up for the books eh, Bert?" asked Hillman, grinning from ear to ear and rising to shake Norris warmly by the hand as he entered the office.

"Nothing short of miraculous, Dylan, if you ask me."

"Hey, you're not going all religious on me, are you?"

"Don't be daft, but some strange quirk of fate or divine intervention led that little guttersnipe to my door last night. If it hadn't been for little Lillie, we'd never have had him in custody right now."

"The dog? Come on, Bert, you've got to tell me the full story."

So Norris did, from the advertisement in the newspaper to Drago turning up at the door, demanding the return of his dog, and Norris recognising him right away, by virtue not just of his face, though somewhat aged, but by Drago's eyes. He described the mêlée that followed, his success in holding on to Drago until Constable Fellows' arrival and the subsequent questioning of the killer in cell number four in the early hours of the morning.

"Well, that was a night to remember, for sure," said Hillman, when Norris fell silent at the end of his narrative.

"You're right about that, old chum. I've waited so long, and had so many sleepless nights because of what Drago did, and now, thankfully, it's over. I feel like a great weight's been lifted from me, Dylan, really I do."

"So I should think. You know, I've always told you not to feel bad about what happened. None of it was your fault."

"Easy enough to say, but not so easy to do, Dylan. You're one of the few people to know the whole truth about that night. I felt I owed it to you to know who you were working with, right from the start."

"And I appreciated you telling me, Bert, even though there was no need. Like I said, Vane knew the risks when he took the job. We all do. You weren't to know that Drago had a gun, or that he'd be stupid enough to actually use it against you and Vane."

"Thanks. I'm not going to debate it, though. At least we've got the murdering little bastard now. Better late then never, eh?"

"Too true. He'll swing for sure, once a jury hears all the facts."

"He'd better. I'd be willing to assist the hangman, too, given the chance. I'd happily pull the lever to open the trap under him and watch him drop."

"At least you can sleep better now, eh, Bert?"

"Yes, and so will Vane's mother. I'm going to see her later, after work. Her husband died a few months before Vane was killed, in an accident on the docks where he worked. It was a double tragedy for her at the time. She gave up her home and went to live with her married daughter soon afterwards. I've kept in touch a bit over the years, so I know she'll appreciate knowing we've got her son's killer behind bars at last."

"That's nice of you. I didn't know you'd kept in touch with her."

"No one does, apart from Betty and a couple of others."

"You're a bit of a softie at heart, aren't you?"

"Give over, Dylan. You'll ruin my reputation if you tell anyone that."

"Don't worry, Bert. Your secret's safe with me."

Hillman chuckled and Norris smiled in return, before adopting a more serious tone.

"We've still got these bloody railway murders to solve though, Dylan. I think we'd better stop celebrating and get down to it, don't you?"

"Whatever you say. You're the boss."

Norris pulled a large box file towards him.

"Well, old chum, this is it. Every file, every report and every statement we've taken on the case so far, including those you and the others made during my three days at home. We're going to go through every word on every line of every page, until we come up with a link that takes us down the right road towards finding the killer. It's in here somewhere, Dylan, I know it is. We know Hargreaves can be counted out, so we need to look closely at everyone else who we've looked at and talked to through the weeks. We may have missed something, or concentrated on the wrong man, or men. Now, we cross-check and cross-check again until we come up with something."

"That could take all day," groaned Hillman.

"Well, we'd better get started then, don't you think?"

The two detectives set to work, meticulously going through every file as Norris had requested. Both men made copious notes, trying to tie statements and reports together. Norris felt himself driven by a newly-fuelled enthusiasm and, despite the interference and roadblocks from above that had blighted the case so far, he grew more determined to solve the case with each passing minute.

As the noon hour passed, so they reached the end of the reports and statements pertaining to the Clara Forshaw case and prepared to move on to Ann Cullen. As they did so, however, the door to Norris's office was rudely barged open from the outside and Constable Fry came racing into the office with a look of horror on his face.

"Fry, what the hell's wrong, man?" asked Norris, seeing the shocked expression on the constable's face.

"Oh my God, sir, oh my God. You won't believe it, you really won't."

And with those words, Norris and Hillman found themselves being introduced to the latest horror to be unleashed upon the streets of London. All hell, it seemed to the detectives, had been let loose, and pandemonium set free, with the announcement of the latest and most terrible atrocity yet, perpetrated by The Whitechapel Murderer. Jack the Ripper had struck yet again!

Chapter 30
Millers Court and
Beyond

The historical facts inform us that at approximately 11.45 a.m. on the morning of November 9th, 1888, rent collector Thomas Bowyer peered through the window of 13 Miller's Court, Dorset Street in Whitechapel and saw the horrendously mutilated remains of Mary Kelly. Such were the wounds inflicted upon the poor woman that hardened, experienced police officers, viewing the scene of carnage, broke down in tears at the sight. None of the previous murders attributed to the killer known as Jack the Ripper had come close to matching the sheer barbarity and wanton destructiveness that had been perpetrated upon the body of Mary Kelly. The door to No. 13 was locked and, in the expectation that bloodhounds might be brought to the scene, the door wasn't opened until 1.30 p.m., by which time it had been announced by Superintendent Arnold, head of 'H' Division, (Whitechapel), that no bloodhounds were coming. Despite this fact, news of the horrific find and the gravity of the carnage inflicted upon the victim spread like wildfire through the police stations of the capital, New Street being no exception.

"Apparently, it's the worst yet," said Madden, addressing the assembled detectives at a hastily convened meeting of New Street personnel. "The Commissioner has ordered every station in the city to provide any spare manpower we can to assist with the investigation. I'm sending two constables and two detectives, you and you, Graves and Holliday." He pointed to the two chosen detectives, who nodded their acknowledgment.

"How bad is it, sir?" asked Hillman. "It can't be much worse than what he's already done, surely?"

"From what I've heard, Sergeant, it's like a charnel house at Miller's Court. The poor woman is hardly recognisable as a human being, by all accounts. There are masses of flesh, blood and human organs and tissue strewn all round the room. Most of those who've seen it so far have been physically sick at the sight, so I'm told."

"Bloody hell," said the sergeant, and similar murmurs could be heard around the room from the assembled officers.

"A *bloody hell* sounds a pretty accurate description of what they've found over there," Madden replied. "Anyway, we're going to be four men short here at New Street, so I have to take a man off your case, Inspector Norris. You'll have to manage without Sergeant Lee from now on."

"I understand, sir," said Norris. "Hopefully, we'll have news on our investigation quite soon. Hillman and myself are checking some things right now, and we may just be on to something before long."

"I hope so, Inspector, I really do. We seem to have expended a lot of manpower on this one, without any results so far."

"No more so than the boys on the Ripper case, sir."

"Mmm, yes, quite."

"And they have a lot more men on it than we do."

"Yes, you've made your point, I think, Norris. Now, the rest of you must do the best you can during our own shortage of personnel, and please, let's all pray to God that this infernal Jack the Ripper character is caught before too long, so we can all get back to normal policing."

The meeting over, the detectives collectively filed out of the muster room. A couple of them tried to pump Norris and Hillman for information. Everyone knew they were working on a 'sensitive' case, but details had been withheld, even from their colleagues within the station. The two men managed to stay tight-lipped, and gave nothing away, causing a great deal of speculation to be bandied about over the next few minutes. The majority of their fellow detectives decided by a small majority that Norris and Hillman must in some way be conducting an independent, undercover inquiry into the Ripper killings, running side by side with the official investigation. Neither man said or did anything to confirm or dispel the rumours that quickly reached their ears.

"Let them think whatever they like, Dylan. We're keeping to the rules on this one, and that way, whatever case we eventually make against whoever did this will stick all the better. Madden and those above him want confidentiality? Well, they've got it. I'm not about to let this slimy bastard slip through my fingers. We're getting close to him, old chum, I'm sure of it. I'd love it if we could nab our man before the Ripper boys nail their own murdering bastard."

"So, we get back to the files?"

"Too right we do. Let's snap to it, eh, Dylan? We've got a killer to catch."

The two men were soon back at work, checking the files of the Cullen case, but, before they could get far, a knock at Norris's office door interrupted them.

"What is it now?" shouted Norris, frustrated at this latest interruption.

The door opened, admitting Constable Fry, yet again.

"Sorry, sir," he said, as his head poked around the half-opened door.

"Now, what have you come to tell us this time, Fry? Are you coming to inform me they've caught Jack the Ripper?"

"Er, no, sir. Actually, Chief Inspector Madden said I was to come and get you. He wants to see both of you in his office."

"Oh, bollocks!" snapped Norris. "What have we done or said to upset the man this time?"

"I don't know, sir."

"Sorry, Fry, that wasn't directed at you. It was a rhetorical question."

"Oh, I see, sir," said Fry, refusing to admit he'd no idea what *rhetorical* meant.

A minute later, Norris and Hillman were once again standing before the desk of the Chief Inspector, who sat with a grave expression on his face.

"You look a bit worried, sir, if I might say so," Norris said, as he gazed at the face of his superior. Madden appeared to have aged ten years in the short time since the meeting in the detectives' muster room. "Is there something wrong?"

"I'm afraid so, Bert. I'd only just returned here from the meeting, just got back to work, and a runner arrived. We've had another murder."

"When you say, 'we', sir, do you mean another Jack the Ripper killing, or is this one of ours?"

"Ours, I'm afraid. On the underground, Bert. The body was found about a half hour ago, in the carriage works at Farringdon, stabbed, like the others. Damn it, it seems as if, as soon as word of a Ripper killing leaks onto the streets, our bloody killer strikes again. It's all too coincidental."

When Norris failed to reply immediately, appearing instead to be lost in thought, Madden spoke again.

"Bert, did you hear me, man? We've got another body on our hands."

Norris snapped out of his reverie and replied.

"Yes, sir, sorry, of course I heard you. It's just that I don't hold much with the idea of coincidence. A thought just occurred to me. Back at the beginning of the case, someone, their name escapes me now, suggested that our murders could have something to do with the Ripper killings. I dismissed the idea as being ridiculous. Now, I'm not so sure."

"You're telling me you think that these women could have been killed by Jack the Ripper?"

"I don't know. For one thing, they were travelling towards Whitechapel, rather than away from it, so they can't have witnessed the Ripper murders and been killed to keep them quiet, and the first two victims weren't the sort to be parading around the streets of Whitechapel late at night. But, what if they saw The

Ripper, after the killings, maybe covered in blood, or. . . no, none of it makes sense. Forget it. It's a stupid idea."

"At least you're applying yourself to other possibilities, Bert. That's not a bad thing. You don't seriously think the Ripper and our man are one and the same, then?"

"No, sir, I don't. At least, I'm not sure if there's a connection. But as for other possibilities, none of it's getting us anywhere, is it? Dylan and me had better get on down to the carriage works at Farringdon and take a look at the latest victim."

* * *

"What about the files, Bert?" asked Hillman, as the two men returned briefly to Norris's office before heading off to the Farringdon Carriage Works and the site of the latest body discovery.

"They'll be here when we get back, Dylan. We can't very well tell Madden we'll go and look at the body after we've read through the case files, now, can we?"

"I know that. I meant, do we leave them on the desk or clear them away? Someone may come in and, what with the fact we're supposed to keep this whole thing as quiet as possible. . . "

"Good point, old chum. I don't want to clear everything away and have to get it out again later, not after we've arranged everything in order like this. We'll lock the door when we go. No one is likely to try and break into my office, now, are they?"

In the cab on the way to the carriage works, Norris confided a thought to Hillman that had been bothering him since Madden had informed them of the latest killing.

"Dylan, something doesn't add up with this one, and we haven't even seen the body yet."

"How so, Bert?"

"Well, the other two women were killed on or in the vicinity of moving trains, yes?"

"Yes."

"Well then, how come all of a sudden a body turns up in the carriage works? Trains do not carry passengers to that place, even I'm certain of that, and I'm no expert on the underground railway.

If this poor woman was killed on a train, it had to be some way from where she was found, and the killer must have carried her body to the carriage works in order to dump it there, to be found. It doesn't fit with the previous killings."

"Are you thinking it may be another killer, unconnected with the first two?"

"I don't know what to think, Dylan, at least, not yet. I'm reserving judgment until we see the body and the surrounding scene. And another thing; I'd have thought the carriage works would be pretty much out of bounds to the general public. How did our killer get in there with a body?"

"Maybe he works there, Bert, or for the railway in some capacity and therefore has access to the carriage works."

"Mm, maybe," said Norris as he fell into deep thought, and Hillman, recognising his inspector's need for silence, held his tongue for the remainder of the relatively short journey to the carriage works.

As the two men stepped from the cab a few minutes later, Dylan Hillman waved in response to a hail from a constable waiting near the vaulted entrance to the carriage works, where myriad railway tracks appeared to run into the dark interior of the works, almost like snakes tunnelling their way into an underground grotto. As they walked towards the entrance, Norris broke his silence.

"You know, Dylan, I've got a feeling that we're very close to nabbing this bastard, but, somewhere along the way, we've missed something very obvious, and possibly very simple, that would have pointed us in his direction. Maybe he'll have been considerate enough to leave us a real clue this time, eh?"

"We'll find out soon enough, Bert," Hillman replied, as they followed the constable into the depths of the Metropolitan Railway's Farringdon Carriage Works, where the latest victim's remains waited to greet them. The vast, arched roof housed myriad carriages and other rolling stock, most awaiting some form of repair or maintenance. As Norris peered into the gloomy interior, which appeared to stretch almost as far as the eye could see, he made out dozens of railway carriages, standing ghost-like in the darkness, silent sentinels awaiting the attention that would see them returned to full productive use. Occasional gas lamps set high in the walls cast a thin, watery glare on the coachwork of one or two of the carriages, adding to the almost ethereal nature of their appearance in the half light.

The acrid and noxious stench of the underground railway lingered here in the carriage works, too, even though they were set aside from the main tracks that carried the rails through the network of labyrinthine tunnels that networked across the city. Norris and Hillman both grimaced as the aroma of smoke, sulphur, coal dust and stale water vapour assaulted their nostrils once again.

* * *

As in the previous two cases, the duty police surgeon doctor who'd been called to the murder scene was Doctor Marcus Roebuck. Norris recognised his distinctive tall frame and immaculate black suit from a distance, even though the physician was hunched over the body as he and Hillman approached. Two uniformed police officers stood in attendance, both known to Norris as being from the Moorgate Street Police Station. The doctor looked up at the sound of the detectives' approaching footsteps and rose to meet them.

"Inspector, Sergeant, I wish I could say it's a pleasure to see you again."

"Afternoon, sir," said one of the sergeants.

"Hello, Doctor, and, er, Sergeant. . . ?"

"Merrydew, sir, and this is Sergeant Crump," said the older and slightly taller of the two officers. "We got here as soon as we got the call from that gentleman over there." Merrydew pointed in the direction of a man dressed in workmen's attire, standing about thirty yards away, in the company of a constable Norris had previously not noticed. Behind them, another gathering stood, comprised of about ten or twelve railway employees, all agog at the scene being played out before them.

Some chance of keeping this lot quiet, thought Norris.

Roebuck's voice broke into his thoughts.

"This one's a bit different, Inspector."

"How so, Doctor?"

"She struggled, or at least put up something of a fight. Her hands show signs of defensive wounds, as if she tried to ward off the fatal blow from his knife. Her face is slashed, too, as though he struck out at her in an effort to shock or subdue her long enough for him to plunge the knife into her chest, poor woman. Another thing, she's been dead for a number of hours. The blood on her clothes is congealed, and her skin too pale for this to have taken place recently. She's also gone into rigor. I'd say, at a guess, she was killed last night or in the early hours of this morning. I'll know more when I do the post mortem examination, of course."

"So she may have been murdered before the latest killing by Jack the Ripper?"

"I've heard about that one, and yes, that's possible. Is it significant?"

"It could be," said Norris, thinking again of the possible, though highly unlikely link between the railway murderer and Jack the Ripper. *If this woman died before the Ripper's latest victim, then it's unlikely the killers are one and the same. What motive could he have for killing her prior to killing the prostitute in Miller's Court? Then again, if he had two differing agendas, one personal, one against the whores of Whitechapel in general, anything is possible.*

Norris and Hillman now drew close to the body of the latest victim. The woman, her body spread face-up across the tracks of one of the lines leading into the carriage shed, appeared to be around twenty-five to thirty years of age, dressed respectably in a shawl, green pinafore dress and clean brown boots that displayed little wear and tear. Her hair, messy in death, was blonde, very long, well-tended, and appeared tainted by the stains from the oil and coal dust that infected the ground on which her body now lay. As the doctor had said, there were visible wounds on her face and on her hands, giving a clear indication that the woman had attempted to ward off her killer before he struck the fatal blow to her chest with his knife. She'd been pretty in life, that much was clear, and Norris felt a pang of regret that he had failed so far in his attempts to bring this vicious killer to justice.

"Any idea who she was?" asked Norris of anyone and everyone present.

"There's a purse, sir," said Sergeant Merrydew. "It was over there, under that carriage. There was a small daily diary inside with her details written in it. She was Amy Cobbold, of Verney Street, sir."

"Well done, Merrydew. Now, did she drop it there? Or did he throw it there? Why? We've never had a clue before. Either our man is getting sloppy, or he bloody well wants us to catch him, Dylan."

"I don't believe he'd want to be caught, sir, so that leaves sloppy, if you ask me," Hillman replied.

"But why get sloppy now? He's been careful so far, made us jump through hoops and still not come up with anything. Why leave us such an obvious lead to her identity when we've had to struggle to find out who the others were by visiting the church and getting the vicar to identify them, or... Wait a minute, old chum. I've got it!"

"Eh? Have you? Got what exactly, Bert?"

"You remember I said we'd missed something? Something simple? It's just come back to me. We need to get back to the station right now, Dylan. It's there, in the notes. We've got him, I know we have."

"What? How?"

"Listen," said Norris, turning to Merrydew. "Let Sergeant Crump attend to taking statements from the railway employees, including Mr. Whatever-his-name-is who found the body. I want you to go and inform this poor woman's relatives of her death. I'd say she was living with her parents and that she attended St. Giles's Church, and also belonged to The Reverend Martin Bowker's Bible Study Group, as I'm sure her parents will confirm, if they're at home. If they do, I want you to come right around to New Street and tell me so. Do you understand?"

"Yes, sir," said a slightly bemused Sergeant Merrydew. "But my own Inspector..."

"Would that be Inspector Hall?"

"Yes, sir, he'll be here soon. He was delayed by another case."

"Don't worry about that. Tell Crump to inform him I've been here on Chief Inspector Madden's orders and that this is now my case. He'll understand, I assure you. Now go, Sergeant. There's not a moment to lose."

"Yes, right away, sir," said Merrydew, who promptly trekked over to where Crump was interviewing the small gathering of railway employees. A minute or so later, he departed and Norris turned his attention to Doctor Roebuck.

"Please, Doctor, get the body to the morgue as soon as you can and commence the post mortem examination. I'll be along as soon as I can, but Sergeant Hillman and I have something very important to attend to."

"Yes, of course. But, please, Inspector Norris, why the sudden departure? Surely you wish to survey the scene for further clues and evidence? I've never seen you quite so animated and agitated, if I may be so bold as to say so."

"All in good time, Doctor, all in good time. I've just remembered something that might save us all a lot of time and trouble here, and put a killer in the hands of justice, too."

"Well, it's all very irregular of course, but..."

"Doctor, please, I do know what I'm doing."

"Then of course I shall do as you request."

"Thank you. Come on, Dylan."

Norris grabbed hold of Hillman and physically began to drag him from the carriage works.

"Okay, Bert, I'm coming. What's the rush?"

"I'll explain as we go, but hurry. I believe we can lay our hands on the killer today, unless I'm very much mistaken. But first, we have to confirm my idea and I think we'll do that when we've read what I'm sure we'll find in the notes."

"Bloody hell, Bert, slow down!" exclaimed Hillman, as Norris ran ahead and the sergeant found himself trailing in the inspector's wake. Truly, if ever there was a man with a mission in mind, and the total desire to carry it put, it was the newly rejuvenated Albert Norris at that moment.

"Now, Bert, what's this all about?" asked Hillman, as the cab sped them through the streets of London back towards the police station and Norris's office, where the notes and reports on the case awaited them on the desk where they'd left them. "You said you'd explain as we went."

And so, Norris did.

Chapter 31
Denial

"No, no, and no again! You surely cannot be serious, Inspector." Chief Inspector Joshua Madden was almost apoplectic in his rage, his face flushed red, his eyes burning with anger.

"But, sir. . . ."

"But sir, nothing! I've never heard anything so preposterous in my life. You should be at the Carriage Works, searching for evidence in this latest murder and instead, you come here, throwing your ridiculous theory in my face as if it's irrefutable proof. It just won't do, Norris. It really won't."

Norris was himself becoming angry at the chief inspector's refusal to listen to him, and to accept what Norris felt to be the solution to the case.

"Sir!" he shouted, feeling that a show of belligerence was the only way he was going to get through to his boss. "Do you really think I'd have left the scene at Farringdon if I hadn't good cause to do so? Hillman and I spent all morning sifting through the reports and statements from the murders of Clara Forshaw and Ann Cullen and I knew there was something there that I'd missed – a discrepancy that didn't show up right away, but was waiting for me to find it. Well, that's why we came back, because I knew where to look. I'd remembered, don't you see? And now, there is the proof sitting on your desk, and you refuse to accept what I've brought you, because it doesn't sit well with what you and everyone else have probably been hoping I'd find in this case."

Norris and Hillman had indeed returned to the station and quickly found what Norris was looking for. When all the statements had been combined and cross-checked, certain things had shown themselves to Norris in the various witness statements and in the words of the congregation of St. Giles's church and the members of the Bellhaven household. Oddly enough, it had been a fairly innocuous remark contained within one of those statements that had set a train of thought in motion within the inspector's brain. This had then lurked and lingered at the back of his subconscious mind, waiting for the moment to reveal itself. That moment had presented itself to him as he'd looked at the body of the newly deceased Amy Cobbold, on the tracks of the Farringdon Carriage Works.

It hadn't taken long for Norris and Hillman to find what they sought, once the two men set to work. Hillman, although shocked at Norris's theory as they'd travelled back to New Street, had soon come to wholeheartedly believe in his inspector's hypothesis. Everything seemed to fit, and Hillman even felt a little mad at himself for not spotting the telltale clue during the three days Norris had been on his enforced 'sick leave.'

Now, the sergeant could only join in his inspector's frustration as the pair stood together before Joshua Madden, only to be told that the chief inspector would give no credence to Norris's idea.

"And just what do you mean by that, Inspector?" asked Madden. "Don't you think I want to find the killer as much as you do?"

"I don't know, sir," said Norris, chancing his arm far further than prudence allowed. "I told you once that I'd like to know if you wanted me to find the real killer, or if just anyone would do. Well, now the time has come when I think I've discovered who the killer is, and you won't even bloody well listen to me."

"That's enough!" Madden shouted, and Hillman was certain the whole station could have heard him.

Norris fell silent, and Madden appeared to be either breathing very heavily as he took stock of the situation, or on the verge of experiencing a heart attack, so red in the face had he grown in the few seconds it had taken Norris to deliver his damning indictment.

His chest appeared to be rising and falling with ever greater rapidity and Hillman waited, along with Norris, for whatever would come next. It would either be a very swift dismissal, Norris knew, or a considered and, hopefully, optimistic response.

Albert Norris had always known that Joshua Madden, despite his apparent bluster and conformist exterior, would go out on a limb for his officers if he felt they had something worth going out on that limb for. He hoped Madden would now see this as one of those times. He'd weathered the storm of the chief inspector's temper, and now Norris knew he must wait to find out if the expected calm would arrive, and, if it did, would he get the response he'd wanted?

"I cannot under any circumstances endorse you running amok and accusing all and sundry of being this heinous murderer, Inspector, you should know that. Allow me an hour to review what you've brought me, and I promise you, if I feel you are anywhere near reaching a solution to the case as a result of what you've presented here, then I'll discuss the next step with you. Is that clear?"

"Quite clear, sir, and thank you. Under the circumstances, I can't ask for more. I do assure you, though, that I'm sure he's our man."

"And like I've always said, Bert, I need proof, hard evidence, before making any sort of move against a man like that. Go, do what you have to do, and come back in an hour."

Norris and Hillman withdrew gracefully from Madden's office and stopped to collect two mugs of tea from the canteen before returning to their office.

"Are you sure about all this, Bert?" asked Hillman, as they sat sipping their hot tea, both pleased not to have been hauled over the coals a little more dramatically.

"You've seen it for yourself, old chum," Norris replied. "All we had to do was add it all together. The clues were there, the little discrepancies that just needed adding together. He was clever, Dylan, bloody clever, always one step ahead of the game, but I'll tell you now, my friend, he's the most vile and vicious beast we could hope to meet upon the streets of London."

"I know, Bert, and I accept what we've found. But, what if Madden *won't* accept it? What are we going to do then?"

Norris fixed his friend with a steely glare as he replied. "Dylan, old chum, I'll tell you what we're going to do. If Madden won't let us proceed with our case, then I'll go to the bloody Commissioner myself if I have to, and if *he* won't help, then. . . then I'll bloody well go and deal with this murdering bastard anyway!"

"I was kind of hoping you'd say that, Bert!" Hillman grinned. "And for now, what do we do until Madden's read through it all?"

Norris smiled a knowing smile, looked out of the window at the gunmetal sky hanging over the bustling city, turned back to his sergeant and replied, "More tea, sergeant?"

Chapter 32
New Respect

Norris and Hillman, having wiled away an hour rechecking their findings, were about to leave the office and return to Madden's when they were disturbed by a knock on the door.

"Come in," Norris called, a little irritated at having to suffer an interruption just as he felt he was about to coax Madden into allowing him to make a bold move in the case. His irritation dissipated, however, as Sergeants Merrydew and Crump entered the office, closing the door behind them.

"Sergeants," said Norris. "I wasn't expecting you so soon. Do you have anything to report that might be of significance?"

"We do, sir," Merrydew responded, acting as spokesman for the pair. "As you requested, I visited the home of Miss Cobbold and sadly, there is no family at her address. I spoke to a neighbour, who told me the woman had lived there for about two years, since her parents died, soon after each other. As far as Mrs. Walker next door was aware, there are no other living relatives, or so Miss Cobbold had told her in passing conversation."

"So, no one to mourn the victim, eh? Sad news indeed, Merrydew. Anything else?"

"Yes, sir, and that's thanks to Davey, here." Merrydew nodded to Crump, who took up the conversation.

"Sir, you asked me to take statements from the railway people at the carriage works. Well, it was quickly plain that most of them had nothing to tell at all, but one of them, a Mr. Evan Jones, was on duty at around three a.m. when he heard a strange noise

225

from the road that runs alongside the north fence of the carriage works site."

"A noise, Crump? What kind of noise?"

"He says it was the sound of hooves, sir, and the unmistakable sound of a carriage as it rattled on the cobbles. The streets around the carriage works aren't the best paved in the city, so it's rare for decent carriages to ply their way along there at the best of times, according to Jones. To hear one at three in the morning, well, that was odd, to his way of thinking. Anyway, a little later, he thought he saw a cloaked figure hurrying from the carriage shed, running towards the perimeter fence. He'd seen nothing in between the original sound of the coach and the sight of the running man, as he'd been busy working on a track repair, but he told me he'd swear to the little he did see, sir."

"Very good, well done, Crump," Norris replied, as Crump ended his report. The inspector looked across at Hillman and gave the sergeant a knowing wink. "This is the first time anyone has seen or heard anything," he remarked. "It looks as if things are finally beginning to fall our way, eh, Dylan?"

"Certainly looks that way, sir," Hillman replied.

With Merryweather and Crump dismissed with a great vote of thanks from Norris, he and Hillman made their way back along the corridor to the chief inspector's office. Norris knocked and entered, without waiting for a response from his boss.

Joshua Madden was sitting with his head resting on his hands as the two detectives made their entry. He looked up, said nothing about Norris having failed to await a response to his knock and instead, his face appeared to exhibit a grave, solemn, almost crestfallen look.

"Sir?"

"Ah, Norris, Hillman, come in. Sit down, both of you."

Surprised at the invitation, the two men did as ordered, and sat on the two straight-backed wooden chairs that served as visitors' chairs in the chief inspector's office. Madden cast his eyes down at the documents Norris had left with him earlier, shuffled a couple of the papers in a quick rearrangement, as though putting off the moment when he'd have to say something, then looked up at the inspector and his sergeant.

"These files give me great cause for concern, Bert, though of course, as I'm sure you're aware, they constitute no more than circumstantial, rather than substantive evidence, and supposition, strong though it may be."

"True, sir, but we now have this as well."

Norris passed the hastily written copy of Evan Jones's statement, as provided by Sergeant Crump. Madden read it quickly, and placed it on top of the other documents on his desk.

"I don't suppose there's anything I can do to stop you taking this further," said Madden. "I told you to catch the murderer and, if you're correct about this, then we must let the law take its course, no matter what the consequences may be for others."

"I've been trying to tell you that all along, sir, with all due respect."

"I know you have, Bert, but you must try to understand the pressure I've been under. Everyone from the Home Secretary down has been trying to tell me that the case revolved around some mysterious plot to undermine the future of the underground railway, and thus the future of London's infrastructure, as we move towards a new century. Those people are not only influential, but highly intelligent and I had no reason to suppose they could be so far wide of the mark."

"I know all that, sir, but our job as police officers is to uphold the law, without fear or favour, is it not?"

"It is, Bert, and I'm grateful to you for helping to remind me of that."

Madden picked up one particular document, a statement taken by Detective Sergeant Dove during Norris's enforced absence from the case. He held it up so Norris and Hillman could see clearly what he was referring to.

"This statement in particular, taken in the context with which you've suggested it, now becomes rather more damning than at first sight, doesn't it?"

"I have to agree, sir. When Dylan and I went through everything a second and then a third time, it leapt out at me. I knew I'd been missing something, that there was more in those statements than I'd first seen, but until now, I'd been unable to pick upon it. Perhaps because of the Drago thing, and the clear mind it's left me with, I was able to focus on things a bit better than I have for a long time."

"Yes, perhaps you're right. I'm very pleased about that, by the way, Bert. You got lucky, but at least you can probably sleep at night again, eh?"

"Yes, but, how did you know I wasn't sleeping well?"

"There's not much I don't know about the officers serving under me, Bert. At least, give me credit for that. I've seen that look in your eyes, the one that said you were crying out for a good night's sleep, the bags under your eyes and the stoop when you walked. They've all gone, and I have a feeling the old Albert Norris has returned to the fold, unless I'm much mistaken."

"He certainly has, sir," remarked Dylan Hillman. "He's been fair wearing me out lately, what with his sudden enthusiasm for everything we've been doing. His mind's a damn sight sharper, too... er, if you don't mind me saying so, Bert."

Norris smiled, and Madden spoke again.

"I don't think he minds at all, Sergeant, do you, Bert?"

"Pleased that you've noticed the change, old chum," said Norris, and Hillman breathed a sigh of relief. He had, after all, spoken a bit out of turn, speaking about Norris in front of the chief inspector as he'd just done.

"Now, as for this. . . " Madden held up the document once again. "Taken together with the other files you've given me, it's now clear to me that we must proceed as you've suggested."

"Thank you, sir. I appreciate your confidence in me."

"It's maybe been a long time coming, Bert, but it's a confidence you've earned and deserved. I'm sorry if you feel I've not been as supportive as I should have been."

Albert Norris was flabbergasted. Never in a thousand years would he have expected such an admission and an apology from the normally hard-hearted and stiff-upper-lipped Joshua Madden. When he spoke again, it was with a new-found respect for his boss.

"Forget it, sir. You had a job to do and so did me and Dylan. It was the same job, but you were being led in one direction by the brass while we were getting the true picture from the streets. How do you wish me to proceed, sir?"

"How do you *want* to proceed, Inspector Norris?"

Norris rose from his chair, reached across the desk and took hold of the statement, which Madden had realised was now of great importance.

"May I, sir?"

Madden nodded as Norris took the document and passed it to Hillman, who folded it and placed it in the inside pocket of his jacket.

"With your permission, Chief Inspector, Hillman and I will be on our way."

"You haven't actually answered my question yet, Bert."

"Oh, the one about how I wish to proceed?"

"Yes, that's the one."

Madden and Norris had returned to their normal stance of verbal sparring, though now there were smiles on both men's faces as they indulged in their roles.

"Oh, right, of course, well, yes, sir. If you don't mind, Dylan and I will be on our way, as I said, first stop, Lewisham Place, Holborn, where I intend to have a rather serious conversation with our friend Mr. Roland Soames, esteemed butler to Mr. Laurence Bellhaven!"

Madden said nothing, merely nodding as Norris and Hillman took their leave of his office. Shuffling the rest of Norris's case files into a neat pile, the chief inspector leaned back in his chair, a weary sigh passing his lips as he did so. Whatever happened in the next day or so would, without doubt, have a profound effect on many futures. One thought raced through his mind over and again as he contemplated the potentially disastrous outcome on his own future, if Norris had got the whole case terribly wrong.

For God's sake, especially for God's sake, for He will have the final say in this when justice is meted out, and for yours and mine, Albert Norris, I hope you're right.

By then of course, it was far too late to stop the chain of events that Norris had now set in motion, even if Madden had wanted to – but then, in a moment of supreme pride, he realised that he *didn't* want to. Norris was *his* man, damn it; and a bloody good detective, too, and he was right, the job came first, and the rest of them, Home Secretary and all, could go to Hell as far as he, Joshua Madden, was concerned.

Chapter 33
An Uncomfortable Visit

The afternoon daylight appeared to be giving way to a premature evening as the cab pulled up outside the Bellhaven home on Lewisham Place. Heavy clouds rolling in from the east partially obscured the weak, autumn sunshine, casting their shadow of grey over the streets of the city. The sky seemed to carry a malevolence in keeping with the mood of the day, as far as Norris was concerned. He certainly felt no desire to be here, and knew that his case, though drawing to a close, was about to reach what he always called the 'messy' stage, when people and events could jump one way or another, often with extremely varying results.

Norris and Hillman alighted, and Norris looked up once more at the grandiose façade of the house's front elevation. He no longer felt the minor sense of awe he'd previously experienced when viewing the grand exterior of the house. Built on the proceeds of wealth as it may be, the home of Laurence Bellhaven was, Norris now knew, no different from any other dwelling within the city, or in the world, come to that. The trials, tribulations and manipulations of one's fellow human beings, the keeping of secrets and the machinations and sexual deviations that take place behind closed doors, are much the same in such homes as in the poorest dwellings, he'd concluded.

He and Hillman stood on the familiar steps and waited for a response to Hillman's loud application of the ornate brass door knocker.

The door slowly swung open a few seconds later, to reveal, not, as expected the dapper figure of Roland Soames, but a younger, similarly attired man, tall, clean-shaven, with dark, wavy hair, and an air of superiority about him that identified him as an archetypal butler.

"Yes?" the man inquired of the unexpected visitors standing on the threshold of his domain. "May I help you, gentlemen?"

"I'm Detective Inspector Norris, and this is Detective Sergeant Hillman, of the Metropolitan Police. I was expecting to see Mr. Soames."

"Ah, my predecessor, Detective Inspector. I'm afraid Mr. Soames is no longer in Mr. Bellhaven's employ. Hence, my presence."

"Quite," said Norris, rather taken aback by the surprising appearance of a new butler at the house.

"Perhaps, in that case, I could have a word with Mr. Bellhaven?"

"The master is not at home, Inspector. . . Norris, did you say? I believe he will return from his office in an hour or two. You may contact him there if you wish, of course. I can give you the address, if it is a matter of any urgency."

It was clear to Norris that this new man knew little, or nothing, of the events surrounding the case. He held no desire for long conversations with the new Bellhaven butler.

"I know the address, thank you, Mr. . . ?"

"The name is Lawton, sir. Just Lawton will do."

Butler or not, this man is a pompous ass, Norris concluded.

"I've no time to travel all the way to the offices of the Metropolitan Railway, Lawton. I shall speak to your mistress in his stead."

"I'm not sure if the Mistress is at home to visitors, sir."

"She'll be at home to me, Lawton. Now, please go and inform Mrs. Bellhaven that the police wish to speak with her. Tell her it is a matter of urgency, and that we shall not take up too much of her valuable time."

"Very well, though I'm sure the mistress will view this as a great intrusion," said the butler. He turned on his heel and left the detectives standing in the marbled hallway as he disappeared up the staircase towards the first floor.

While they waited, Norris prowled the entrance hall while Hillman stood quietly awaiting the reappearance of the butler, hopefully with his Mistress in tow. Norris found himself next to the hall stand, on which there rested a number of envelopes – probably, he thought, letters awaiting posting. His natural inquisitiveness as a detective saw him quietly lift the top item and slowly sort through the small pile. Of the six envelopes on the stand, four were written in a strong hand and, from the addressees on the envelopes, obviously written by Laurence Bellhaven to business or personal contacts. The other two, contained in smaller envelopes embossed with a delicate, violet-hued floral pattern in the top left corner, were in a different, lighter hand, obviously that of the lady of the house, judging by the fact that the envelopes were both addressed to ladies in two differing London locations. He thought it extremely unlikely that Laurence Bellhaven would be corresponding with a Mrs. Lorelei Grafton, or Lady Menzies of Leith, and certainly not on floral decorated stationery.

Before replacing the last of the envelopes, he beckoned to Hillman, who walked across to join him by the hall stand.

"Look at this," Norris whispered, holding up one of the envelopes for Hillman to examine.

"What am I supposed to see?" asked Hillman. "It's an envelope, Bert."

"I know it's an envelope, old chum, but look at this."

Norris withdrew a paper from the inside pocket of his jacket and passed it to the sergeant, who looked closely at it for a few seconds.

"Well, I'll be. . . "

"Shush," Norris cautioned, as he caught sight of the butler's highly polished boots preceding the rest of the man as he walked slowly down the staircase. Florence Bellhaven walked about three stairs behind him, immaculately attired in a green day dress, a three-strand pearl necklace decorating her pale, slim neck. Norris quickly arranged the pile of letters in approximately the same order as he'd found them in, though he doubted anyone would be checking them after he'd gone.

"Good day to you once again, gentlemen," said Florence Bell-haven, reaching the bottom of the stairs and walking across to Norris, offering her hand as she did so. Norris took the proffered hand gently and released it almost as quickly, refusing the invitation to lift and kiss the hand as a gentleman might do. "Lawton informs me you wish to speak to me on a matter of urgency concerning... er, Soames, of all people."

"That's correct. We wished to ask him some more questions, but it appears he's no longer in your employ?"

"Please, not here in the hall, Inspector," said the lady of the house, conscious that Lawton, the new butler, remained standing to one side, awaiting instructions. "Come into the sitting room. We'll talk there."

Then, to Norris's horror, she made a bee-line for the hall stand, where she quickly swept up the pile of letters, passing them immediately into the hand of the butler.

"I shall be quite safe with these gentlemen for a few minutes, Lawton. Please take these and place them in the posting box while I'm engaged."

"Yes, of course, Ma'am," said Lawton, who then withdrew to make his departure via the servants' entrance. Norris realised that even the butler was denied the use of the front door for his own comings and goings, even on the official business of his master and mistress.

With Lawton gone, Florence Bellhaven led the two detectives into the sitting room, where they politely waited until the lady was seated. She declined to invite them to join her, so, standing by the fireplace, a few feet away from where she was sitting, Norris began.

"I had wished to speak to Soames, or in his absence, Mr. Bell-haven, but I appear to be hampered on both counts."

"My husband is at his office, Inspector, going about his lawful and gainful business. As for *Mister* Soames, that man is indeed no longer employed by my husband. He showed disloyalty and betrayed our confidence, contrary to all his position allowed for."

"In what way?" asked Norris, already only too aware of what answer to expect.

"Why, by revealing private household information to you, of course."

"But, Mrs. Bellhaven, Soames was replying to police questions relating to a murder inquiry – the murder, I might remind you, of your own husband's private secretary."

"I'm aware of that, Inspector, but Soames was our butler, which is a trusted position, you must agree. When a man like that enters service, he is well aware of the fact that the privacy of the household is of paramount importance. Revealing gossip and tittle-tattle overhead by way of eavesdropping at a door, even to the police, is certainly not what one would expect of a man in his position. What our servants do in their own time and outside these walls, is their own business, but once they close the doors and are contained within these walls, which form not only their place of employment but their home, too, then they must abide by the confidentiality imposed upon them by my husband's strict rules of the house."

"How long had Soames been with you?" asked Hillman, standing a little way from Norris, near the slowly ticking grandfather clock.

"Ten years, Sergeant. Why?"

Bloody hell, thought Norris. *She can dismiss ten years of faithful service just like that.*

"What about his wife? She was your cook, if I'm correct."

"Yes, but of course, it would not have been acceptable to keep Mrs. Soames in service at the same time as dismissing her husband. They were both asked to leave, though of course, Mrs. Soames received an adequate reference, whereas Soames himself did not."

Norris knew that Roland Soames would never find another position in his chosen employment without a good reference from his previous employer, and he marvelled at the hard-heartedness displayed by this woman, who looked and sounded so genteel. After all, the man had simply responded to police questioning, and had hardly betrayed some deep family secrets. Now, more than ever, Norris was certain that this household held secrets which those within it would prefer stayed hidden behind its elegant façade.

"It's vital we speak to Soames, Mrs. Bellhaven. Do you have a forwarding address for him and his wife?"

"I do not, Inspector. They left rather hurriedly, as you might imagine, and this had been their home for ten years, so they'd hardly have anywhere to go at the drop of a hat, would they? So, as to where they may have gone when they departed, I can be of no help whatever."

Callous to the core, thought Hillman, echoing precisely the thoughts of Albert Norris.

"There was another murder last night," said Hillman quietly, from his position by the grandfather clock.

"I'm aware of that, Sergeant. That was partly the reason for my husband being in his office so late in the day. The company is most concerned that this latest murder will result in a degree of negative publicity for the Metropolitan Railway, and they are meeting now to discuss ways of minimising the effects, so I believe."

I'll bet they are, thought Norris. *And looking for more ways to keep the whole affair quiet, too.*

"A woman is dead, as a result of an act of wanton violence, Mrs. Bellhaven. That is my first and only concern. Soames holds information that I require and I must locate him."

"You think perhaps he is your killer?"

"I cannot discuss my theories regarding such matters, as I'm sure you understand. Would any of the other servants know where Soames has gone?" Norris was growing impatient and it was beginning to show in his clipped sentences, as Hillman was very aware.

"I believe he sometimes went to the pub, The Crooked Man, with Peacock, the gardener. Maybe he knows where Soames has gone."

"Thank you," was Norris's curt reply. He'd had enough of this woman for the time being.

"You're welcome, Inspector," she replied, though he was sure she didn't mean it.

"Is Peacock at work today?" asked Hillman.

"He was, Sergeant, but he finished his hours some time ago. In fact, you'll possibly find him in The Crooked Man already, if I know the man."

"We'll be going now, Mrs. Bellhaven, but please inform your husband on his return that we will be wanting to speak to him very soon."

"But surely I've told you all you need to know? What can my husband possibly add, Inspector?"

"That'll be between me and Mr. Bellhaven, Ma'am. Now, we'll be taking our leave. Don't bother ringing for Lawton. We can find our own way out."

Leaving Florence Bellhaven almost open-mouthed at the apparent gross social impropriety of not allowing themselves to be seen out by the butler, Norris and Hillman quickly withdrew from the room, crossed the hall and exited through the front door, Hillman giving it a specially hard slam behind him as he closed it and followed Norris down the steps to the pavement.

"Phew, she's a hard nut, that one, Bert. I'd never have thought it of her."

"I know, Dylan. And then there was that bloody envelope."

"I could hardly believe it. You know what this means, don't you?"

"Only too well, old chum, only too well. Things have just got a bit more complicated, don't you think? We may have to wait a day before we end this case, after all."

Hillman looked grave, as he and Norris both allowed themselves a few seconds to absorb the enormity of the discovery they'd just made while waiting for Florence Bellhaven to attend upon them. Hillman looked at Norris and asked, "And now?"

"Now, Dylan," Norris replied, as he raised his hand, summoning their cab from its waiting position at the end of the strect, "we head for The Crooked Man. As a matter of fact, I could do with a pint myself."

Chapter 34
The Crooked Man

The Crooked Man public house, situated as it was, something over a mile from the Bellhaven residence, in a less than salubrious street far removed from the genteel surroundings of Lewisham Place, was, nevertheless, a haven of fervent activity. As Norris and Hillman entered through the double doors that led into the saloon bar, their nostrils were immediately assaulted by the heady smell of beer, spirits and other less tangible aromas. Music filled the smoke-laden air as a lone pianist sat banging out a succession of raucous melodies in keeping with the establishment's credentials, the piano desperately in need of retuning, and many of the less than sober denizens of the pub were doing their best to sing along, whether or not they knew the actual words to the songs.

Norris and Hillman surveyed the scene, trying their best to locate Peacock, the Bellhaven gardener, through the smoky haze. Hillman was the first to see their man. He touched Norris on the elbow and pointed to a table in the far corner of the room, where Peacock was sitting with two other men, both around his own age, neither of whom was Roland Soames. The two police officers picked their way through the maze of closely gathered tables, assorted staggering drunks and outstretched legs, until they arrived, unscathed, at Peacock's table.

Sensing the presence of the newcomers, Peacock and his two cronies looked up.

"Why, if it isn't Inspector Morris!" said Peacock, who'd obviously imbibed a couple of pints or more of beer already.

"That's *Detective* Inspector *Norris*," Hillman corrected, in a voice loud enough to be heard over the raucous din of the room.

"Right, Norris it is then. 'Ow can I 'elp you, Inspector?"

"I'm trying to locate the whereabouts of Roland Soames, Mr. Peacock. Mrs. Bellhaven thought you might know where he'd gone after his dismissal from the Bellhaven household."

"You mean you 'aven't 'eard?"

"Heard what?" asked Norris.

"Old Roland's dead, Inspector. Snuffed it, 'e 'as. Threw 'imself in the Thames, over by Burrell's Wharf, a couple of days ago. Couldn't live with the shame of gettin' the old 'eave 'o from 'is position, that's what I reckon."

Shock filled the faces of the detectives. News of a suicide at The Isle of Dogs, a few miles down river from their own location, certainly wouldn't have filtered through to New Street, at least not if there were no suspicious circumstances attached to the case.

"How do you know it was Soames?" asked Hillman.

" 'Cause 'is own missus told me, didn't she? She were in 'ere last night. Bereft, she were. Came specially to tell me, she did, me and 'im bein' friends as we were, like."

"And how did the police know it was Soames, and how did they find his wife so quickly?" asked Hillman.

"E 'ad 'is wallet on 'im when 'e went in the river. 'Im and the wife 'ad moved into her cousin's 'ouse, on Richmond Road, and old Roland 'ad put 'er address down in 'is wallet."

"And they said it was a definite suicide?" Norris asked.

"No doubts, as far as I know."

"Poor Missus Soames," said one of Peacock's companions.

"Aye, poor indeed. That's what she'll be, without 'er 'usband to support 'er," said Peacock gloomily.

"I'm sorry to hear of Soames's death," Norris ventured. "I was hoping he could help me."

Peacock grimaced.

"Last time 'e did that, it cost 'im 'is job, didn't it? Mind you, Mrs. Soames said as it wasn't your fault. Them Bellhavens turned right nasty after you and your other people 'ad visited us at the 'ouse. Held a real inquisition, they did, wanting to know who'd told the police about the row old man Bellhaven 'ad with Clara. Soames, bein' more of a gent than Bellhaven 'imself, owned up right away. Said as it were the right thing to do under the circumstances. Well, Bellhaven went off the deep end, 'e did. There were some shoutin' behind the closed doors of the study a bit later and next thing I knows, old Soames and 'is wife were gone the next day, and now, this. Terrible tragic it is, terrible tragic. Old Soames came in 'ere the following night, after getting' dismissed, and told me 'as 'ow 'e could 'ave said a lot more. I asked 'im what 'e meant and 'e told me 'e could have let slip just where the master went in 'is carriage when 'e went out at night. Seems old Bellhaven didn't just exercise 'is 'orse, Inspector. 'E liked to play around with the ladies, accordin' to Soames and used to pick up prossies in the carriage and screw 'em in it, before goin' 'ome to 'is little wife. Anyways, that's what Soames said."

"Well, thank you, Mr. Peacock. That's all very interesting, but of course, no one can verify that piece of information, now Mr. Soames has gone, can they?"

"Bellhaven can," the old man grumbled.

"Yes. Well, we'll maybe have a word with him about that."

Norris looked at Hillman, who nodded in reply to the inspector, acknowledging the signal to leave.

There being little else they could extract of value from Peacock or his friends, Norris threw a few coins on the table. "Have a drink on us, boys," he said, as he and Hillman beat a retreat from The Crooked Man. Only when they'd reached the street did he turn to Hillman and say, "Well, we never got our pint, Dylan, old chum, did we?"

"We didn't get much at all, except for a damn good shock, eh, Bert? Who'd have thought Soames would have done himself in, or that Bellhaven visits prostitutes in his spare time?"

"Do you really believe it was suicide, Dylan?"

"You mean, you don't believe it was?"

"I don't know, Dylan. I'd like to know if he went into the river at Burrell's Wharf and died where he was found, or whether he went in upriver and was carried down to the wharf by the current. If he went in at the wharf, I'd put it down as suspicious, because why would he go all the way to the Isle of Dogs to drown himself when he could have gone in from much nearer home? Richmond Road is miles from the Isle. As for the prossies, I think Soames was telling Peacock the truth, although I don't know how he knew what his employer was up to."

"So you think he may have been killed to prevent him from talking to us?"

"I could be wrong, but I see it as a possibility, yes."

"Then what do we do next?"

"We go back to the station and see if Madden's still there. We tell him everything we've come across today, especially about that bloody envelope, because Dylan, as you and I both know, that envelope has just thrown a great big complication into our case. If what you and me now believe to be true really *is* true, the cat will certainly be among the pigeons when the boss hears the news."

"Well, he and the top brass always said it was a conspiracy, didn't they?" Hillman smiled.

"They did, Dylan, but I doubt they ever expected it to be a conspiracy such as we've just discovered."

"The thing is, Bert, why kill the third girl, Amy Cobbold? She can't have had anything to do with it, can she?"

"I doubt the second girl, Ann Cullen, had anything to do with it, either. I think they were both killed as smokescreens, Dylan, to make us think we were dealing with a bona fide serial killer, another Jack the Ripper. For God's sake, we could still be dealing with Jack the Ripper, for all we know. No, Clara Forshaw was the sole genuine target in this case Dylan, old chum, I'm sure of it. The others. . . well, like I said, smokescreens, a ploy to throw us off the real scent, and it very nearly worked."

"Bloody cold-hearted as they come, eh, Bert?"

"Oh yes, cold-hearted, all right. But I'll tell you this, Dylan. They'll damn well swing for this, if there's any justice in the world."

* * *

Evening had already usurped afternoon by the time they pulled up outside New Street once again. The clouds that had gathered over the city earlier, continued to hang heavily over the city and the air felt dank and stale, as though the day itself had grown tired and was ready to surrender to the onrush of night. Norris and Hillman emerged from their cab, dismissed the driver and the two stood and stretched their aching limbs almost in unison as they stood on the steps of the police station. It had been a long, hard day, and they'd discovered much, and now they knew who the killer was and, with what they hoped would be the blessing of Chief Inspector Joshua Madden, they fully expected to close the case by the end of the following day. Norris felt lucky when the sergeant on duty at the desk told him that the Chief Inspector was indeed still at the station, working late in his office.

This time, Norris knocked and waited. Madden bade him enter and looked up as he and Hillman trudged rather wearily into the office.

"Well, Bert, you look like you've had a long day. Have you confirmed what you suspected earlier?"

"We have, sir, but there's more, much more, I'm afraid. I don't think you're going to like hearing what we've found, but not only do the sergeant and me now know who the killer is, we also know who his accomplice is, too."

"Accomplice?" Madden sounded shocked.

"Yes, sir. You see, the killer wasn't acting alone, but had help, from a most unexpected quarter, I must say. This was a conspiracy, as you told me the top brass suspected, but not one against the railway, sir."

"Then what, Bert. What's it all been about?"

And so, as the gas lights hissed quietly in the background and the evening stretched into night, Albert Norris laid out his beliefs to Joshua Madden, who sat ashen-faced as the true nature and motive for the crimes of the Underground Railway Killer were brought to savage life by the words of the inspector.

Chapter 35
Norris's Dénouement

First, Chief Inspector Joshua Madden listened with shock to the news of Soames the butler's death, realising the significance of this latest tragic event in light of the information Norris had laid before him.

"I think you'd better tell me everything now, Bert," he said, in a quiet and thoughtful tone, then he sat back and allowed Norris to relate his version of events.

"Clara Forshaw was the reason all this happened," Norris began. "From the very beginning, the dead girl's link with Martin Bowker and the Bible Study Group at St. Giles's Church led me to believe Bowker was in some way connected with the crime. When Ann Cullen, another member of Bowker's class, became the second victim, my belief grew stronger, as you know, sir. It was you who then reined me in from my pursuit of Bowker, and forced me to widen my inquiry, and I have to say I'm grateful to you for doing so.

"When we looked deeper into the case, it became apparent that we were being led to believe in a conspiracy against the Metropolitan Railway – though in fact, I always believed Clara Forshaw's murder was a personal killing, with its origins in an affair she'd become embroiled in with a married man, and nothing to do with any political agenda to force the railway to cease its expansion plans. Having said that, only someone with easy access to every part of the railway system could have come and gone on the underground with such ease, and apparent anonymity. Gradually, I came to believe that the truth of the matter lay somewhere behind the walls of the Bellhaven home on Lewisham Place. Again, you tried to lead me away from that idea, calling it a preposterous theory, but, as I've now shown you, I believe I was right to follow that line of inquiry, sir.

"Laurence Bellhaven is, without a doubt, the killer of Clara Forshaw and the other women, though Ann Cullen and Amy Cobbold were mere window-dressing, a feint to throw us off the true scent. I'm sure that when we question him and face him with the facts we've accumulated, he'll admit to being the father of Clara's unborn child. Laurence Bellhaven is a cold-blooded, evil killer, sir, as bad as any thug from the streets of Whitechapel or Spitalfields.

"The argument the butler, Soames, overheard was nothing to do with a renewal or renegotiation of Clara's contract, but was likely Clara trying to make Bellhaven keep to some promise he'd obviously made to her. Like many men before him, he'd probably promised to leave his wife for her, as a means of getting her to sleep with him, and then, when she realised that was never going to happen, she threatened to tell his wife about their affair, and the child. Perhaps she even threatened to make his indiscretion public, in a bid to shame him into taking care of her as he'd promised, but I'm afraid all that did was release the murderous side of Bellhaven's nature.

"In a statement given to Sergeant Dove during my absence, Reverend Bowker stated that Clara, as a professional secretary, volunteered her services as administrator of his Bible Study class, and therefore held a list of all the ladies who made up the membership of the class. It was an easy matter for Bellhaven to get his hands on that list, probably when Clara was absent from her room, and identify the other women who attend the class with Clara, hence giving him a convenient means of selecting future victims.

"Bellhaven was in the habit of taking late-night carriage rides, and I believe he used the carriage to travel to a location near the church, where he met Clara on the night of her death. I don't know how he got her to board a train with him – perhaps it was by saying it would be less conspicuous – but she did as he asked and he selected an unoccupied carriage, where he murdered the poor girl in cold blood. He slipped from the train as it stopped at Aldgate, knowing that no one would pay any heed to passengers going about their business. It often pays to be part of a crowd, invisible among the many, and Bellhaven exploited that fact.

"Of course, Bellhaven knew that the railway board would do all they could to suppress news of the killing and, as a member of the board, he was in a prime position to perpetuate the theory and force it down the throats of the Police Commissioner and even managed to influence the Home Secretary. So, we were given instructions to ensure the case was investigated with a minimum of fuss, and little press coverage. He thought to hamper us by making sure we allotted minimum resources to the investigation. A clever man indeed.

"Then, he realised he needed more in order to convince us that there was indeed a conspiracy against the railway. Another murder would suffice to advance his mad plot nicely. Ann Cullen was selected from Clara's list, and he somehow managed to persuade her to travel with him. Perhaps he just waited on the platform and joined her in her carriage before killing her and throwing her body on the tracks. Remember that the carriages are not connected, so, if he and the girl were the only ones present, no one in adjoining carriages could have seen what took place. Again, there would have been no reason for anyone to take notice of a lone man leaving the train when it arrived at whatever station he chose to alight from."

Norris paused, cleared his dry throat and continued, noting the rapt attention on Madden's face.

"Now, we come to the letter. When it appeared to Bellhaven that I wasn't quite falling for the political or terrorist conspiracy, the letter became a way of attempting to push us back in that direction. To be truthful, sir, I never accepted it as such. It was all too convenient, it turning up just at that time. It wasn't until I saw the letters on the hall stand at Bellhaven's home, however, that I realised he hadn't operated alone. The envelopes addressed to the two lady friends of Florence Bellhaven were written unmistakably in the same hand as the letter we received from the killer. That meant only one thing. Florence Bellhaven was in this with her husband right from the start. She wrote the letter, not him. Perhaps they assumed we might recognise his handwriting from official documents or something, but of course, we'd have no reason to look at his wife's writing, unless we suspected her, which, until a few hours ago, we didn't. Hillman will confirm that we both checked the writing on the envelope with that on the letter from the killer, which I had in my pocket at the time."

Hillman nodded his agreement as Norris continued to sum-up the reasoning that led them to suspect Bellhaven of the murders of the young women.

"Amy Cobbold is the biggest slip-up he's made so far. I don't know where the poor girl was killed, though I'll find out from Bellhaven soon enough, believe me, but for some reason it wasn't on a train this time. He had to maintain a connection with the underground, though, to convince us to go on with the ridiculous terrorist theory. So, he carried the body in the carriage, which was heard by a witness pulling up on the street outside the carriage works. The same witness later saw the figure of a man disappearing over the boundary fence. Bellhaven had simply dumped Amy Cobbold's body on the tracks leading into the carriage shed, and scurried back to his carriage, and eventually home, as fast as he could. I'm betting we'll find bloodstains somewhere in the carriage, no matter how careful he might have been."

Norris paused for breath and Madden took the opportunity to make a couple of observations.

"The wife, too, Bert? It's simply incredible! I'd never have believed it, but of course, you do know it's all circumstantial, as I said before. And what about this business of the butler's death?"

"Soames knew too much, sir. As a good butler, little that happened in the house escaped his attention. He knew about Bellhaven's late night forays to the streets of Whitechapel and his penchant for prostitutes. Maybe Soames himself had gone down that particular path and seen his employer 'at it' at some time. However he found out, it was dangerous knowledge, especially once Bellhaven discovered that Soames had told us certain things about life behind the closed doors of 24 Lewisham Place. First, Bellhaven dismissed him from service, and then probably discovered that Soames wouldn't go quietly, and was shooting his mouth off in the pub. Either way, I believe he waylaid Soames, rendered him unconscious, and ferried him to the Isle of Dogs in his carriage, where he dropped the poor bugger in the river and left him to drown."

"And Jack the Ripper?" asked Madden suddenly.

"You mean, could Bellhaven be Jack the Ripper, sir?"

Madden said nothing, merely nodding as a wave of tiredness swept over him.

"I honestly don't know, sir. He likes the company of prostitutes and uses their services regularly, which I'll bet his wife doesn't know about, by the way, but whether he could slaughter a woman in Whitechapel and then compose himself enough to drive his carriage to various locations to commit the railway murders, I just don't know. We'll soon get the chance to ask him, though."

Madden sighed and held up a hand, stopping Norris from going any further with his narrative. He stood up, pushing his chair back as he did so, then turned and stared out of the window for a few seconds, lost in thought. Turning back to face the two detectives, he finally spoke.

"Bert, if you're sure of all this, as I think you are, and I must say you've prepared a highly tangible case against the Bellhavens, then we need to bring them in, obtain confessions, and then I can inform the Chief Superintendent, who will have the less than pleasant task of transmitting the results of our inquiry to the Commissioner and upwards. Do you think you can get them to confess?"

"When Dylan and I confront them with all we know, and I think Florence Bellhaven's handwriting will prove decisive in this, then I'm sure they'll collapse under questioning. They are, after all, wealthy members of society and not our usual hardened criminal type. They'll cough all right, sir, you can count on it. Once I get going on them, I won't give up until we have them bang to rights."

Madden looked to Norris as though he'd aged ten years in the short time it had taken him to relate his version of what he believed to have taken place. The Chief Inspector spoke again.

"What a cold-blooded and unfeeling pair they must be. To kill Clara Forshaw was bad enough, but to use and murder two other innocent girls as mere cover for their vile act, to try and create a conspiracy where none existed, shows pure evil at work. And then to murder the butler, if indeed they did! It beggars belief, Bert, it really does. What makes me angry is that they manipulated the establishment right to the top, and had us tied up in knots in a ploy to make certain we'd never get close to the truth. Only your diligence and pig-headed determination, if you'll forgive the phrase, drove you on to ignore all the smokescreens and interference from above, and from me, I'm sad to say. For God's sake, they even had Special Branch doing their dirty work for them!"

He sighed again, then, with a look of grim determination on his face, Joshua Madden instructed his inspector, "Go and get them, Bert. Sod their wealth and position. They're no better than Drago and his like. Bring those murdering bastards in."

Norris and Hillman were out of the office in seconds!

Chapter 36
Return to Aldgate

Prior to leaving New Street, Norris and Hillman slipped into the inspector's office, where Norris walked to a small safe positioned at the side of his desk, twiddled the dial this way and that as the numbers of the combination did their work and, as the safe opened, he reached into its interior, removing a box, which he placed on the desk. Extracting a small key from his pocket, he opened the locked box, revealing the menacing shape of the small handgun within, and beside it, a box containing the bullets that would turn it from a benign, inanimate object into a lethal weapon, capable of ending a man's life with one well-placed shot.

"Are you sure you want to take that with you, Bert?" asked Hillman, his face covered in concern. The use of handguns by the police was a rarity in the Victorian era, and Hillman knew that Norris had never fired a gun in anger, his experience with such weapons having been restricted to a few practice shots on a firing range.

"I made a huge mistake once before Dylan, old chum," Norris replied, harking back to the death of Peter Vane, "and I don't intend to compound that error by being unprepared this time. Belhaven has killed three, maybe four people. He's a bloody dangerous killer, and if he resists arrest or tries anything violent, I'm going to be prepared and, if I have to, I'll shoot the bastard where he stands."

"Be careful, Bert, that's all I'm saying. You don't want to end up being the one charged with murder, if you shoot him down without good cause."

"Don't worry, I know what I'm doing, and I know the rules. I'll only shoot as a last resort, and if he gives me no alternative. I don't intend to be the one in a cell by the end of the night. That particular accommodation's reserved for Laurence and Florence Bellhaven."

"I still can't believe his wife's been a part of it all along, Bert."

"You know what they say, Dylan. The female of the species can be far more deadly then the male. I'll lay odds that Bellhaven admitted all to his wife and she, not wanting to face public disgrace or lose the financial security her husband provided, agreed to help him in his wild and ill-thought out scheme to rid themselves of the problem. She's as guilty as he is, and just as deadly, believe you me."

Opening the ammunition box, Norris slowly and carefully inserted the bullets into the chamber of the gun, until it was fully loaded. After taking care to ensure the safety catch was in place, he placed the gun in his right-hand pocket and patted it gently through the fabric of the jacket.

"Ready, Dylan?"

"Ready as I'll ever be," the sergeant replied.

"Let's go and arrest a pair of murderers, then."

Sharing a look of determination and a desire to bring the case of the Underground Railway Murders to an end, the pair exited the office and made their way along the corridor towards the street. As they were about to walk through the front doors of the police station, Constable Fry came rushing in, his face flushed from running.

"Where's the fire, Fry?" asked Norris, as the constable almost bowled him over in his exuberant rush through the doors and into the station's reception area.

"Sorry, sir. You're just the man I wanted to see. I ran all the way, hoping you'd still be here."

"Well, here I am, Constable. Now, what's so urgent to have you perspiring like this so late at night?"

"There's been an accident, sir, at Aldgate Underground Station."

"What sort of accident, man? Come on, it must be important if you needed me in particular."

"I was on patrol, sir, and heard a police whistle, and when I followed it, it was coming from the entrance to the underground station. Constable Medley was standing there, and he told me a man had fallen under a train as it came into the station."

"And you, of course, went to take a look, Fry?"

"I did, sir. When I got to the platform, members of the public were gathered in a huddle, obviously shocked by what they'd witnessed. They pointed me towards the end of the platform, where a train stood, the engine belching smoke and letting off steam. I ran along, followed by Constable Whitely, who'd likewise responded to Medley's whistle and followed me down a few seconds behind me, and then we saw it. At the rear of the train, under the very last carriage, a man's body was visible. The train had been arriving at Aldgate when the man must have fallen from the platform right at the spot where the train appeared at the end of the platform. The driver must have braked quickly, but there had been no way to avoid the man. He was crushed under the wheels of the locomotive and his body was then run over by the carriages. Whitely and me jumped down between the platform and the train, and got close enough to take a look at the body. It was a real mangled mess, sir, I can tell you. Fair turned my stomach, it did. But you see, sir, when I looked closely, despite the injuries the dead man had sustained, I could make out enough of his face to know who it was. I'd seen him before, you see, even been to his house while you were on sick leave."

Norris's face fell, as he instantly realised exactly who Fry was speaking of.

"Are you going to tell me it was Laurence Bellhaven?"

"Why, yes, sir. It was. I thought, under the circumstances of the case you're working on, you'd want to know right away, so I left Whitely there and ran all the way back here in the hope of catching you before you left for the night."

"And I'm very glad you did, Constable. Thank you. Please get back to Aldgate, and Sergeant Hillman and I will follow you very soon. We need to speak to the Chief Inspector before we join you."

"Yes, sir, right away, sir."

"And Fry?"

"Sir?"

"Allow no one, and I mean no one, near that body until we get there. Is that clear?"

"Yes, sir, of course."

Fry departed as quickly as he'd appeared, leaving Norris and Hillman standing in the doorway.

"Bloody hell, Dylan. The bastard's gone and cheated the hangman after all."

"Do you believe it was an accident, Bert?"

"No, I damn well don't. Somehow, Bellhaven has been one step ahead of us almost all the way through this case, and it wouldn't surprise me if he got wind of the fact we were on to him and took it into his mind to do away with himself, rather than face justice in front of a judge and jury, and the obvious disgrace and ignominy that a guilty outcome and a hanging verdict would bring upon his so-called good name. My guess is that we'll find someone on that platform who saw him jump under the wheels of that train. It would have been travelling fast enough to kill as it first ran into the station. Those underground trains take quite a bit of stopping, I've heard, and under normal circumstances, after braking just before arriving at the platform, the loco would have ended up right at the far end. Bellhaven knew just where to stand to make sure he'd be killed by the impact."

"So we're too late to get him. He's managed to cheat the hangman after all, eh?"

"Yes, Dylan, he has, but his bloody cold-hearted bitch of a wife hasn't. She's got a lot of talking to do before she swings on the end of a rope, and we're going make sure she does just that. But for now, we'd better go and give Madden the bad news."

* * *

"Well, I can't say I'm surprised, Bert," Madden remarked, as soon as Norris finished informing him of the demise of Laurence Bellhaven. "Suicide was probably preferable to man like that. Can you imagine the scandal that would attach itself to a murder trial involving one of the board of directors of The Metropolitan Railway?"

"Bit of a coward though, sir, leaving his wife to face the music."

"He probably thought we haven't made the connection to Florence, Bert. Maybe he thought she'd get off scot-free once he was dead and out of the picture."

"He was wrong then, wasn't he?" Hillman remarked.

"Yes, Sergeant, he was. I suggest you two get on over to Aldgate with all haste, gentlemen. Verify your suicide suspicions if you can, Bert, and then make your way straight to Lewisham Place and pick up Florence Bellhaven. She's got a lot to answer for, and it's our job to see justice done. With her husband gone, she's going to have to take the whole blame herself."

"At least I shouldn't need this now," said Norris, removing the gun from his pocket and placing it on Madden's desk. "Perhaps you could look after it till I get back, sir."

"I see," said Madden. "You weren't taking any chances, were you, Bert?"

"No, sir, I wasn't. I couldn't take a chance on Bellhaven springing any nasty surprises on us, but somehow, I don't think Mrs. Bellhaven is likely to try and do anything stupid once we confront her."

"You're sure about that, are you, Inspector?"

"Well, not entirely, sir, but I don't think I've got it in me to shoot a woman, murderer or not."

Madden thought for a moment and then pushed the gun back across the desk towards Norris.

"Take it with you, just in case. She may not try anything, but if she does, you'll have it to use as a deterrent. Hopefully, if you wave that bloody thing at her, she'll give in, always assuming she does try something stupid of course. It's my hope she'll come quietly, especially when you inform her of Bellhaven's death."

"If you say so, sir," said Norris, pocketing the gun once more.

"I do, Inspector," said Madden gravely. "Take no risks, understood?"

"Understood."

"Then be off with you, and I'll see you when you return with your prisoner."

"You're not going home, sir? It's getting late."

"I'm aware of the time, Bert, but you don't think I'd send you two out to bring in our sole surviving suspect, and not be here when you return, do you?"

"No, sir, of course not, and... thanks."

"Oh, go on, get out of my sight!" Madden grinned, a little embarrassed by Norris's gratitude. After all, he'd been one of those who'd tied Norris's hands, metaphorically speaking, right from the beginning of the case. Now, his inspector had been proved right all along, and yet was thanking him.

"See you later, sir," said Hillman, as the pair disappeared from Madden's office in double-quick time and headed for the streets once again.

As opposed to thirty minutes earlier, however, instead of heading in the direction of the Bellhaven home in Lewisham Place, they set off for the site of Laurence Bellhaven's final act, Aldgate Underground Station, where the whole case had begun so many weeks previously with the death of Clara Forshaw.

Chapter 37
Death at Aldgate

A strange feeling of déjà vu crept over Albert Norris as he and Hillman descended into Aldgate station once again, returning the salute of Constable Medley, on patrol at the entrance, as they did so.

"It's maybe appropriate that he ended it where it all began, eh, Bert?" asked Hillman, echoing the inspector's thoughts.

"You're right, Dylan, though I think it really all began between a pair of crisp white sheets in the Bellhaven house while Mrs. Bellhaven was occupied elsewhere."

"Right enough. Strange how these upper class nobs can't keep their dicks in their pants, isn't it? Always chasing the servants and the hired help, as far as I can see."

"Not just them, Dylan. I daresay there are lots of married men indulging in a little slap and tickle outside the marital bed nowadays, but I suppose the rich and wealthy have more opportunities, that's all."

"Well, this time it didn't do old Laurence Bellhaven much good, did it?"

"Definitely not, old son."

The body of Laurence Bellhaven still lay where it had been deposited by the braking underground train. Constable Whitely stood at the edge of the platform, looking down to where the police surgeon on duty, Doctor Donald Feldman, was examining the remains. For once in this long and tangled case, Doctor Roebuck hadn't been on call when the body was found.

"Hello, Doctor," Norris called down to the medic, who was doing his best to examine the body in its tangled position beneath the carriage.

"Hello, Inspector," he called up to the inspector. "Not much to tell, really. The man died from massive trauma caused by being hit by a moving train. Not much more I can say now, or even later after a post mortem, I'd say. There are massive injuries to the chest and legs, and one arm has been severed completely and is over there." He pointed a little way forward from the body's position. Norris bent down and followed his pointing arm and sure enough, he caught sight of the severed limb some twenty feet away, lying in the middle of the track.

"Nasty," said Norris.

"Gruesome," remarked Hillman.

"Definitely fatal," said the doctor.

"Was it a quick death?" asked Norris.

"Oh, I think so," the doctor said. "He'd have been dead in seconds from those wounds."

"Shame," said Norris.

"I beg your pardon?"

"Oh, ignore me, Doctor, just thinking aloud. We'd better go and talk to the witnesses."

"Right, well, I'll send you my report as soon as I've done a post mortem, shall I?"

"Yes, please. You do that, Doctor."

Norris and Hillman walked off towards the other end of the platform, where another constable had arrived to keep order amongst the gathered witnesses.

After speaking to a mere three men who'd witnessed the death of Laurence Bellhaven, it became clear to Norris and Hillman that this was indeed a case of suicide, and no accident. Each witness repeated almost the same tale. The dead man had been seen standing right at the end of the platform, leaning forward and peering along the tracks, as though watching intently for the arrival of the train.

As the train was heard approaching the station, Bellhaven was seen to stand tall, bracing himself, so the witnesses thought, until the train was a mere twenty yard or so from the platform. At that moment, the man pitched himself forwards, hands outstretched, and landed immediately in front of the approaching locomotive. The driver of the train stood no chance of avoiding the inevitable, and the man was heard to utter one loud scream as his body was hit by the locomotive and then dragged under the train, being repeatedly hit by the wheels and undersides of the carriages as his body bounced from the various impacts.

Hillman duly noted the names and addresses of the witnesses and asked Constable Dobbs to obtain full statements from the three men and anyone else who'd visually witnessed Bellhaven's death, with instructions to deliver his notes to New Street as soon as he was relieved.

* * *

"No doubt about that then, Dylan, old chum."

"None at all, I'd say. We have enough witnesses to confirm it, so, suicide it is."

"Yes, which means the murdering sod has escaped justice, and met his end in his own way by his own chosen method. It's up to us to make sure his lying, murderous wife doesn't get the same opportunity."

"I take it we're heading for Lewisham Place now, eh, Bert?"

"Too right we are, Dylan. We may have missed out on putting the collar on Bellhaven, but dear Florence will be a different matter. Come on, let's get out of here. I can't stand the smell of these damnable places any longer."

As they exited the station, Norris noticed something and motioned Hillman to stop. After staring across the street for a moment, he led Hillman to where a horse and carriage stood, apparently deserted by its driver. The vehicle, a beautifully polished black Brougham 'Victoria', gleamed, even under the pale, ghostly light of the streetlamps. The horse stood patiently, its head moving in a gentle nodding motion as it waited for the return of its driver.

"Bellhaven's?"

"I'll stake my life on it," Norris replied to Hillman's question. "Let's take a look."

Hillman pulled open the nearside carriage door and the two men peered inside.

"It's too dark to tell, but I'll wager a week's pay that if we have this examined in detail, no matter how much he's cleaned it, we'll find some trace of blood, somewhere inside. I'm pretty sure this is where he killed his last victim, and possible Roland Soames, too, before dumping their bodies."

"If only the horse could talk, eh?"

"Yes, if only. Better just go back and ask Constable Dobbs to arrange to have the carriage collected and taken to New Street. They can keep it in the yard and feed the horse, or do whatever they have to do with horses, until we can have it examined."

Hillman disappeared to speak to Dobbs, returning five minutes later. Thus, after much delay and with the determination that had been growing stronger within both men throughout the evening, they set off at last for Lewisham Place. Florence Bellhaven was about to receive unexpected visitors.

Chapter 38
Florence Confronted

Lawton, the new butler, expressed surprise at having to answer the door to the police at such a late hour. Not only was this their second unannounced call of the day, but it was now after 9 p.m. and most of the household was preparing to retire for the night.

"Is your visit absolutely necessary, Inspector Norris? Do you know what time it is?"

"I'm well aware of the time, Lawton. This is police business and I must speak with your mistress this very minute. No arguments now, there's a good man. Go and tell her we're here."

In the gaslit glow of the doorway, Lawton's face bore an almost ghostly pallor as he replied, "I'm sorry, but that won't be possible. Mr. Bellhaven has not as yet returned from his office, and the mistress does not wish to be disturbed."

Norris cast a glance towards Hillman.

"I *shall* speak with your mistress, Lawton. Please ask Mrs. Bellhaven to join me immediately."

"This is most irregular, Inspector. It is late, and..."

"And you will do as I ask, without delay. As I said, this is a police matter of the utmost importance. Now, please fetch Mrs. Bellhaven. We'll wait in the hall."

Norris pushed his way past the butler, closely followed by Dylan Hillman who slammed the door shut behind him, and the two officers simply stood in the middle of the marble-floored hall, waiting. Lawton, realising there was nothing to do but comply with Norris's demand, walked in silence past the detectives and strode up the long staircase. "Wait there," he said as he reached the halfway point, as if his words would allow him to regain a little of his lost composure.

Mrs. Florence Bellhaven descended the stairs some five minute later. Her face betrayed no emotion, no sign that she had received any prior notice of Norris's visit. Her husband, if he had intended to protect her, would have decided not to give her advance notice of his intentions, Norris decided. Lawton was nowhere to be seen, and Norris concluded he'd gone about his business using the servants' stairs at the rear of the house.

Dressed in a grey dress with pink embroidery at the neck, and wearing no jewellery, probably due to the late hour and her readiness for bed, Florence Belhaven appeared agitated by the late intrusion by the officers.

"Really, Inspector Norris, this is a most unseemly hour to come calling. My husband is not yet home and whatever you wish to discuss with him can surely wait until morning."

Norris got right to the point, without preamble.

"Your husband won't be coming home tonight, or any other night, Mrs. Bellhaven," Norris said, in his most official-sounding voice.

A look of shock and bewilderment passed swiftly over Florence's face, before she appeared to regain a degree of composure.

"Whatever do you mean by such a remark, Inspector?"

"Quite simply that your husband, Laurence Bellhaven, is dead."

Florence almost collapsed on the spot, and Hillman moved quickly across the hall to offer her a supportive arm before her legs gave way from under her.

"What on earth do you mean? How can he be dead? He's at his office, working."

"Your husband was killed when he threw himself under the wheels of one of his own trains at Aldgate Station a short while ago. You must know of Aldgate Station, Mrs. Bellhaven. It's where he killed and left the body of poor Clara Forshaw, after the two of you decided to get rid of her, to prevent her disgracing and possible socially destroying you when she became pregnant by your husband."

Florence held a hand to her face, the back of her hand swiping across her brow as the shock of Norris's words hit home. She was on the verge of fainting, but held her composure as she tried to brazen the situation out.

"I've no idea what you're talking about. First, you tell me my poor husband is dead and now you accuse him, and me, it appears, of murder, too."

"Don't try to deny it. We know most of what happened, Mrs. Bell-haven. You husband had a dalliance with Clara. She fell pregnant, maybe demanded money to keep quiet about it, and together, the pair of you hatched a plot to get rid of her. Your husband murdered her, and then proceeded to create a so-called conspiracy against the Metropolitan Railway in an attempt to deflect suspicion, so that her death wouldn't appear to be a cold-blooded personal attack on an innocent girl. So, he killed Ann Cullen and then, when it looked as if your plans were going wrong, he added Amy Cobbold to the list.

"Oh yes, and somewhere along the line, he realised that Soames possibly knew too much about his activities with the prostitutes of Whitechapel and he did away with him, too, just in case he spoke to us and we caught on that he wasn't quite the pillar of society he appeared to be, and caused us to investigate him further. Last of all, probably because he realised we were closing in on him, he took his own life as a means of escaping the true justice of the law. We know you were in on it with him from the start, because you wrote the letter that was sent to Scotland Yard."

Florence's face fell at that last remark. Seeing it, and sensing a weakening in her resolve, Norris carried on, in full flow now.

"Yes, we saw your mail when we called the last time. Your letters to your lady friends were waiting to be posted and I compared your handwriting to the letter you sent to the police. They matched, so we know your husband drew you into his plot and that you were a willing participant and accessory to the murders. Now please,

Mrs. Bellhaven, before I arrest you and take you to the police station, have I missed anything out?"

At that point, it appeared to Norris and to Hillman that Florence Bellhaven underwent an extraordinary change. The quiet, mild-mannered lady of the house disappeared, to be replaced by a snarling, vicious-faced woman who now laughed in their faces as she exploded in anger.

"Oh, you are a clever man, Inspector Norris. You think you've got it all worked out, don't you? Well, you have, but not with any great degree of accuracy. Do you really think Laurence could have thought up such a plan himself? That buffoon was incapable of such meticulous planning. It was all my idea, don't you see? That little harlot tried to blackmail us. She really thought he'd leave me for her, and then, when she realised he wouldn't, she tried to squeeze money from him to take care of her bastard brat when it was born, as if we'd have allowed that to happen.

"She didn't know that I'm the money in this house. My family are very, very wealthy, and Laurence earned barely enough to keep me in the style to which I was accustomed before our marriage, despite his high position in the company. He owed everything to my father and there was no way I was going to condone that bitch trying to take money, or my husband, from me. You see, he may have been an adulterer and a philanderer, but he was still my husband, and we had to maintain appearances for the sake of our social position.

"I spent two weeks planning the murders. The names of the other girls I obtained from Clara's Bible Study class file. Laurence found it easy to pick them up and offer to escort them home. He was, after all, known to them as Clara's employer, whom they'd often seen at church. The last one was a problem, though. She seemed to sense he was up to no good and tried to run away. He had to chase her in the carriage and killed her in it. He said she tried to fight him off, but of course his manly strength prevailed. There was a large quantity of blood on the seats and the floor which I later told him to have cleaned off as soon as he could. He panicked then and dumped her on the nearest railway premises he could think of, which were the carriage works. I told him he'd made a big mistake and that it wouldn't look right, not leaving her on a train or near a station, but it was too late. The damage was done.

"Soames? Yes, we killed him, too, or at least Laurence did, on my orders. My husband was a weak man, Inspector. My health has never been good. I'm not very strong and things in the bedroom were never good between us. I didn't mind him lingering with those filthy whores in Whitechapel just so long as he kept it to himself and didn't touch me, and infect me with their terrible diseases. Sadly, Soames saw him one night, leaving one of those vile brothels, and then again carousing with a filthy harlot in an alleyway, of all places, near the Britannia Public house, I believe. When Soames spoke to you and your people, and broke the confidence of our home, we thought it would be only a matter of time before he told you of my husband's infidelity with the whores and that you would then presume he was also the father of Clara's child. I ordered Laurence to kill him and dispose of the body a little way from here, so as not to draw suspicion back to us and our home.

"Apart from those few minor inconsistencies, you were almost correct in all your assumptions, Inspector. You must realise that, as people of society, we had to do all we could to protect ourselves and our good name. So, what happens now?"

It was all Norris could do to say anything at all, faced with the barefaced and cold-blooded testimony Florence Bellhaven had just provided. As confessions went, it was as concise and damning as any prosecuting Queen's Counsel could ask for, but of course, what she'd said in the last few minutes was simply a verbal confession and not admissible in court. He'd have to hope that Florence Bellhaven would reiterate every word when they took her to New Street and questioned her further, when everything would be written down and she would have the opportunity to sign her own confession. At length, he composed himself and delivered the reply Florence stood waiting for.

"Ah, yes, well, what happens next, Mrs. Bellhaven, is that we shall place you under arrest and take you to the police station, where you will be formally charged and further questioned. You will be asked to make a statement such as you have just given to me and the sergeant. You will sign it, and you will then be placed in a cell for the night. Tomorrow, you will be arraigned before the magistrate who will in all likelihood remand you to a women's prison to await trial for murder, as you have freely admitted to being the prime mover in these events, which places equal blame on you and your husband, who you deem to have been a mere pawn in your own self-admitted murder plot. It is my belief that you will eventually be brought to trial, and, if found guilt by a jury, you will ultimately be hanged by the neck, until you are dead. Have I missed anything out, Sergeant?"

As Florence Bellhaven visibly blanched at the closing sentences of Norris's blunt appraisal of her future within the justice system, Hillman simply replied, "No, I don't think so."

Florence Bellhaven gathered her wits once more and spoke in a firm, clear voice, betraying none of the fear and trepidation Norris would have expected from her by that point in time.

"Perhaps you will permit me one last favour, Inspector, and I in return will do the same for you. I should like to leave a short note for my family, telling them of events in brief, and where they might find me. My butler can then deliver it to them on the morrow. I have writing paper and ink in my dressing room, where I have also kept a diary of recent events. I'm sure you would like to possess it, as it details everything I have told you, scrupulously."

Stunned by the cold and calculating manner in which the woman conducted herself, Norris felt obliged to allow her to leave the note, if it meant she would provide them with yet more evidence against herself. It appeared to him that, now that her husband was gone, Florence Bellhaven felt she had nothing left to lose and was thus unafraid to consign herself to whatever future fate and the courts of justice might have in store for her.

"Very well, Mrs. Bellhaven, but we must accompany you to your dressing room."

"Of course you must, Inspector. Follow me, please."

Florence Bellhaven led the way up the staircase to the first floor and along the landing that led to her small sitting room. She spent five minutes in writing the note intended for her parents, which she placed in an envelope such as Norris had seen on the hallstand and which had given her away as the writer of the letter to Scotland Yard.

"Please ask Lawton to deliver this to my parents, won't you?" she asked.

Thinking she'd find it embarrassing to ask the butler to do so herself, while leaving the house in handcuffs, Norris readily agreed.

"And the diary?" he asked.

"Of course." Florence next went to the safe, opened it and took out the leather-backed diary. She produced the key and opened the lock on the cover, passing the book to Norris. "It's all in there, Inspector Norris. Every detail you need to know, diligently recorded in chronological order. I hope you will find it satisfactory for your purposes."

"I'm sure I shall, Madam," he replied. "Now, if you please, we must go."

"Oh, I'm sure you must, but, please, do forgive me if I don't accompany you."

With that, Florence reached inside her dress and brought out the diminutive glass vial she'd taken from the safe along with diary, unseen by the two men. Before they could move to stop her, she'd removed the small cork and, in a flash, tipped the contents of the vial into her mouth.

"Bloody hell, Dylan. She's taken poison!" Norris shouted and the pair moved quickly to try and remove the vial from her hand, but it was too late. The vial was empty.

"Cyanide," she gasped, as the effects of the poison began to take effect almost instantaneously. "A large dose, I'm afraid. You can do nothing."

Within a few seconds, Florence Bellhaven began to show signs of the effects of cyanide poisoning. The poison began to shut down the consumption of oxygen by her body tissues. She started to feel sick and clutched at her head as a terrible headache began to beat in her brain. She began to gasp for breath. Her eyes took on a wild, staring expression, and she reeled on her feet before falling to the ground, her body convulsing and twitching until, in less than two minutes from the ingestion of the poison, she fell into unconsciousness.

Norris bent down and did his best to try and revive her, but he knew that there was no chance of recovery as soon as he smelled the distinctive scent of bitter almonds that emanated from the woman, confirming, as she'd said, the use of cyanide. Less than a minute after she'd fallen into her unconscious state, Florence Bellhaven's heart and lungs collapsed, and death wrapped her in its icy grip.

"Oh, God," said Hillman. "I've never seen anyone die like that, have you?"

"No," Norris replied, as he stared at the lifeless figure of the woman he'd come to arrest.

"She's cheated us, too, hasn't she?"

"Yes, Dylan, old chum, she has. Two murderers, and not a single one to hand over for the hangman to mete out the judgement of law."

"What's Madden going to say?"

"There's not a lot he can say, Dylan. We couldn't have foreseen her doing this, could we? Anyway, once he sees this diary, he'll not have much to complain about. We've solved the bloody case, Dylan. Against all the odds and with all the bloody pitfalls they laid before us, we've solved the bloody case! Now, you'd better go and see Lawton, tell him his mistress is dead as well as his master, and send him for a doctor and a constable. Oh yes, and give him this, too," said Norris, passing Florence's final note to her parents to the sergeant.

Hillman left the dressing room, leaving Norris alone with the body of Florence Bellhaven. As he waited for his sergeant to return, Norris sat in the chair in front of the dressing-table and looked down at the body of the woman who had masterminded the monstrous and cold-blooded plan that had led to four innocent deaths. At length, he spoke his final few words to the corpse that lay before him.

"Rot in hell, Florence."

Chapter 39
Aftermath, Two Days
Later

"Sir, what do you mean, 'case unsolved'? We solved the bloody case, didn't we?"

Norris and Hillman stood in their familiar place in front of Joshua Madden's desk, as the chief inspector delivered what was for them a crushing blow.

"I know you solved it, Bert, and you too, Sergeant, but listen. You must understand that this case holds political and economic ramifications that reach far beyond the walls of Lewisham Place. Try and imagine the potential loss of confidence in the Metropolitan Railway, if it became public knowledge that one of their senior board members and his wife had indulged in a killing spree on the railway in order to settle a personal grievance with his secretary. Apart from the loss of public confidence in the underground railway, the economic impact on the system would result in a total collapse of its finances. The future of the underground railway, and therefore the proposed improvements to London's infrastructure, would be brought into serious doubt, with effects that may never be recoverable from.

"I'm sure you already know that Sir Charles Warren has resigned as Police Commissioner, ostensibly, I believe, because of the failure to capture Jack the Ripper, but his personal involvement in this case may have been a large consideration in his decision, I'm sure. Many other people in high places face great embarrassment over this case, gentlemen, myself included, and you two are probably the only ones to come out of it with any degree of credit.

"That being said, however, it has been decided, at the highest level, that the following communiqué will be delivered to the press today, for general release."

Madden picked up a sheet of paper from his desk and began to read:

"*It is with sadness that the death is reported of Laurence Bell-haven, Director of the Board of the Metropolitan Railway. Mr. Bell-haven suffered fatal injuries when falling from the platform at Aldgate Underground Railway Station, and into the path of an oncoming train. He died almost instantly. Such was her grief on hearing of his death, that his wife of twenty years, Florence Bell-haven, neé Birchall, ingested a large dose of potassium cyanide, kept in the home as a weed killer, and died almost instantly. The members of the Board of Directors of the Metropolitan railway wish to express their personal sadness at this double tragedy, and extend their sympathies to the families of both deceased.*"

"Sadness at a double tragedy? They were a pair of cold-blooded killers, for God's sake!" Norris shouted, almost losing his self-control completely.

"I know, Bert," Madden replied, "But the matter is out of my hands. As I said, this decision has been taken at the very highest level, and that's an end to the matter. You did a superb job, both of you, and at least we know there will be no more killings on the Underground as a result of your perseverance in the face of many unfortunate hurdles."

"But, what about the victims' families, the witnesses to Bell-haven's suicide, all the people we've come into contact with during the case?" asked Hillman.

"Special Branch will deal with that side of things, Sergeant. They'll all be sworn to secrecy, on grounds of National Security, or some such reason. I've not been made privy to that information. Maybe they'll be told the killer was an unidentified foreign seaman who has since left the country, or some such concoction. Special Branch are good at that kind of thing."

"So, it's keep silent or face a trial for treason, is it?" asked Norris, with a look of derision on his face.

"Something like that, probably, Inspector," said Madden, looking as sad and crestfallen as he actually felt.

"So, that's it, is it?"

"Yes, Bert, that's it. Congratulations on a terrific job of detective work, but it can go no further."

"And no one will ever know?"

"*We* know, Bert, and that will have to suffice. We saw off two killers, maybe not in the way we'd have liked, but their suicides saved the government, the Metropolitan Railway and even the Commissioner of Police, from a great deal of public embarrassment. You must take heart from the fact that, in the course of the case, you found and nailed the killer of Constable Vane, and also helped rid the world of two highly despicable and disreputable people. Let's face it, they were so wealthy, a good barrister may even have helped them escape a death sentence. This way, they must both meet their maker and face judgement from a far higher authority than exists here on Earth."

"Speaking of God, perhaps I should pay a visit to Martin Bowker. I think that perhaps I owe the vicar an apology for being so hard on him."

"Er, Bert. . . " said Madden, with a note of caution in his voice.

"Oh well, maybe not," said Norris. "Will there be anything else, sir?"

"No, Bert, that's it. Case closed, nothing more to be said."

"Then, if you don't need us any more?"

"No, you can go, and. . . well done, Bert. You too, Sergeant Hillman."

The detectives departed Madden's office with heavy hearts. Both knew that all their hard work, although resulting in the demise of the killers they'd sought, amounted to nothing in the eyes of officialdom. 'Unsolved' stamped on the official case file meant that, as far as the authorities were concerned, the investigating detectives had failed to identify or apprehend the murderers; not exactly a glowing recommendation to place on their personal records. However, they also knew they could do nothing to change the situation, when everyone from the Prime Minister down to the Chief Constable knew the truth, but were determined to keep that truth a closely guarded secret, for all time.

As the pair left New Street and headed for the teeming, bustling streets of London once more, Hillman turned to the inspector and asked, "What now, Bert?"

"A pint at the Spotted Hound, Dylan old chum, then I'm going home to walk the dogs. Sod the lot of 'em!"

Chapter 40
Postscript

The case of the Underground Railway Murders left a sour taste in the minds of everyone connected with the investigation, but no more so than in the mind of Detective Inspector Albert Norris, who firmly believed that Laurence Bellhaven, in addition to committing the murders of Clara Forshaw, Ann Cullen, Amy Cobbold and Roland Soames, may also have been none other than the Whitechapel Murderer, renamed by history as Jack the Ripper. Bellhaven's propensity for visiting the prostitutes of Whitechapel and his weakness when confronted by member of the opposite sex, combined with his surprisingly submissive role within his marriage, led Norris to believe that the man possessed all the psychological attributes necessary to fulfil the role of the notorious Ripper. It seemed clear to Norris that Bellhaven nursed an intense hatred of women, and that hatred could have led him to slake an intense bloodlust by indulging in the ferocious and constantly escalating murders and mutilations perpetrated by the Ripper.

Sadly, it is unlikely that we will ever know if Norris's beliefs had any basis of fact, but it is perhaps significant that no further Jack the Ripper killings took place after the date of Laurence Bellhaven's suicide. Coincidence, perhaps? But Albert Norris never believed in coincidence. I leave it to you, the reader, to ponder Norris's thoughts...

About the Author

Winner, Best Author, The Preditors & Editors Readers Awards 2009, and also Winner of Best Children's Book, and Best Artwork for *Tilly's Tale* (under his Harry Porter pseudonym), and with a Top Ten Finisher Award for his thriller, *Legacy of the Ripper*, Brian L Porter is the author of a number of successful novels. His works include the winner of The Preditors & Editors Best Thriller Novel 2008 Award, *A Study in Red – The Secret Journal of Jack the Ripper* and its sequels, *Legacy of the Ripper* and the final part of his Ripper trilogy, *Requiem for the Ripper*, all signed for movie adaptation by Thunderball Films (L.A.), with *A Study in Red* already in the development stages of production. Both *A Study in Red* and *Legacy of the Ripper* were awarded 'Recommended Read' status by the reviewers at CK2S Kwips & Kritiques.

Aside from his works on Jack the Ripper, his other works include *Pestilence, Purple Death, Glastonbury, Kiss of Life* and *The Nemesis Cell*, and the short story collection, *The Voice of Anton Bouchard and Other Stories*.

Brian has also become thoroughly integrated into the movie business since his first involvement with Thunderball Films LLC and is now also an Associate Producer and Co-Producer on a number of developing movies, as well as being a screenwriter for many of the movies soon to be released by Thunderball.

Two sequels to *Behind Closed Doors* are planned, both featuring Inspector Norris and Sergeant Hillman. Watch out for *A Tainted Inheritance* and *An Unfortunate Recuperation*.

He is a dedicated dog lover and rescuer and he and his wife share their home with a number of rescued dogs.

For more about *Behind Closed Doors* please go to www.inspectornorris.webs.com.

From International Bestselling Author Brian L Porter

Thrillers by Brian L Porter

Mersey Murder Mysteries
A Mersey Killing
All Saints, Murder on the Mersey
A Mersey Maiden
A Mersey Mariner
A Very Mersey Murder
Last Train to Lime Street

A Study in Red - The Secret Journal of Jack the Ripper
Legacy of the Ripper
Requiem for the Ripper
Pestilence
Purple Death
Behind Closed Doors
Avenue of the Dead
The Nemesis Cell
Kiss of Life

Dog Rescue

Sasha
Sheba: From Hell to Happiness
Cassie's Tale

Short Story Collection

After Armageddon

Remembrance Poetry

Lest We Forget

Children's books as Harry Porter

Wolf
Alistair the Alligator, (Illustrated by Sharon Lewis)

With Diana Rubino

Sharing Hamilton

Coming soon

Tilly's Tale
Dylan's Tale
Charlie the Caterpillar, (Illustrated by Bonnie Pelton)
Hazel the Honeybee, Saving the World, (Illustrated by Bonnie Pelton)
Percy the Pigeon, (Illustrated by Sharon Lewis)

As Juan Pablo Jalisco

Of Aztecs and Conquistadors

42407008R00166

Made in the USA
Middletown, DE
13 April 2019